She'd always had a crush on her brother's best friend, and now he's back in town!

All Out of Love

"So there's absolutely no chance you'd consider going out with me?"

She raised her head, drilled a hole straight through him with those amazing blue eyes of hers. "Not if you were the last man on earth."

"Lace Bettingfield," he said levelly, holding on to his calm against the barrage of endorphins lighting up his body. "I'm warning you right now."

She tilted up her sassy chin. "Warning me about what?"

"Don't issue me a challenge, woman."

"Why not?"

"Because I will surely take you up on it." He hitched his fingers through his belt loops, turned, and walked away. Wished he had spurs on so he could hear them jangle.

"Oh yeah?" she hollered at his back. "What do you intend on doing about it? Kill every man on the face of the earth?"

A grin split across his face. Ha! A crack in her armor. He'd gotten to her. Pierce spun back around. "Sweetheart, that won't be necessary. You'll be begging me to take you to bed long before it comes to that."

By Lori Wilde

ALL OUT OF LOVE
LOVE AT FIRST SIGHT
A COWBOY FOR CHRISTMAS
THE COWBOY AND THE PRINCESS
THE COWBOY TAKES A BRIDE
THE WELCOME HOME GARDEN CLUB
THE FIRST LOVE COOKIE CLUB
THE TRUE LOVE QUILTING CLUB
THE SWEETHEARTS' KNITTING CLUB

Available from Avon Impulse
THE CHRISTMAS COOKIE CHRONICLES:
CARRIE
RAYLENE
CHRISTINE

LORI WILDE

ALL OUT OF *Love*

A CUPID, TEXAS NOVEL

AVON
An Imprint of HarperCollinsPublishers

AVON BOOKS
An Imprint of HarperCollins*Publishers*
10 East 53rd Street
New York, New York 10022-5299

Copyright © 2013 by Laurie Vanzura
Excerpt from *Somebody to Love* copyright © 2014 by Laurie Vanzura
ISBN 978-0-06-221896-4
www.avonromance.com

First Avon Books mass market printing: July 2013

Avon Trademark Reg. U.S. Pat. Off. and in Other Countries, Marca Registrada, Hecho en U.S.A.
HarperCollins® is a registered trademark of HarperCollins Publishers.

Printed in the U.S.A.

10 9 8 7 6 5 4 3 2 1

This book is dedicated to Diana Coyle. Thank you so very much for all your help. I can't believe I waited so long to acquire a beta reader. I feel like I found a diamond in the sand.

Acknowledgments

WHILE writing is a solitary effort, publishing is not. For a story to become a successful book it takes a team. Spinning a good yarn is only part of the equation. Without strong publisher support, sharp editors, talented cover artists, a go-getter sales force, dedicated copyeditors, keen-eyed proofreaders, and dynamic publicity and marketing departments, a book doesn't stand much of a chance. And yet, these essential team members rarely get the accolades they so abundantly deserve. I want to express my humble gratitude to have found such a magnificent group. From the bottom of my heart, I say, "Thank you" to Avon—there is a reason you are the leader in quality romance—and to my most awesome agent, Jenny Bent. I know you are the people who have made my career.

$$\mathcal{P}rologue$$

Millie Greenwood High School, Cupid, Texas, May 25, 2001

Dear Cupid,

I am crazy in love with my older brother's best friend, Pierce Hollister! You should see him in his gym shorts when he's out on the football field running sprints. Omigod, he's got the most amazing thighs. Of course that's nothing compared to the way his butt looks in Wranglers. Be still my pounding heart!

And his eyes! Brown with intriguing green flecks.

He made direct eye contact with me once. It was a moment I will never, ever forget until my dying day. I'd dropped my books in the crowded hallway and I was fumbling to pick them up when suddenly, out of nowhere, I see a pair of black cowboy boots and a hand reaching out to help me.

I looked up and it was him!

I got tingly all over and honest to God, I

thought I was going to die right there on the spot! This is no ordinary boy. He's the quarterback of the football team! He dates cheerleaders! His daddy owns the biggest ranch in Jeff Davis County and here he was helping me!

And I'm nobody. I'm pudgy (Mama calls me fluffy) and I wear glasses and I stutter. I've had speech therapy, but I still can't speak without stammering and that is in a relaxed atmosphere. Believe me there was nothing relaxed about this. Every muscle in my body was tuned as tight as the strings on a concert violin and I couldn't have said a word if my life depended on it.

His eyes met mine and he smiled.

Smiled! At me!

"Here you go," he said, handing me my biology book (it had to be biology, didn't it?), and our knuckles brushed. I don't know how I kept from bursting into flames. "Have a nice day, Lace."

And then he was gone, leaving his heavenly sunshine and leather scent lingering behind, as I stared after him with my mouth gaping open.

Pierce Hollister had smiled and touched my hand and said eight whole words. To me!

I have no chance with him. I know that. He's a senior. I'm a freshman. He's handsome as a movie star. Way out of my league. He's filet mignon and I'm day-old bread. Okay, so I am a direct descendant of Millie Greenwood, but so are practically half the people in this town. It's not a unique claim to fame.

It's silly of me to wish and pine, I know. But Cupid, I just can't stop thinking about him, no matter how much I try. Every night before I go to sleep, I imagine what it would feel like if he were holding me tight against his muscled chest, our hearts beating in perfect time together. Beating as if we were one.

That's why I'm writing to you, Cupid. I'm miserable with love for him. I want him to love me back so badly that I can barely breathe. Please, Cupid, please let Pierce Hollister fall in love with me. I know I'll have to wait for him. I am only fourteen after all and he's got a girlfriend and a football scholarship to the University of Texas, but one day? Someday? Please!

> *Yours in total despair,*
> *Hopelessly Tongue-Tied*

Lace Bettingfield stood frozen in freshman homeroom, half in the doorway, half out of it, with her backpack slung over one shoulder.

Seated in front of her were seventeen students, and every single one of them was reading the current issue of the school newspaper, the *Cupid Chronicle*.

Ominously, hairs on the nape of her neck stood up.

The fact that *everyone* was reading—including the stoners and the jocks—was odd enough, but when they all looked up at her with what seemed to be perfectly choreographed smirks, Lace's stomach took the express elevator to her Skechers.

In a split second, her gaze darted to the student nearest her. It was Toby Mercer, her biology lab partner.

Toby was six-foot-six and weighed the same as Lace, a hundred and sixty-two pounds; on him the weight was gaunt, on her it was zaftig. He possessed strawberry blond hair and skin so pale it had earned him the nickname Casper way back in kindergarten. She'd known him her entire life. His family lived just down the block from hers. She'd comforted him when kids had picked on him. They'd attended each other's birthday parties. They'd dissected frogs together.

But right now, Toby was looking at her all narrow-eyed and smug, like she was a dilapidated barn and he was a wrecking ball.

She flicked her eyes from Toby's face to the paper he held in his hand, and there it was.

Dear Cupid,
    I am crazy in love with Pierce Hollister!

It was the letter she'd written to Cupid, her private letter that had never been meant for anyone's eyes but her own, printed on the front page of the school newspaper!

Her letter. Front page. Declaring her love for Pierce. How? How had this happened?

Unlike the tourists who came to Cupid, wrote letters to the Roman god of love, and deposited their letters in the special letter box in the botanical gardens (expecting them to be answered by the town's volunteers and published in the weekly Cupid Chamber of Commerce circular), Lace had never intended for anyone to see this letter.

She'd written it in study hall three days earlier as she gazed out the window, watching the football team practice. She'd carefully folded the letter and tucked it into the side pocket of her notebook with every intention of burning it in the patio chiminea that weekend when her parents were out of town at a cutting horse event.

Reality hit her like a fist to the face.

Mary Alice.

Mary Alice Fant, her second cousin, who was also the editor of the *Cupid Chronicle*. Pierce had recently dumped her for the head cheerleader, Jenny Angus. Two nights ago, Mary Alice and her parents had come over to Lace's house for dinner, and at one point, Lace had caught Mary Alice snooping around in her bedroom.

Oh God!

Now everyone knew about her secret crush. Her life was ruined. Nausea splashed scalding bile into her throat. Her entire body flushed hot as August in the Chihuahuan Desert.

One heartbeat later, and the class erupted into a feeding frenzy.

"Do you imagine she calls out Pierce's name when she's touching herself?" sniggered Booth Randal, a smart-assed stoner who spent the bulk of his time in detention.

"P . . . Pa . . . Pa . . . Pa . . . Pierce," another boy stuttered in a fake falsetto, "Yo . . . yo . . . yo . . . you . . . ma . . . ma . . . make me so hot."

Moaning and breathing heavily, the two boys pretended to kiss and fondle each other, while the other students hurled derisive catcalls like stones.

"Poor me," wailed Tasha Stuart, whose mother worked in the teller cage next to Lace's mom at Cupid National Bank. "I'm sooo in love with the most popular boy in school and he doesn't know I exist."

"Who knows," someone else called out. "She might stand a chance. Pierce could be a closet chubby chaser."

"Na . . . na . . . na . . . not unless she can sta . . . sta . . . stop stutt . . . stutt . . . stuttering." Toby stabbed her in the back.

"Yeah, who wants a girl whose tongue is hopelessly tied?"

"One day. Someday."

"Please, Cupid, please, please, please."

The words slapped her harder than any physical blow. She knew these people. Was related to some of them. Had thought many of them were her friends, but they'd turned on her like hyenas.

The only one who looked at her with anything other than ridicule was Pierce's younger brother, Malcolm. He slunk down in his seat, pulled his collar up, sank his chin to his chest, and kept his eyes trained on his hands folded atop his desk. He was embarrassed for her humiliation.

Blindly, Lace spun on her heels, and almost crashed into the teacher, Mr. Namon.

He put up his palms, "Whoa, slow down, what's going on, Miss Bettingfield?"

Head ducked, Lace shoved past him and fled down the corridor.

But there was no sanctuary here.

The hallways were lined with students, several of them holding copies of the *Cupid Chronicle*. Some laughed. Some pointed. Some made lewd gestures. Some threw out more catcalls. A goth girl was slyly singing "Crush," a song about a stalker.

Everyone was going to think she was a stalker.

"Hey, Tongue-Tied, drop thirty pounds and maybe you can land your dream man."

"Reality check. No guy like Pierce could ever love someone like you."

"Yes, he touched your hand, but I heard he washed it off in Lysol afterward."

Lace plastered her hands over her ears, willed herself not to cry, but it was too late, tears were already streaming hotly down her cheeks.

Nightmare. It was a living nightmare.

And just as in a nightmare everything moved in slow motion. It felt as if she was trying to run through knee-deep mud. Her lungs squeezed tight. Her heart pounded so hard she thought it was going to beat right out of her chest.

Good. If her heart beat out of her chest she would die.

It seemed to take hours to traverse that hallway. She kept her head down, didn't once make eye contact with anyone. She was headed for the exit, desperate to find a place to lick her wounds.

The morning sun glinted against the metal bar in the middle of the exit door. Almost there. Salvation was just a few steps away. She rushed forward, her legs breaking through the slow-motion morass.

Her hand hit the bar and she gave a hard shove.

But fate, that vicious bitch, wasn't done with her yet.

The door smacked into something solid. Someone was coming in at the same time she was trying to get out. Trapped. She was trapped. No exit. *Knock 'em down if you have to. Just get the hell out of here.*

She raised her head and found herself staring into Pierce Hollister's brown eyes.

Her heart literally stopped and a whimper escaped her lips.

For Mary Alice to print her letter in the school paper was a horrible betrayal. The bullying by classmates she thought she knew was unbearable. Breaking down and crying in front of everyone was humiliating, but nothing that had happened to her that morning was as bad as what was written across Pierce's handsome face.

Utter, abject pity.

Chapter 1

*Inflorescence: a group or cluster of
flowers arranged on a main stem.*

Twelve years later . . .

Aunt Carol Ann's pleasant reaction to the devil's
tongue blooming near the Cupid fountain should have
served as fair warning.

At seven-thirty A.M. on Monday morning in late
July, Carol Ann Spencer minced through the back gate
of the Cupid Botanical Gardens in four-inch heels, a
size four gray pencil skirt, and a lemon yellow blouse
with capped sleeves that showed off her toned biceps.
Even though she was over fifty, her hair was still a soft
honey brown achieved by the alchemy of her colorist.

Carol Ann carried an oversized canvas tote bag to
collect the letters that had been deposited over the weekend in the locked, white wooden box with "Letters to
Cupid" stenciled on it in red. To the right of the letterbox
was a list of rules posted on a glassed-in bulletin board.

1. All letters should be submitted using an anonymous pseudonym.
2. Letters will be answered within one week.
3. Letters of a sexually graphic nature will not be published.
4. The letters are for entertainment purposes only.
5. Cupid is not to be held responsible for what the letter writers do with the advice.

Lace Bettingfield, PhD, was kneeling in the soil behind the five-foot stone fountain of the Roman god of love, enthusiastically pruning *Hersperaloe parviflora,* commonly known as red yucca, even though it wasn't actually yucca. She wore military-grade kneepads over her blue jeans, and a long-sleeved, red-plaid cotton shirt. She tilted her head back far enough to watch Carol Ann from underneath the wide brim of her straw hat as she clicked the wrought-iron gate closed behind her.

Usually, it was her cousin Natalie who retrieved the correspondence for the tri-weekly meeting of volunteers who answered the letters from the lovelorn. Hmm, what was their aunt doing here instead?

Her glasses had slid down on her nose and she pushed them back up with the pinky finger of her gloved hand. Sweat beaded her brow, but she barely noticed. Perspiration was a tool of the botanist's trade.

Carol Ann's heels clacked against the terra-cotta

pavers. She cast a sideways glance at the flies swarming the devil's tongue blooming in the large mosaic pot.

Lace's new assistant, Shasta Green, had insisted they decorate the terra-cotta planter with remnants of other broken pots to create the mosaic. Shasta's rationale had been, "If it's gonna smell like a dead rat, it at least needs a pretty pot to bloom in."

She had to admit that while Shasta might not be the deepest bulb in the garden, she did have an eye for design. After she twice caught the girl sleeping in the potting shed, she'd hired Shasta and let her stay in the garage apartment over the Craftsman-style house that Lace had recently bought on Manlow Avenue. Shasta claimed she was nineteen, but Lace had her doubts. The kid was probably a runaway, but Lace respected other people's privacy and hadn't prodded her for details about her circumstances. Better to have her working where Lace could keep an eye on her, than slipping around getting into trouble.

And when the girl had announced, "Name's Shasta, like the daisy. *Chrysanthemum maximum*. My mama used to work in a flower shop and she named me after the hardiest flower she could think of," it had cinched the deal.

Carol Ann cocked her head, and studied the devil's tongue with rapt interest. Lace expected her aunt to twist her face into a mask of revulsion and whine, *What's that disgusting smell coming from that hideous-*

looking thing, but her nose didn't even twitch at the fetid stench.

Was something wrong with her olfactory perception? That had to be it. She'd lost her sense of smell.

To Lace, the aroma of *Amorphophallus konjac*, aka devil's tongue, aka voodoo lily, aka snake plant, was the sweet smell of success. She'd been trying for four years to get it to bloom. She'd planted this one from a tuber while she was getting her PhD in plant science from Texas A&M and she'd brought the aroid back home with her when she'd been hired to run the Cupid Botanical Gardens three months ago after the previous director, Miss Winnie Sparks, had retired at age seventy-six. Miss Winnie had been holding on to the position until she could get her degree and take over.

Sometimes, she wondered if coming back home to Cupid had been a mistake, especially since people here saw her as she'd once been, not whom she'd become. But she loved this job and her roots ran deep in her hometown community snuggled in the foothills of the Davis Mountains.

Humming "Everything Is Not What It Seems," Carol Ann stopped in front of the white box and leaned over to twirl the numbers on the combination lock.

Apparently her aunt hadn't seen her. She would have happily put her head back down and kept on pruning, but she had to admit, her curiosity was piqued.

"Seriously, Auntie," she drawled, "Selena Gomez?"

Carol Ann let out a shriek, threw the tote bag over her shoulder, and clasped both hands over her heart. "Oh my Lord, Lace! You scared the living daylights out of me. What are you doing lurking about?"

"I work here." She pointed the tip of the pruning shears at the red yucca.

"You should have cleared your throat or said hello or something so I would have known you were there. You always were a sly child."

Whenever Carol Ann said that within her mother's hearing, Colleen Bettingfield would lean over and whisper to her, "Not sly, just smart and shy. Big difference."

She smiled an apology. "Sorry, Auntie. I didn't mean to give you a cardiac arrhythmia."

"Don't you have workers who can do that?" Carol Ann waved a hand at the yucca. "You're the director. You should be taking meetings and doing research and planning budgets and things like that."

"I'm also the curator," she reminded her. "Which means managing the plants. Besides, I already did the budget. Manuel is out sick and we don't have enough in the coffers to hire extra gardeners."

"Isn't that what your assistant is for?"

"For one thing, she's getting minimum wage. Plus, she's just a kid, still learning the ropes."

"Why didn't you say things were that tight?" Carol Ann sank her hands on her hips. "We can always start charging admission. I'll put it on the next city council agenda."

"Please don't mention it to the city council. I'm proud of the fact we don't charge admission so that everyone can enjoy the garden. I'll find the money in the budget." If she had to use her own salary to fill in the holes, she would.

But that was only a stopgap solution. She did have to find a way to raise money if she wanted to implement the improvements she had in mind for the gardens. Her ultimate dream was to win the annual Lady Bird Johnson city garden beautification award, but that was a long ways off.

"Well, if you're sure."

"I'm sure."

Carol Ann stepped toward the devil's tongue.

Wow, she was actually getting closer to the stinky plant? Lace couldn't believe it.

At four feet tall, *Amorphophallus konjac* was a sight to behold, although nothing like its giant cousin, *Amorphophallus titanium* (common name corpse plant, which gave some idea of how bad *it* smelled), which had been known to grow as tall as twenty feet and took a decade to bloom. She'd always had a secret longing to grow titanium. Nursing one to full bloom demanded a level of commitment she'd as yet been unable to make, but one day she'd do it.

This plant possessed a florid burgundy inflorescence, so plastic-like that if it were not for the smell, it might be mistaken for artificial. In the center was a single elongated "tongue," known as a corm, and decidedly phallic in appearance. A purple leaf curled up around the corm like the collar of a vampire's cloak. The overall effect was both sinister and oddly elegant.

It was a fascinating specimen and kids loved it because of its foul fragrance and demonic appearance, which was the main reason she'd moved it from the greenhouse into the garden. She loved getting children interested in botany. In spite of the reeking odor, it was a sight worth seeing.

"Is that konjac?"

Lace raised an eyebrow. "You know what it is?"

Carol Ann stuck her chin in the air. "I might not have a PhD, but I'm not stupid."

"I didn't mean anything derogatory by the question, it's just that you don't even like gardening. Where did you hear about konjac?"

"Dr. Oz. He said it's a fabulous weight loss substance, safe and effective."

Ah. Now it was all making sense.

"So I did a little Googling and saw a picture of the konjac plant. They did say it was very stinky and now I see why." Carol Ann waved a hand in front of her nose. "Stinky is a kind way of putting it. Smells like the meat that went bad in our mountain cabin after the freezer went out."

With the mystery of her aunt's interest in *Amorpho-phallus konjac* solved, Lace turned back to the yucca.

"And those flies are quite annoying."

"Flies are what pollinate the konjac. That's why it smells the way it does. To attract them."

"I see." Carol Ann tilted her head. "Which part is the corm? I read that's where they get the food source from."

"The part that looks like a porn star's penis." Okay, it was flippant, but seriously, her aunt had it coming.

Carol Ann made a chuffing noise and her thin nostrils flared. "There's no need to be crude, young lady."

Lace rolled her eyes.

"I saw that."

" 'Penis' is an anatomically correct word," she pointed out.

"That may be true but it's not a word to be used in polite company."

"It's just you and me here. There's no one else around to judge us. No ghosts of Fants or Greenwoods past."

Carol Ann picked up the tote bag she'd dropped earlier and returned to unlock the letterbox. "Well, in spite of the fact you need your mouth washed out with soap, I *am* glad to see you're taking proactive steps to do something about your weight."

Lace blinked. "What?"

"Although honestly, you could just purchase the konjac pills at a health food store. It's called glucomannan. I know you love to dig in the dirt and you do have your father's hippie tendencies, but you don't have to grow and harvest and compound your own weight loss aid."

Silently, she counted to ten. If Carol Ann said, *You have such a pretty face, if you'd only lose thirty pounds, you'd have guys flocking all over you*, she was going to scream.

She had been skinny once. She'd had guys flocking all over and she had allowed the attention to go to her head. Lace cringed, remembering the wild coed she'd become when she, like Carol Ann, had worn a size four. She liked her weight the way it was now, liked being a size fourteen. The sturdiness made her feel powerful, grounded, substantial, and in control.

"Honey, you do have such a pretty—"

"Don't you have to be at work by eight?" Lace cut her off. Her aunt was a CPA and she'd just been asked to take over the books for the town of Cupid after their last accountant left unexpectedly.

"Oh my, yes." Carol Ann glanced at her wristwatch. "Thank you for the reminder." She scooped the letters from the box, tucked them into her tote, reset the lock.

She clipped the yucca, enjoying the *snip-snip* sound of the shears.

Carol Ann cleared her throat. "Oh, by the way, we're moving the noon meeting from the community center."

"Where to?"

"The rehab wing of Cupid General Hospital. They

moved Aunt Delia there yesterday and the doctor said it was fine to hold our meeting in her hospital room. He thought it would cheer her up to feel useful again."

A month earlier, Lace's feisty great-aunt Delia had fallen in the tub and broken her hip. "I'll be there."

Carol Ann stood there a moment as if expecting more conversation. Lace didn't give her any. "Well, I'll leave you to it."

"Have a nice day," she said without looking up.

Her aunt *click-clacked* her way back to the gate, paused, and turned around. "Oh, sweetie, I almost forgot what I came here to tell you."

Lace suppressed a sigh and raised her head again. She had to see her aunt three times a week at the volunteer meetings, no point in stirring the pot, although it took a lot of tongue biting to keep from smarting off. "What is it, Auntie?"

"Pierce Hollister has come home."

Boom!

Carol Ann dropped the bomb and walked away without even looking around to see the results of her detonation.

With a trembling pinky finger, Lace pushed on the bridge of her glasses again, even though they hadn't fallen back down, as her heart climbed into her throat. This was it. The very thing she'd spent the last twelve years dreading.

The prodigal athlete's return.

SOME THINGS NEVER changed. Life in Cupid, Texas, was one of them.

People tipped their Stetsons, and nodded hello to friends and strangers alike. Folks sat out on their front lawns, waving to whomever went by. Kids ran laughing and squealing through water sprinklers. The ice cream truck rolled through the neighborhoods offering its wares of fudge bars, Nutty Buddys and Push-ups to the Pied Piper warble of "Pop Goes the Weasel."

Pierce Hollister drove his F–150 King Ranch luxury Ford pickup truck down Main Street and took a left on Pike. He cruised past the botanical gardens and the Bettingfield livery stable, the smell of horses in the air. It had been a long time since he'd been on the back of a horse.

If it weren't for the leg, he'd saddle up a stallion when he got to the Triple H and go for a gallop. Pierce leaned over and pressed a hand to his left shin, and he could feel the ridges of the scar even through the heavy denim of his Wranglers.

The sky was brilliant blue, the air a dry eighty-nine degrees; the Davis Mountains squatted behind him, as solemn as Zen masters, knowing everything but saying nothing. He had a coach once who'd required them to meditate before a game. He bitched about it as much as the next player, but secretly he'd loved the silent practice and came to look forward to it. Too bad he couldn't seem to get back to that quiet inner peace.

He passed by the high school, the parking lots vacant except for the one near the football field filled with pickup trucks and SUVs. The players were running the bleachers, the coach stood on the field, hands on his hips, whistle in his mouth. Year after year, football practice started in July. The players changed, but the ritual never did.

His leg twinged again and melancholia, bittersweet as pickled watermelon rind, rolled across his tongue. He could taste the shadow of his youth mocking him. Who's the big shot now?

Shake it off. Next thing you know you'll be puttin' on Springsteen and wailing to "Glory Days." Back. He was going to get it all back. By this time next year, the media would be calling him the Comeback Kid. Well, maybe not Kid. At thirty, he certainly wasn't a kid anymore.

The Dairy Queen was still across the street from the high school, although it had a new paint job since Pierce Hollister's last thunderclap visit to his hometown two years ago.

The same day he'd made quarterback of the junior varsity; he'd copped his first feel behind that Dairy Queen in his battered old 1978 Chevy pickup with Mary Alice Fant. His hands up under her sweater, palms skimming her belly, his mouth on hers. A few weeks later, they'd gone all the way on the chaise longue on her parents' back patio.

Ah, Mary Alice.

Pierce grinned, until that memory led to another one and he remembered the mess Mary Alice had caused by publishing that sad little Dear Cupid letter written by his best buddy Jay's younger half sister in the school newspaper. That had been damn vindictive of her. Mary Alice had done it to embarrass Pierce for breaking up with her so he could date the head cheerleader, Jenny Angus, but what she'd ended up doing was humiliating her own cousin.

Grimacing, he shook his head. He'd had no idea that Lace had been crushing on him. If he had known how she felt, he wouldn't have tweaked her hair and called her "brat" for tagging along after him and Jay.

He still recalled the way Lace had looked the last day he'd ever seen her, barreling through the door of the high school in shame, tears streaming down her face. He'd had an impulse to pull her into his arms and soothe her, tell her everything was going to be okay, but that would have just made things worse for both of them. So he'd just stood there at the door watching her run down the sidewalk as fast as her legs would carry her.

Coward.

The incident had happened at the end of the school year and Pierce was relieved to avoid any blowback by going off to the University of Texas, while Jay had been accepted to Texas Tech. They'd kept in contact for a while, but with him on a football scholarship and Jay pre-med, well, they simply had different interests and they'd eventually drifted apart.

Oh, they still called each other once in a while—Jay had phoned with his condolences when Pierce was in the hospital after the Super Bowl disaster where he'd broken his fibula and tibia and lost the game—but they never brought up Lace's name.

Silly, in retrospect, to let something like that cause a ripple in their friendship, but the fact was, it had. Sad because when they were teenagers they'd been like peanut butter and jelly.

Didn't really matter now. That was twelve long years ago, so much water under the bridge.

He braked at an intersection. La Hacienda Grill sat on the corner as it always had, a garish mural painted across the front featuring a platter of tacos and a pitcher of margaritas inset over a pink hibiscus flower, along with four smiling mariachis. Smoke poured from the metal chimney on the roof, punctuating the lunch hour with the smell of sizzling skirt steak.

A gaggle of giggling teenage girls in halter tops and short shorts strutted in front of his hood. Once upon a time, he would have been chasing after them with a wink and a crook of his finger. Now they just made him feel old. Young bucks leaned against the side of Greenwood's Grocery, flexing and posturing for the girls. Cocky and full of themselves, so certain their youth would last forever. Funny how things that had once seemed so important barely mattered now.

Pierce snorted. The light turned green and he eased off the brake.

He had bigger things on his mind these days than which girl he could lure into his bed. In fact, he'd sworn off women for the foreseeable future. His girlfriend Amber had done a number on him when she'd broken things off after his accident and then promptly took up with the quarterback who'd replaced him on the team. To compensate, he'd thrown himself one hundred percent into his rehab and had made tremendous progress.

Up ahead, the blue "Hospital" road sign pointed the way to Cupid General. He braced himself for the institutional scent of antiseptic, overheated linen, and powdered eggs. It was a smell he'd grown far too familiar with over the last five months.

Temporary.

All his setbacks were temporary. While the media had shown the sack repeatedly—that point of impact where the linebacker's hit had broken his leg—and compared him to Joe Theismann, his injury had not been quite that severe. His doctors had assured him that it was entirely possible that he could make a full recovery and return to the NFL. Pierce simply wasn't the kind of guy who could stay sidelined for long.

In fact, if his old man hadn't gotten sick, he would still be in Dallas getting physical therapy.

But his old man *had* gotten sick and Pierce had come home. Not to lick his wounds, but to help his brother, Malcolm, run the family ranch while Dad was laid up.

Soon as his father was on his feet again, Pierce would be headed back to Dallas. By then, he should be off the disabled list and ready to hit the ground running.

He pulled to a stop in the visitors' parking lot and got out, but he'd taken no more than two steps when from behind him a woman shrieked.

"Oh. My. God! As I live and breathe, it's Pierce Hollister!"

A few more females squealed, then came the sound of stampeding high heels, and the next thing he knew, he was surrounded by two blondes, two brunettes, and a redhead, all young and gorgeous and sweet-smelling.

Pierce tipped his Stetson back on his head, gave his patented smile, and drawled, "Hello, ladies."

They erupted into fresh squeals.

"I told Tiffany that was you!" the taller brunette said. She had big, wide Bambi eyes and a nose that looked like she'd had it whittled down until it was too small for her face. She was holding a Mylar balloon that said: "It's a Boy!"

One of the blondes, who resembled the actress Hayden Panettiere—Pierce had once sat next to Hayden at a celebrity charity event—twittered. She had a box, gift-wrapped with blue paper, tucked under her arm. "It wasn't that I didn't believe you, I just couldn't imagine why Pierce Hollister would come back to this one-horse town."

"Cupid is my hometown," Pierce chided. Hypocrite. When he was her age he'd felt the same way, but he wouldn't earn any community brownie points by saying so. "Don't dis it, Tiff."

Tiffany wilted like a delicate flower in the hot desert sun. "Oh, I am so, so sorry. I didn't mean anything by it. Cupid is my hometown too, it's just that it's so dinky and nothing ever happens here—"

"Be proud of where you're from." *But get out while the getting is good.*

The buxom redhead darted out a hand, quickly stroked his forearm, snatched her hand back, and giggled. "Look at me, I just touched Pierce Hollister!"

The second blonde, whose hair was so fine and thin her ears poked out through it, whipped out her cell phone, snapped a picture of Pierce, and with lightning-fast thumbs was already sending it off to social media sites.

The others immediately followed suit. Pierce's smile was fading.

"Can I have an autograph?" asked the shorter brunette, her ponytail swishing as she dug in her oversized purse. "I got a pen and notepad in here somewhere."

"Forget the paper." The redhead whipped out a Sharpie from the back pocket of her tight-fitting jeans, thrust it at him, and then pulled open her blouse, revealing an impressive set of tits. "Sign these."

Yes, some things never changed.

Pierce suppressed a sigh, uncapped the Sharpie, and autographed her cleavage. Of course, after that, they all wanted their boobs signed and then they had to take pictures of his signature and tweet it too.

"We are so sorry about your leg," the first brunette said when the Sharpie and smart phones had been put away. "We hope you heal real soon."

"You'll be back better than ever!" the redhead enthused.

"The Dallas Cowboys aren't the same without you," Tiffany said.

How would she know? Preseason didn't start for another month. The Cowboys might just be fine and dandy without him. Immediately, Pierce stomped on that thought, ground it out. He couldn't allow self-doubt to take root and grow. The redhead was right. He would be back better than ever.

Uh-huh. Go ahead, blow smoke up your own ass.

"If you ladies will excuse me." He motioned toward the hospital and started moving slowly in that direction. If he moved carefully enough, he could keep from limping.

"Oh, we're going that way too," said the tall brunette. "Our friend just had a baby. We'll walk with you."

"Who are you visiting?" asked the thin-haired blonde, falling into step beside him.

"My dad," he said, feeling his lips stretch tight.

"Oh yes, your dad owns the Triple H, right?"

Pierce nodded. "He does."

The redhead laid a hand on his shoulder. "I hope he gets well real soon."

Not half as much as Pierce did. "Thank you."

Tiffany rushed ahead and opened the door for him. "You know, you're a lot more handsome in person than you are on TV."

How was a guy supposed to respond to that? He just smiled.

Heads turned as he and his entourage entered the hospital. People whispered and pointed. Feeling like Pimp Daddy, he kept the smile shellacked on his face all the way to the elevator.

"We gotta go," the shorter brunette said wistfully.

"The maternity ward is on the first floor," explained the redhead.

"It was sure nice meeting you," said the other three in unison.

He tipped his hat, winked. "You ladies have a nice day."

They giggled. The elevator dinged. Reluctantly, they bid him good-bye, all five of them walking backward so they could watch him until he disappeared from sight.

The door slid open. The Muzak of Vivaldi's Four Seasons—Summer spilled out.

Pierce stepped quicker than he should have, eager

to get on the elevator, and plowed right into a pair of plush, pillowy breasts.

"Ooph." The woman coming off the elevator took a step back.

"I'm so sorry." Pierce put out a hand to cup her elbow and stared straight into the bluest eyes he'd ever seen framed by a pair of small, rectangular, black-rimmed glasses.

A soft hiccup escaped lips the color of roses in full bloom. Jet black hair, cut to fall just below her chin, arched around her face in big silky curls. Her skin was smooth and pale as Ivory soap, her eyelashes long and thick.

Call central casting at Disney. He'd found Snow White.

In that moment Pierce experienced the most overwhelming sensation of . . . Well, what in the hell was this sensation?

He had no words to describe it. The only comparison that seemed even remotcly apt was how it felt to be sacked by a human steamroller at the exact same moment the wide receiver who'd caught his Hail Mary pass ran into the end zone for the game-winning touchdown. Lying on his back, vision blurry, breath knocked out, charley horse squeezing his gut, grinning like a Texas opossum at the crowd's wild roar, knowing that all the pain was worth the victory.

Sweet heaven.

Sweat broke out on his forehead.

She jerked her elbow away, tossed her chin in the air, and pushed past him. Her palm made contact with his rib cage. Instant heat spread up his body, warmed his chest.

"Excuse me," she said brusquely.

She was built like a brick house with a beautiful plump rump that his hands tingled to latch on to, and he thought, *Cadillac, ripe Bartlett pears, Versailles, curvy cellos.*

He knew this woman but for the life of him, he could not place her. He stepped out of the elevator to watch her spectacular ass bounce down the hall, his heart hammering strangely. The elevator door whacked him in the side, but he barely noticed. He blinked and finally recognized her. She was the younger half sister of his best buddy in high school.

Lace Bettingfield.

All grown up.

Stunned, Pierce staggered to the rear of the elevator, braced his shaky arms on the railing, and leaned his head back against the wall as violins wept through the piped-in sound system. He stood like that for a good two minutes, his breath quickening along with the crescendo of Vivaldi's honey-coated summer before he realized he'd forgotten to push the button.

Yes, some things never changed. But Lace Bettingfield sure had.

Chapter 2

Crown: part of a plant where the root and stem meet.

IN a haze, Lace pushed through the front door of the hospital and stood outside on the sidewalk, blinking in the sunlight. Her pulse pounded in her ears. So what if Pierce was moving back to Cupid? She didn't care. She'd gotten over him years ago. She'd done just fine there in the elevator. She'd held her head high and kept on going. Fine, huh? So what was she doing out here when she was supposed to be in Aunt Delia's room?

Pivoting, she walked back into the hospital. Using a technique she'd learned while undergoing therapy to treat her stutter, she recited basic botanical terms. The trick never failed to calm her. *Stem, node, internodes, bud, stipule, rhizome, root, bulb.*

A bright-face candy striper stuffed her hands into the wide pockets of her pink pinafore, and grinned at Lace. "You saw him too, huh?"

"Who?" Lace asked.

"Pierce Hollister. He's so hot." She melted against a cart loaded with pots of *Dianthus caryophyllus*, the ubiquitous get-well carnations, that was parked outside the hospital gift shop.

The pots wobbled and Lace quickly put out a restraining hand to keep them from toppling over. "Why would you say that?"

" 'Cause this is the second time you walked past here in the last five minutes looking dazed and confused. What else would have you looking like that?"

"It's not Pierce Hollister," Lace snapped.

"Oh yes it is. My daddy is a huge fan of the Dallas Cowboys and Pierce is from Cupid. And believe you me, it was Pierce. I even snapped a picture of him on my cell phone." She pulled the phone out of her pocket. "Wanna see?"

"I do not want to see." Lace had meant that it wasn't Pierce Hollister who'd caused her to rush into the hospital twice, but she was lying about that. She'd spotted him in the side visitors' parking lot surrounded by beautiful women.

Shocker.

To avoid him, she'd driven around the other side of the building, parked there, and rushed through the front entrance before he could untangle himself from the groupies. She'd thought she was safe until the elevator opened on the third floor where Great-aunt Delia's room had been and rushed in only to find it empty, before she remembered Carol Ann had told her that Delia had been moved to the rehab wing.

She'd hopped back on the elevator, hell-bent on getting to the rehab wing ASAP. As rotten luck would have it, Pierce had been there waiting on the elevator.

But she'd been cool. Hadn't given away that she recognized him. Prayed he hadn't recognized her, and she'd walked right out the front door. She was not going to allow that man to have any influence over her feelings. None whatsoever. That mess was a long time ago. Ancient history. She'd put it all behind her. He was nothing but high school foolishness.

Lace waved a hand at the candy striper. "Where's the rehab wing?"

This was rich. She'd been born and raised in Cupid. Been inside the hospital numerous times. She should know her way around. But hey, they'd remodeled Cupid General while she was away at college.

"Take a left at the next corridor." The candy striper pointed.

"Thank you."

Lace found Delia's room easily enough. Once she got to the rehab wing, all she had to do was follow the laughter. The door stood ajar and everyone was already there.

Every Monday, Wednesday, and Friday at noon the volunteers met to answer the letters written to Cupid. There were eight permanent Cupid volunteers, plus a dozen others who showed up periodically or filled in for the core group when they went on vacation, experienced illnesses, or had family obligations.

The Cupid letter-writing tradition had started in the 1930s after the Depression hit and the town had a desperate need of extra income and they were doing anything to generate tourism. Lace's grandmother Rose had spearheaded the campaign, gathering some of the local women to answer the letters that people left at the base of the Cupid stalagmite inside the Cupid Caverns. At first, the replies to the letters were left on a bulletin board posted outside the caverns, but that became unwieldy and in the 1940s someone had the idea of doing away with the bulletin board and instead printing the letters and "Cupid's" reply in a free weekly newspaper that was paid for, and distributed by, local businesses.

Great-aunt Delia was propped up in bed wearing a puckishly gamboge knit cap over short-cropped, cement-colored curls. She was the family matriarch, the last surviving member of Millie and John Fant's eight children. The over-bed table was positioned across her lap. The hospital lunch sat untouched on a tray, while Delia munched a drumstick.

"Best fried chicken ever," Delia sang out. "Tell Pearl she has my undying gratitude. If I had to survive on that hospital tuna casserole, I'd shrivel up and die."

"I'll tell her," Cousin Natalie said.

Pearl worked for Natalie at her bed-and-breakfast, the Cupid's Rest, and she was inarguably the best cook in town.

"Should you really be eating that, Delia?" Carol

Ann asked. She sat in a blue plastic chair drawn up to Delia's bedside and her legs were primly crossed at the ankles, her knees pressed together, a tablet computer in her lap.

Mignon delicately stripped the skin from her chicken, and pushed it to a pile on the paper plate. Mignon was Delia's daughter-in-law. She and Delia's son, Michael, ran Mon Amour, one of the three vineyards on the outskirts of Cupid. Mignon had been born in Loire, France. She had dark hair, almost as black as Lace's own, and everything she did seemed utterly sophisticated and elegant. Mignon and Michael had no children and had never wanted them. "Children have a way of ruining passion," Mignon was fond of saying, usually with a suggestive wink.

Sometimes, if she and Michael were having trouble with the vines, they consulted Lace on how to improve the crop. "You are the plant whisperer," Mignon told her once. "Whenever you speak to them, the grapes flourish."

It was the nicest thing anyone had ever said to her.

"Lace, sweetie, are you feeling well?" asked Aunt Sandra. She sat to Mignon's right. "You look flushed."

"Fine." She put a hand to her face. Her cheeks were warm, but it was *not* from running into Pierce Hollister on the elevator. "I've been in the sun all morning."

"Have something to eat," Sandra invited. "It will make you feel better."

Sandra was Delia's sister-in-law, but twelve years Delia's junior. Even at sixty-five, her cocoa-colored skin was still flawless. She loved to eat and it showed in her matronly figure, just made for hugging her numerous grandchildren. Sandra was the connector of the group, the one who smoothed things over when feathers got ruffled, although Natalie did that as well. Sandra's favorite saying was "You can't push a river."

After that humiliating incident in high school, Sandra was the first one to show up. She knocked on Lace's bedroom door. "Honey child, I made you a big ol' bowl of banana pudding."

Lace had refused to come out of her room or talk to anyone for two days, freaking her mother out. But she slid off her bed and cracked the door open for Sandra and motioned her in. They sat on Lace's bed eating the most heavenly banana pudding in the world, and Sandra never said a word about the newspaper letter or Pierce Hollister. She didn't tell Lace that one day she would look back and laugh at this the way her mother and father had.

They ate the entire bowl of pudding, then Sandra got up, kissed Lace's forehead, and whispered, "Love just plain hurts sometimes, but we can't let that stop us from loving. Love is the only thing in the world that really matters."

She still wasn't sure about that one. Did love of plants count?

"Lace?" Sandra handed her a paper plate, breaking her from the memory.

"Fine," Lace repeated, and moved to where the food was laid out on a short dresser, but for once after heavy gardening, she wasn't hungry. *Oh no, you're not going back there. Eat something.*

Cousin Zoey reached over and plunked a chicken breast and a big spoonful of potato salad on Lace's plate. "There you go."

"Thanks," she said tightly.

Today, Zoey was dressed in playful black pleather shorts that showed off every bit of her long tanned legs, a floral silk raspberry blouse that had flowy ruffles at the scoop neck, and black and raspberry wedge-heeled espadrilles. In contrast to her chic clothing, her finger-nails were ragged and unpainted, reflecting her new interest in archaeology. Zoey had an explorer's enthusiastic spirit, and the spunk of a chipmunk, eagerly hopping from one fascinating discovery to another. Lace sometimes wondered if her cousin had an attention deficit disorder.

After "the incident," Zoey, who'd only been ten at the time, trotted over to Lace's house with a Raggedy Andy and a box of pins. "Let's pretend this is Pierce and make a voodoo doll out of him." She handed Lace a straight pin with a big red head. "Go ahead, stick it where it'll hurt."

Bloodthirsty kid. But Lace had done it. Ramming

the pin right into Raggedy Andy's heart. Immediately, she'd felt bad about it and yanked the pin out. After all, it wasn't really Pierce's fault that he had not loved her. She'd been the stupid one, writing that letter in the first place.

Now Zoey spontaneously wrapped an arm around Lace's waist, laid her head on her shoulder, and whispered, "It'll be okay."

Lace froze, her hand gripping the paper plate. *Organic fertilizer.* Did they all know that Pierce was back in town?

She turned back around to see everyone staring at her with a mixture of concern and fascination, like a huddle of doctors consulting on a mysterious illness, ready to poke and prod. Yep. They knew.

"People," she said. "It's no big deal that Pierce Hollister is back in Cupid. I do not care. He means *nothing* to me."

The concerned fascination turned to sympathetic disbelief.

"There's no shame in still having feelings for him," said Junie Mae Prufrock from her spot beside Sandra. Junie Mae was the only volunteer who was not related in some way by either blood or marriage to Millie Greenwood Fant.

Junie Mae resembled Dolly Parton when she was in *Steel Magnolias*—big blond hair, even bigger boobs, and that slow Southern twang. She ran the LaDeDa

Day Spa and Hair Salon next door to Natalie's B&B. She decorated her place with artificial plants, which set Lace's teeth on edge. "I was born with the blackest thumb around," Junie Mae pronounced when Lace had tried to give her an ivy plant. "If you don't want that poor plant to rest in peace in the Dumpster by the end of the week, take it back."

Lace slowly blew out her breath. They meant well. She knew that. "I do appreciate your concern, but truly, I'm fine. Can we get down to work?"

They all exchanged looks.

Although she dearly loved her huge extended family, sometimes they could be a serious pain in the keister.

Delia kicked the foot of the leg on the opposite side of where she'd broken her hip. "Sit on the end of my bed, Chantilly."

Her great-aunt had fun calling her the names of different types of lace. Gingerly, she sat on the end of the bed and balanced her plate on her knee.

Cousin Natalie, who was sitting at the folding table between Junie Mae and Mignon, reached for a letter at the top of the pile. Natalie had an air of ethereal peace about her that had intensified since she'd fallen in love with former Navy SEAL–turned–cowboy Dade Vega. The two were so lovey-dovey it was enough to make a single woman hurl, but Lace couldn't resent Natalie's happiness. Poor girl had been through a helluva lot in her life, losing both her parents in a plane crash when she was nine and left with the responsibility for her kid sister, Zoey, and a permanent limp. Now in the throes of new love, she positively glowed.

Natalie was the one who waited while the rest of the family had rallied around her after "the incident," even though the last thing Lace wanted was for people to keep trying to make her feel better about it. Natalie seemed to understand that.

After things finally died down, Natalie drove up in their grandmother Rose's car one Sunday afternoon. Lace had been sitting on the front porch reading a book on botany.

Natalie rolled down the window. "Get in."

She shook her head. She'd avoided leaving the house. "I'm good."

"Lace," Natalie had said patiently but firmly. "Get in the car."

She hesitated, but the look on Natalie's face persuaded her. She closed the book, opened the front door, and called to her mother, "I'm ga . . . ga . . . going to hang out with Natalie."

"Have a good time," her mother hollered from the kitchen. "Be back in time to set the table for supper."

She'd closed the door and walked up to the driver's side window. "Wh . . . wh . . . where are we going?"

"You'll see."

"Don't wa . . . wa . . . wa . . . wanna be around pa . . . people."

"We won't."

It wasn't like Natalie to be cryptic. Intrigued, she had gotten in. Her cousin had driven them to the entrance to Cupid Caverns.

"The caverns are closed on Sunday," Lace said.

Natalie dangled a key on a scarlet ribbon in front of her face. "I sneaked the key out of the teacup on Gram's hutch."

"Natalie!" Lace giggled at her daring.

"Get the tote bag out of the backseat."

Lace retrieved the tote bag. Inside she found two flashlights, two slingshots, and a bag of black-eyed peas.

Curiouser and curiouser.

Natalie shouldered the tote and led the way. They entered the caverns. It was spooky all alone inside, but Lace wasn't afraid of the dark. They played the flashlight beams over the path that wound around to the cavern containing the Cupid statue on which the town legend was based.

The fable started before Cupid became a town, when a charming outlaw named Mingus Dill, on the run from a posse for stealing a horse, took refuge in the cavern. It was just after the Civil War and there was an odd law on the books in Trans-Pecos territory that a man could be saved from being hanged for any crime, except murder, if any single woman claimed him for her husband.

Mingus stumbled into the dead-end cave that housed a stalagmite that looked exactly like Cupid. As the sounds of the pursuing posse filled his ears, Mingus dropped to his knees and prayed to the Roman god of love to send an arrow through the heart of some local woman to save him from being hanged. And it happened just as he prayed when a childless spinster, Louisa Hendricks, saved him from the noose. He and Louisa fell madly in love, and although they never had any children, they had a long and happy life.

The romantic tale was cemented when their great-grandmother, Millie Greenwood fell in love with her employer's brother, the richest man in Cupid, John Fant. John loved Millie too, but he was betrothed to another. On the day before John's wedding, a broken-hearted Millie wrote a letter to Cupid, asking him to intervene, and she carried it to the caverns in the dead of night on Christmas Eve and laid the letter at Cupid's feet. John Fant ended up leaving his betrothed at the altar in order to marry Millie. Thus spurring the letter-writing tradition.

"Da . . . da . . . damn that Millie and her st . . . stu . . . stupid letter," Lace stuttered, for about the thousandth time since her letter had ended up in the school paper.

"That's why we're here," Natalie had said cheerfully as they entered the Cupid cave.

Natalie shone her flashlight over the stalagmite and

they'd stood there in awe. Whether she wanted to admit it or not, it was an impressive sight.

The stalagmite was over seven feet tall and almost touched the ceiling of the cave. Cupid appeared to be running, one leg on the ground, the other bent at the knee, a quiver on his back. He held what looked enough like a half-cocked bow with an arrow strung in it that you didn't even have to squint to see the resemblance. The top of Cupid's head was graced by what looked like a three-pointed crown, three thin knobs of stone standing up less than an inch tall. Cupid's face was just a green-orange blob of stone formed from years of steady dripping, but it was easy enough to see why the stalagmite had captured everyone's imagination.

"Here." Natalie held out a closed fist to Lace. "Open your hand."

Lace put out a palm.

Natalie dumped a handful of black-eyed peas into it. "Stick those in your pocket."

She did that too.

Natalie took their flashlights and propped them up so they would illuminate the stalagmite, passed a slingshot to Lace, and kept one for herself. "Load up."

"You mean sh . . . sha . . . shoot Cupid."

"I do." Natalie put a pea in the leather pocket of the slingshot, pulled back on the stretch rubber, and let a pea fly. "Take that, Mary Alice for publishing Lace's letter in the school paper!"

Lace had been a bit shocked. Cupid was such a town icon and Natalie was generally such a goody-goody, her actions seemed like sacrilege.

"Your turn," Natalie said cheerfully.

She cast a glance over her shoulder. It wasn't that she was afraid to let Cupid have it, but rather she feared that once she got started, she wouldn't be able to stop.

Natalie nudged her in the ribs with her elbow. "Go on. You'll feel better."

"Here goes nothing," she muttered, nestled the pea in the pocket, raised the slingshot to her face, closed one eye, Cupid in her sight, pulled back, and let go, and the pea did fly with a zing that rocketed around the cave and shook through Lace's arms.

Cupid didn't flinch.

"Mary Alice, you're a bitch." She loaded up another pea and sent it sailing. It hit Cupid's bow, bounced up and hit him where an eye would be if he had one.

She shot another pea and another and another, calling out the names of the students who'd laughed and ridiculed her, faster and faster. She rummaged through her pocket, through the knots of humiliation and lint balls and loose change, searching for one last pea to fling. When she found it, hidden underneath a dime, she pinched it between her fingers, last shot, make it count.

"Take that, Millie Greenwood!" she hollered. The last syllable echoing throughout the cave—*wood, wood, wood.*

Then aiming right at Cupid's head, she pulled back the leather strap and released the pea.

It catapulted, whizzed gracefully through the air, and slammed into the middle tine of Cupid's crown, breaking it off with a brittle *clink*.

"Oh shit," Natalie said.

Lace had never heard her curse.

Her cousin grabbed up the flashlights, tossed one to her. "Let's get the hell out of here."

Holding hands, they ran giggling for the entrance.

It was only when they were outside again that she realized, not once during the roll call of the black-eyed pea shootout, had she uttered a single stutter.

"Yo, daydreamer!" Zoey's voice snapped her back to the present. She was dangling a letter in Lace's face. "You want this or not?"

"Yes, sure, I'll take it." She snatched the letter away from Zoey, crumpled it in her fist.

"Lace?" Sandra asked. "Are you sure?"

Uh-oh. Damn, she should have been listening. Lace shrugged. "Sure, why wouldn't I be?"

"It's a letter about . . ." Junie Mae trailed off.

Without even looking, Lace knew from the expression on everyone's faces what the letter was about. "Go ahead, Junie Mae, you can say it."

Junie Mae shook her head.

"Unrequited love," Lace finished for her.

Junie Mae poked at her potato salad with a plastic fork.

"It was twelve years ago! You people can stop treating me with kid gloves. I got over the stutter and I got over Pierce Hollister. I was a dumb kid with a dumb crush. You guys are the ones who made a bigger deal of it than it was." Blatant lie, but that was her story and she was sticking to it. Although she had eventually worked through her feelings and gotten them properly sorted out.

"We just don't want to see you hurt." Natalie's eyes were gentle.

"So I got humiliated in front of the entire high school. I survived. Can anyone here say they've never been humiliated?"

"Got it," Carol Ann said brusquely, and typed into her iPad. "I'll mark you down to answer Hero Worshipper."

They went on like that, divvying up the letters to be answered, until they got through the entire pile. Sandra got up to clear away the food. Natalie slipped the letters Delia said she would answer into her own purse. Zoey snatched up the last piece of chicken and headed for the door with a jaunty wave of her hand.

Carol Ann was zipping up her iPad in her briefcase when her phone dinged, signaling she had a text message. She glanced down at her cell. "Oh my goodness, what a surprise."

"What is it?" Junie Mae asked, putting the lid back on the potato salad bowl.

"Melody is coming home for a visit."

Melody was Carol Ann's oldest child and only daughter. At twenty-eight, just eighteen months older than Lace, she was a big-wheel ad executive on Madison Avenue. Although Lace and Melody were the closest in age of Grandmother Rose's four granddaughters, they were polar opposites in both looks and personality.

While Natalie and Zoey had tried to cheer Lace up following "the incident," Melody had told her to suck it up and stop being a crybaby. She'd resented her cousin for years because of that blunt opinion. But now? She conceded that Melody's advice had been spot-on.

"We should throw a party for her at the vineyard," Mignon said.

Lace tuned out. Parties were not her thing. She shouldered her purse, murmured her good-bye, which no one paid much attention to, and slipped out the door. She'd just stepped out the front entrance again when she realized she'd left the letters she'd agreed to answer back in Aunt Delia's room.

Venus frigging flytrap.

Sighing, she went into the hospital for the third time that day.

"Pierce Hollister fever." The annoying candy striper grinned. "It's going around and it looks like you've got it bad."

Chapter 3

*Corolla: the part of a flower that
constitutes the inner whorl.*

ABE Hollister's appearance was shocking. His skin
was pasty, his normally sharp eyes glassy. He'd always
been a lanky man, but now he was so skinny that the
gold band on his bony fourth finger looked like it would
fly across the room if he suddenly waved his left hand.
But lethargy had a strong hold on him. No sudden hand
waving going on here. His frail body sank deep into the
hard mattress.

Pierce stood in the doorway of his father's hospital
room, the hyper-edginess of intense sexual attraction
that had overcome him in the elevator draining away.

His father wore a paper-thin hospital gown the color of
misery. House shoes with worn-down heels were tucked
underneath the foot of the bed. A metal walker parked
beside the bed with the maroon robe Pierce had sent him
for Father's Day thrown over it. Dad lifted a weak hand
to his stomach, pressed his lips together into a grimace.

Pierce's throat constricted and his gut twisted. Ah

damn, ah damn. This was not good. No easy solutions. No quick get things straightened out and get back to the gridiron. No magic wand.

The last time he'd seen his father had been five months earlier when Abe had come to visit him in the hospital in Dallas. In February, he had been the one in trouble. Now it was Dad. How could his father's health have deteriorated so rapidly?

His brother, Malcolm, was seated in a chair beside their father's bed, keyboarding on a laptop computer. He was small-boned and blond like their mother. He wore what every rancher's son in Jeff Davis County wore, the same thing Pierce had on—Wranglers, Western-style shirt, cowboy boots. Except Malcolm's boots were dusty and scraped, whereas Pierce's were shiny, new, and cost ten times more.

Abe hacked a raspy harsh cough that shook his spine.

A dark word carved into Pierce's brain, in a big, red neon glow of ugly.

CANCER.

Air hung in Pierce's lung. He curled his hands into fists. Ah man, no, no. Not again. Cut and run! His father hadn't seen him yet. The impulse to flee was mutinous. He just might have done it too, if Abe's gaze hadn't flicked toward the door.

Instantly, his father's face brightened. "There he is! My number one son! C'mon in here, boy. Let me see you."

"The big shot he remembers," Malcolm muttered. "But the son who works side by side with him every day? Not so much."

Alarmed, Pierce flung a glare at his brother. What did he mean by that crack? Was Dad's memory going too?

Malcolm lifted one pale eyebrow, gave a tight, one-shouldered shrug.

His father opened his arms slowly, like a leggy sand-hill crane unfurling his wings for flight.

To keep from limping, Pierce took his time crossing the room and then allowed his father to envelop him in a weak-muscled hug. "S'up, Dad?"

"Not a damn thing. I sure am glad to see you." He sank back against the pillow, his arms drifting down to his sides. "But why aren't you at practice getting ready for preseason? You boys are gonna win the Super Bowl this year, I just know it."

"Broke my leg, Dad. Remember?" Pierce touched his left leg.

His father's face clouded. "I don't remember that."

"Sure you remember Pierce's Joe Theismann moment. They showed it on TV over and over and over." Malcolm sounded damn cheerful about it.

"Joe Theismann. Yeah, yeah. Lawrence Taylor got him on the blitz." Abe grimaced.

"When it comes to football, memory as big as an elephant's balls." Malcolm closed his laptop, stood up, and settled the computer in the seat he'd just vacated.

"Do you have to do that in front of Dad?" Pierce kept his voice low and his tone even.

"What? Speak the truth?"

"Be disrespectful."

Malcolm's mouth dipped in a sulk. "Don't worry. He never listens to me anyway."

"Theismann was never the same." Abe shook his head woefully. "Taylor's sack ruined his career."

Pierce's leg twinged.

"I rest my case." Malcolm folded his arms over his chest.

"Do you need to take a walk?" Pierce asked.

"Matter of fact, I do. I'm going for a sandwich." Malcolm headed for the door. Paused. "You want anything?"

Pierce raised a palm. "I'm good."

"I want for Pierce to bring home that Super Bowl ring," Abe sang out.

Pierce sucked in his breath. That's all his father had ever wanted from him. It had started with the football Abe had given him for Christmas when he was five. Pierce never knew if he really did have an exceptional passing arm as the sportscasters claimed, or just an exaggerated need to please his old man.

Malcolm looked put out, grunted, and left the room.

Abe's eyelids lowered and he was breathing shallow. Asleep already? Pierce took the seat Malcolm had been sitting in, settling the laptop on the window ledge.

His father's eyes popped open. "How's that throwin' arm?"

"Good."

"Good?" Abe glowered, grabbed the bedrail, and pulled himself upright. "Boy, good ain't near good enough."

"I know, Dad."

"To have a prayer of making the junior varsity your arm has to be great."

"Uh-huh." *Better than great.*

"Better than great. You have to be excellent. Never forget, this is football in West Texas! Now, get back out there and practice your throwin'. Make me proud."

"Yes, Dad."

What was going on here? Now his father thought he was still in high school?

Pierce felt the same pang in his stomach that he'd felt when he'd heard the lecture the first five million times. Usually when it was well after dusk and his throwing arm was aching so hard that all the ibuprofen and mentholatum rub in the world couldn't soothe it.

Abe's eyes were bright, his breathing too quick and raspy. "You're gonna be the next gawddamn Roger Staubach one day. Just as long as you don't cloud your mind with girls."

"You're right."

He shook a finger at Pierce. "No girls. You got that?"

"Dad, I already made it, remember," he murmured wearily. "I played in the Super Bowl for the Dallas Cowboys."

His father looked startled and for a moment, clarity flashed in his eyes, but then his expression turned wily. "Then lemme see that Super Bowl ring."

"I don't have a ring. We lost the game."

His father dropped back against the mattress, waved a dismissive hand. "You're no Roger Staubach."

"Don't I know it," Pierce mumbled.

He sat there feeling like he was fourteen again and had seriously upset the old man when he didn't make first-string quarterback his freshman year. Always a disappointment, no matter how hard he tried.

It was an old wound he tried not to pick. Abe was proud of him when he won, not simply because he'd done his best. Pierce gulped. He couldn't be resentful. Abe's constant pushing was what had gotten him to the top of the heap. In a way, he was glad his father thought he was still in high school, had forgotten he'd lost the Super Bowl, busted up his leg, and now his entire career hung in the balance.

Abe drifted off to sleep.

Malcolm returned sometime later with a brown paper bag smelling of garlic and marinara sauce. "Picked you up a meatball sub from Franny's. I know it's your favorite."

"Thanks."

"Think quick." Malcolm threw the sack.

He stood up and with an easy one-armed catch, snagged the sandwich in midair, but his left knee crumpled and he stumbled against the bed.

"Huh?" His father jerked awake. "What is it?"

"Sorry, Dad," he apologized.

"Is that a meatball sub from Franny's?" Abe eyed the sack and perked up.

"Sure is." Pierce reached for the controls and raised the head of the bed. He unwrapped the sandwich for his father.

"He won't eat it," Malcolm muttered, moving to the other side of the bed.

Sure enough, Abe took one bite and shook his head. "My stomach hurts."

A lead anchor pressed against Pierce's chest. He couldn't believe the shape his father was in. He met his brother's eyes. "Can I talk to you out in the hall?"

Pulse thumping hard, he turned and stalked out into the hall. Malcolm took his sweet time following him. While he waited, Pierce drummed his fingers against the wall.

A nurse was in the hallway pushing a medication cart from room to room. She did a double take and her eyes widened. She smiled briefly, glanced away, and then peeked back at him again. If he had a dime for every time a woman had glanced at him like that, he'd double his net worth.

Malcolm strolled into the corridor, his eyes unreadable.

Pierce swallowed, reached out, and clapped his brother on the back in a quick, stiff hug.

It took a good three seconds for Malcolm to lift his arms to touch him briefly, and then step back.

"How long has he been like this?" Pierce lifted his cowboy hat, ran a hand through his hair.

"Been going on two months, but he's steadily been getting worse. The memory lapses are fairly new. I'm scared it's Alzheimer's."

"Christ, he's only fifty-eight."

"It's been tough."

"Why didn't you call me before now?" He struggled to temper his tone. His brother bristled easily.

"You know how stubborn the old man is." Malcolm jammed his hands into his front pocket, hunched his shoulders. "Besides, you had a lot on your plate."

He stuck his cowboy hat back down on his head. "He's my dad too. I had a right to know how bad his condition was."

Malcolm's jaw tightened and he ran a hand over his mouth. "If you called once in a while—"

Pierce took a step forward. "I've been recovering myself."

Malcolm raised his chin, held his ground. Pierce was three inches taller and fifty pounds heavier. They stared at each other like two gunslingers on the streets of Dodge City.

"How's your leg?" Malcolm asked through gritted teeth.

"Healing. I should be off the disabled list by October." Okay, that was a best-case scenario, but he wasn't going to tell his brother that.

"Good for you." Malcolm's upper lip curled in a sneer.

He sank his hands on his hips. "What do the doctors say about Dad?"

"Nothing yet. They're still running tests."

"We need to get him out of here. Send him to a specialist in El Paso or San Antonio." Pierce tugged his cell phone from his pocket. "I'll call and make the arrangements."

Malcolm clamped a hand on his wrist.

Nostrils flaring, he narrowed his eyes, put flint in his voice. "What is it?"

"You can't just waltz in here and start ordering people around." This time, his brother was the one to take a step forward until their chests were almost touching.

Don't rise to the bait. Think of Dad. "I'm only trying to help."

"No, you're trying to play the big shot."

Pierce forced his muscles to unclench. "Obviously you need a break. Why don't you go home and—"

"Why don't you stop telling me what to do?"

"Excuse me, Mr. Hollister?"

Simultaneously, he and Malcolm glanced over to see

the medication nurse standing there. She gave a tenuous smile, and extended a pen and notepad toward Pierce. "I know it's probably inappropriate of me to ask," she said, "but could I trouble you for your autograph? My little boy is a huge fan."

The response was so automatic, it took Pierce only a second to find his grin and set it to stun. "Why surely, darlin', no trouble at all. What's your boy's name?"

"Sammy." She was dancing around on the tips of her toes, her hands clutched in front of her.

"Some things never change." Malcolm snorted and went back into their father's room.

The nurse cast a glance at his departing brother. "Is he mad about something?"

"Other than the fact that he wasn't born first?"

"Ah." She nodded. "Sibling rivalry."

He scribbled a short note to Sammy, signed his name, and gave the pad and pen back to her.

She thanked him profusely. "Well, I better get back to work," she said, walking backward toward her medication cart.

"You better watch—" Pierce tried to warn her, but she rammed her butt into the cart before he got the words out.

"Oops." She plastered her hand over her mouth and blushed.

A gaggle of other nurses were peering around the corner of the nurses' station, all giving him the eye.

Pierce suddenly felt allergic to his own skin. He had to get out of here. Clear his mind. Think about what to do about his father without stepping all over Malcolm's toes.

To his left, a green exit sign mounted over the door to the stairway beckoned.

To his right lay a herd of salivating women in blue scrubs.

Ah hell. Pierce pulled his Stetson down over his forehead and took the easy way out.

LACE STOOD BESIDE her ten-year-old Corolla—okay, the model bordered on being a cliché, but what could be a more fitting car for a botanist?—which had been her first and only car, in the parking lot of Cupid General, pawing through the contents of her oversized handbag, searching for her car keys. She shoved aside the rubber-banded letters she'd been given to answer, dug past her wallet, a magnifying glass, a hori-hori sheathed in a leather pouch, a handful of Ziploc bags for collecting plant specimens, and a tube of sunscreen.

"Flytrap," she muttered her favorite faux curse word. Where were her keys? She needed to get back to the gardens. Jeff Davis Elementary was busing in third graders on a field trip at three.

She leafed through the side pockets—a tube of Carmex, her glasses case, a folded ten-dollar bill, an iPod with ear buds attached, cell phone, and a small tin of cinnamon Altoids.

But no keys.

Sighing, she shouldered her bag and patted down her pockets. There were some clippings from the red yucca stuck in her front shirt pocket, but other than that, her pockets were empty.

"Organic fertilizer," she muttered the botanist version of a swearword. She must have left the keys in Aunt Delia's room. She was going to have to go past that smug little candy striper a fourth time. Bracing herself for another smart-aleck comment about Pierce Hollister ruining her brain, she started to head for the hospital entrance, but something compelled her to shade her eyes from the sun with the edge of her hand, and peek past the tint of the driver's side window.

Yep. The keys were dangling from the ignition.

And, of course, the doors were locked.

She groaned and got out her cell phone. She was just about to text Zoey to see if she could swing by Lace's house and bring the spare key, when a brown Ford King Ranch extended cab pickup truck did a U-turn in the middle of the road, drove into the hospital parking lot, and pulled to a stop in front of her.

Her stomach took a roller-coaster ride up into her throat, before plummeting back down to her feet. Without even glancing up, she knew who it was.

"Car trouble?"

She did not want to look at him, but then again not meeting his gaze would make it seem like he affected her. He did not affect her. Not in the least. So she raised her head and locked on to those gorgeous, green-flecked brown eyes that once upon a time had kept her awake at night.

His mouth turned up into a heart-stopping grin.

Her stomach switched rides, sliding from the roller coaster to Tilt-A-Whirl. "Under control," she said smoothly.

"You sure?" He cut the pickup's engine, opened the door, and swung to the ground.

Go away! "Positive."

"I don't mind giving you a hand."

I mind. "I'm good."

He stepped closer, rested his palm on the hood of her Corolla, and leaned in. "What's the trouble?"

Even though she'd met his eyes, she'd managed to steer clear of *truly* looking at him, but now with him crowding her personal space she couldn't avoid it any longer.

It was the first time she'd seen him in the flesh in twelve years, and there was a big difference between watching him fling a football on television and being here with him up close and personal. Inevitable really. Bound to happen. Once she'd decided to make Cupid her permanent home, deep down, she'd known at some point this moment would come.

For a brief time after graduation, she'd considered not moving back for this very reason. She'd even been offered a job working for the Smithsonian. But the only thing she'd ever wanted was to run the Cupid Botanical Gardens and spend her life studying the mesmerizing plants of the Trans-Pecos region.

Her roots ran deep in this arid soil, and family was important to her, in spite of the fact that her parents, numerous cousins, aunts, and uncles could be a royal pain in the butt as often as not. In the end, she simply could not allow some ridiculous incident that had happened when she was fourteen dictate the trajectory of her life.

Even so, the moment that Lace had dreaded for over a decade was finally here.

It was now.

In spite of being braced for it, she was unprepared for the full effect of Pierce Hollister. The good-looking boy had morphed into a strikingly handsome man. He moved with athletic grace, all loose-limbed and easy, while at the same time his muscles coiled tight with potent masculine power.

He had a straw Stetson cocked back on his head and the sleeves of a blue and white Western-style cowboy shirt rolled up to reveal muscular forearms. Thick curly hair, the same honey gold color of pronghorns, was cut close on the sides, but longer on top. He'd grown into the nose that had once been a little too big for his face, although now it crooked a bit to the left, giving him a thoroughly rakish air. Or maybe it was the wicked grin.

Either way, Paul Newman in *Hud* had nothing on him in either the looks or the rascal department.

From a distance, he might be mistaken for an ordinary cowboy—he'd never shaken off that lanky, West Texas gait—but up close, he smelled like sophistication. Lace's nose twitched as she identified the rich notes that composed his cologne. Freshly printed money, suede, rosemary, and a hint of something lighter, frivolous— *Amaryllidacese*, the narcissus flower.

His nails were clipped short and buffed, the cuticles pushed neatly back, making Lace's own garden-roughened hands look pretty ratty in comparison. She thrust her hands behind her back.

"How's Jay?" he asked.

She almost told him, but an impish impulse took hold of her and she bit off her answer and instead asked, "You know my brother?"

He startled, looked confused.

Ha! Gotcha.

"Lace, it's me. Pierce."

The sound of her name vibrating off his tongue was almost her undoing. His voice was deep. Deeper than she remembered, and he put added emphasis on the "la" sound, scraping the tip of his tongue over his palate, ending with a solid lay down against the back of his lower teeth on "ace." The way he said "Lace" made it seem like the sweetest word in Webster's Dictionary and caused her to think far too much about the mechanics of his mouth and tongue.

His smile quickly slipped back. "Aw, you tease. You're yanking my chain."

She glanced over at him, almost lost her bravado in the face of those brown eyes as rich and tempting as pecan pralines, but managed to bluff her way through it. "Your ego simply can't believe that someone doesn't recognize the great Pierce Hollister?"

"Not someone," he said. "*You.*"

He said "you" like he was saying "sex." Slick technique he'd no doubt perfected to ignite the panties of his multitudinous groupies. Well, her panties were staying ice-cold, thank you very much.

Pierce cocked his head, studied her attentively. So attentively, in fact, that it made her itchy. She scratched the back of her hand. The man was a paradox—at once slick and sophisticated but at the same time, down-home country, with a magnetically rugged edge that no amount of urban living could polish.

"It was fun catching up," she said, and wriggled her fingers at him.

He kept standing there.

What the hell did he want from her? "Good-bye."

"Bye." He didn't move.

Neither did she, because where was she going to go? He was blocking her way.

"You're a lot different from how I remembered you," he said.

"You're not."

"You were so quiet and sweet."

Quiet yes, because she stuttered. Sweet? Shows how much he really knew her. "I was fourteen."

"You don't stutter anymore."

"You ever see *The King's Speech*? It was like that."

"You cursed your stutter away?"

Yes indeed, by cursing him and Mary Alice. "Among other techniques."

"I'm impressed."

"Don't be. I didn't cure cancer."

"Dad's sick," he blurted. "I'm scared he might have cancer."

Oh man, why did she have such a tendency to stick her foot in her mouth? Downside of conquering her stutter, she opened her big trap too often. "I'm so sorry to hear about your dad."

He pulled a palm down his face. "I don't know why I said that. It's not your problem."

She wished he hadn't said it either. It made him vulnerable and human. How could she hold a hard-line stance when he was standing there looking all vulnerable and human? "Jay just started the last year of his residency at Johns Hopkins," she said. "You might want to call him about your dad."

"He's a heart surgeon."

"He's also a friend."

"We really haven't been all that close since . . ." He hesitated. "We went off to separate colleges."

That wasn't the big wedge that had been driven between her brother and his best friend and they both knew it. Lace shifted her weight. "I'll keep your father in my thoughts."

"Thanks." He didn't make a move to leave.

Lace massaged her forehead. How to get rid of him without being flat-out rude? That option had been sealed off when he'd told her about his father.

"Ah," Pierce said.

Ah what?

He was looking through the windshield of her car. "You locked yourself out."

"It happens."

His grin reappeared, bright and perky as ever. "A lot?"

"Enough."

"Still a daydreamer, huh?"

"Listen," she said. "I'll have a busload of field-tripping third graders showing up on my front door at three—"

"Gotcha." He winked. "You need in there fast. Hang on."

Great. Now he was determined to help.

He spun on his heel, hustled over to his pickup, rummaged around in the big shiny silver toolbox in the bed of the truck, and returned with a slim jim.

"You keep a tool for breaking into cars in your toolbox? How very gangster of you."

He flashed those straight white teeth again. "Not at all. I keep it for damsels in distress."

She whacked herself on the side of her head with a palm. "Duh. Should have known."

"Make way." He came toward her.

She slipped back, but couldn't really go anywhere, hemmed in by the Lincoln to her left and a yew hedge behind the cars. Twelve years ago if she'd found herself in this close proximity to him, she would have drooped like a tropical orchid in the Chihuahuan Desert. But now, she was tough as a purple sage.

Bring on the heat. She could withstand it.

His scent circled her. He focused on the car, the muscles in his arm flexing as he worked. In under a minute, he had the door unlocked and gestured with a flourish. "Your chariot, Princess."

Oh, she could see why women melted at his feet. All the more reason not to. "Thanks," she said tightly.

"You're welcome. Drive safe." He saluted her, ambled back to his truck.

She took a deep breath, and went to turn the key.

Except it was already turned—in the wrong direction. Not only had she left the key in the ignition, but also she'd mistakenly turned it to the accessory position.

"Please let it start, please let it start," she prayed. She closed her eyes, and twisted the key to the start position.

Click.

Then nothing.

Chapter 4

*Dormancy: the phase of temporary growth cessation
in plants under harsh environmental situations.*

PIERCE knocked on her window.

She rolled it down.

"Need a jump?"

Yes, it was corny, but he couldn't resist. One look into those gorgeous blue eyes and he instinctively shifted into full seduction mode. The thing was she fascinated the hell out of him. On the surface she looked so prim and proper with that wavy, jet black hair, creamy white skin, and bookish glasses perched on her nose, but the lush curves of her body blew prim and proper all to Hades.

She'd always been a beauty, although he'd never allowed himself to really notice. For one thing, she was four years younger, and when you were eighteen those four years were a huge divide. Plus she was his best friend's younger sister and strictly off-limits. It was an unwritten guy rule. No poaching friends' sisters. But, hallelujah, he was certainly noticing now.

Lace heaved a long-suffering sigh. "My car needs a battery boost, yes. Do you mind?"

Wow. Way to make a guy feel like a balloon in a cactus patch and yet, he couldn't seem to stop with the innuendo. "I'd love to give you a spark."

She rolled her eyes.

"Sorry," he apologized. "That made me sound like a douche."

"I'm sure it's a deeply ingrained habit," she said. "No need to go changing your personality on my account."

Zing! It *was* habit. Living up to the playboy quarterback image. No woman had ever seemed to mind his sexual banter before. In fact, the shtick normally worked like a charm, but it only seemed to irritate Lace.

He patted her windowsill. "Be right back."

"Clearly, I'm not going anywhere."

Man, she truly disliked him. Whatever happened to the lovestruck teen who had written that letter to Cupid?

He moved his truck into position so he could give her battery a boost and retrieved his jumper cables from underneath the seat. He might have expected her to be embarrassed since this was the first time they'd seen each other in twelve years or be her usual shy self and not want to speak to him. This snarky wit was new.

But while the change in her caught him off guard, he kind of liked it.

Maybe she had a boyfriend. Maybe that was the deal. Possibly even a fiancé or husband?

A hollow sensation settled in Pierce's stomach. Jay hadn't said she was married. Surely he would have said something if Lace had gotten married. Then again, Jay never brought up her name with him.

Hell, Hollister, why do you care?

He didn't. It might explain the mystery of her bad attitude, but the first thing he did when he got back to her window was look at her left hand.

No ring.

He smiled.

"What is it?" Lace asked suspiciously.

"Nothing."

She made a toggling motion with her index finger. "Could we get this show on the road?"

"Yes, ma'am." He tipped his hat.

She muttered something under her breath. Man, what had happened to that sweet girl who used to follow him and Jay around like a puppy? Puppy grew up and cut a few teeth. She was giving him a run for his money.

Grinning, Pierce set about giving her a jumpstart. Once he got everything hooked and ready to go, he called around the hood of her car, "Go ahead and crank it."

The Corolla engine immediately turned over.

He disconnected the cables, shut the hood, and ambled back to her open window. From where he was standing, he could see right down the neckline of her shirt. The scoop of her white brassiere cupped those plump beautiful breasts. Bullet-hot images of what she would look like out of that shirt burned his brain and he squirmed thinking about her. Once, back in the day when he was hanging out with Jay, he'd spent the night at the Bettingfields' and gotten up early, Lace had come slipping out of the bathroom wrapped in nothing but a fluffy pink towel, an identical pink towel wrapped around her head. He'd been behind her, but made a decision not to notice, until she reached up to secure the towel at her head that had started to unravel, and the other towel slipped off. His jaw unhinged. In one smooth move, she'd grabbed the towel, secured it around her body, and went on to her bedroom. She didn't see him, but he never forgot that glimpse, and now that he had an unobstructed view of her cleavage, it got to him worse than all the bare naked women who'd ever occupied his bed.

"Thank you," she said.

"No thanks needed, but I wouldn't mind a home-cooked meal."

"Then go home and cook one."

He threw back his head and laughed.

"I'm late. Could you please move your truck?" She looked completely disinterested, but the pulse at the hollow of her throat was pumping blood through her veins hard and fast. She was feeling some kind of emotion toward him.

"Got it. You don't cook. All right then, how about I take you out to dinner?"

"Honestly? You're hitting on me?"

"Just a nice dinner between two old friends."

"We were never friends. You barely gave me the time of day."

"A serious oversight I'm aiming to rectify."

"Aim somewhere else."

Why was he flirting with her when she was clearly not interested? *Don't play clueless.* He knew precisely what he was doing. Enjoying the thrill of the chase. It had been a very long time since he had to make an effort to catch a woman's eye. *Be honest. You've never had to make an effort to win a woman.* Usually, all he had to do was smile and wink.

Lace's sky blue eyes peered inquisitively at him through the lenses of her glasses, her face was flushed, and she was breathing just a little bit too hard. Ah, she was enjoying resisting as much as he was enjoying pursuing. But she probably wasn't wondering how close they were to the nearest motel.

"If you'll excuse me." She made shooing motions.

"You mean it? You're just going to drive off?"

"I know it's probably tough for this to sink through your arrogant hide, Pierce Hollister. Yes, once upon a time I was a silly young girl who had a crush on you. But I was a child and you were nothing but a fantasy. I've grown up and moved on. I have not been sitting here waiting for you to show up and sweep me off my feet. I appreciate you getting me into my car and getting it started, but surprise, surprise, I could have handled my car issues just fine on my own if you hadn't insisted on butting in. I do not want you. I don't even *like* you." She finished her rant, eyes brighter, cheeks pinker, and her hands knotted in her lap.

"Feel better now that you got that off your chest?" he asked mildly.

"Argh!" she yelled, and bashed her forehead against the steering wheel.

What was it that caused him to push his luck? The way things had been going lately he should respect the fact that luck wasn't something you could count on. Yes, it had worked for him up until the last five months, but when good fortune hit the skids, it hit hard.

"So there's absolutely no chance you'd consider going out with me?"

She raised her head, drilled a hole straight through him with those amazing blue eyes of hers. "Not if you were the last man on earth."

"Lace Bettingfield," he said levelly, holding on to his calm against the barrage of endorphins lighting up his body. "I'm warning you right now."

She tilted up her sassy chin. "Warning me about what?"

"Don't issue me a challenge, woman."

"Why not?"

"Because I will surely take you up on it." He hitched his fingers through his belt loops, turned, and walked away. Wished he had spurs on so he could hear them jangle.

"Oh yeah?" she hollered at his back. "What do you intend on doing about it? Kill every man on the face of the earth?"

A grin split across his face. Ha! A crack in her armor. He'd gotten to her. Pierce spun back around. "Sweetheart, that won't be necessary. You'll be begging me to take you to bed long before it comes to that."

"OF ALL THE egotistical, arrogant, cocky . . ." Lace was still muttering three hours later after she'd locked the iron gates of the botanical gardens. If she had a time machine, she would zoom back to 2001 and knock some sense into her fourteen-year-old self. Pierce Hollister had never been worthy of her hero worship.

She went inside the research lab located at the back of the main building. The window faced the livery stable her parents owned. Here was where she worked on a pet project involving tracking down the existence of the fabled golden flame agave—a plant that bloomed only once at the end of its hundred-year lifespan. Most botanists believed the legend was absolute fiction, or if by some slight chance it was true, the cactus was long since extinct, but Lace disagreed. There were historical botanist journals, topographical maps of the Trans-

Pecos, climate deviations for as far back as records had been kept and various soil samples arranged and cataloged in meticulous order. Her after-hours work was when she really got to dig in and play, and usually she couldn't wait to get to it even after a full eight hours on the job.

Except for today.

She could already tell she wasn't going to be able to concentrate on her research. Not when she was in such a stew. She might as well call it a day and head home.

"Are you still fussin' 'bout sumpthin'?"

Lace jumped and spun around to find Shasta in the corner sweeping up a week's worth of sand they'd tracked in. She'd been so busy cussing out Pierce Hollister that she hadn't even noticed the girl when she'd come in.

Shasta had put on a little weight in the month she'd worked for Lace, going from scrawny to merely skinny. She had carrot-colored hair she wore parted down the middle and plaited into a single braid that hung down her back. Her freckled skin burned instantly if she dared step outside without sunscreen and a hat.

"You've been riled up ever since you got back from that meetin'. What did your kinfolks do to you?" she asked, bending over to sweep the debris into a yellow plastic dustpan.

"It wasn't them." Lace sighed and dumped her purse on the wooden table with uneven legs, where she had textbooks and scholarly journals opened, paper clipped and highlighted.

The passel of Cupid letters tumbled out of her handbag and hit the floor with a solid plunk. Hero Worshipper's letter was right on top.

There. That was the problem. Silly young women who put love on an impossible pedestal, making it the end-all, and be-all of their existence. Thinking about it lit a spark of anger inside her. Not at Hero Worshipper, but at herself and the foolish girl she used to be.

That encounter with Pierce in the parking lot might have put her off her game when it came to research, but it fired her up in regard to answering the letters.

Industriously, she snagged up the letters and sank down onto the utilitarian folding chair at the table. She took a pen from her purse and rolled the rubber band off the letters. It shot across the room to land in Shasta's dustpan.

"You couldn't do that again twice if you tried," Shasta said. "It must be some kinda sign." Her assistant was big on seeing signs and patterns and omens in everything—clouds, toast, tea leaves, the way a duck's tail curled.

Scientific-minded Lace had been trained against the human tendency to find patterns where none exist, to evaluate evidence and identify true correlations between things. "It doesn't mean anything except a rubber band landed in your dustpan."

Shasta dumped the contents of the dustpan into the trash can by the sink, propped it and the broom in the corner. "Might mean one of those letters is important."

"It doesn't mean that."

"How do you know?" Shasta scratched her nose. Underneath the fluorescent lighting, her skin looked sallow. She wore a funky pair of bubble-gum pink coveralls, the color strangely complementing her orange hair, and a white blouse with puffy short sleeves and a Peter Pan collar. With her first paycheck, she had bought the clothes at Second Chances, the thrift store behind Greenwood's Grocery.

"Because a rubber band can't prognosticate."

"What does that mean?"

"Predict the future." From the top of the stack, Lace picked up the pink envelope that contained Hero Worshipper's letter. The sharp-edged flap sliced her index finger. Ouch! A drop of blood appeared and she popped her finger into her mouth. "Frigging flytrap."

Shasta came over to perch on the old floral sofa that used to belong in Lace's parents' game room and was positioned slightly behind the table where she was sitting. "What is it?"

"Paper cut."

"See." Shasta wagged a knowing finger. "The rubber band was trying to tell you sumpthin'."

"That notion goes against cause and effect. The

envelope cut my finger. The fact that the rubber band landed in the dustpan has nothing to do with it."

Shasta shrugged. "Whatever you say."

"It's not what I say, it's what is."

"Uh-huh." Shasta gave her a shrewd smile that said she knew a big secret Lace could never be privy to.

Fine. She didn't want to be controlled by superstition. Then again, who was she to judge Shasta? No telling what the poor girl had been through. In spite of being something of a social misfit, Lace was loved and supported by her close-knit family—even Carol Ann, who while annoying, meant well at heart—and she couldn't imagine what it must be like to have no one you could count on. It would probably make her latch on to any outlandish belief that seemed to make life easier.

Lace pushed her glasses up on her nose and unfolded the letter. The smell of strawberry-flavored gum wafted out.

Dear Cupid,

I found my Soulmate. He is ~~magnef magnetif~~ awesome and so handsum! But he don't know I even eggist. See he's famous. Real Famous!! If I tole you his name you wood know him. I tried to met him onct, but his Body Guards woodn't let me near!!! I don't know what to do!!!! I wrote him a letter onct and he sent me a pickture. I could tell his singnature was just a stamp!!!!! He prolly never saw my letter and some secreterry jest stamped it. But I sleep with his pickture under my pill low. How can I show him we are mint to be if I cain't get close to him? Please Cupid tell me how to let him know I am here!!!!!!

—Hero Worshipper

Obviously, Hero Worshipper was either very young or uneducated or, most likely, both. She was tempted to write back: *Snap out of it! Get over him! Forget the dude. Get on with your life. Don't build your world on an illusion. It'll never happen, not in a million years. Stay in—or go back—to school. Find someone real to love you.*

But this was a tender, aching heart. The progressive use of exclamation marks that multiplied the more she used them illustrated the letter writer's growing despair.

Hero Worshipper's pain lodged in the center of Lace's chest as big as the legendary Pecos Bill's fist. Boy howdy, she'd been there. Knew how difficult it was to let go of a fantasy, and even though she'd learned the hard way that the quickest route to getting over a fantasy was to have life kick you in the teeth, she couldn't bring herself to be the one to put on the hobnail boots.

Organic fertilizer. Why had she agreed to answer the letter? She would just give it back to Carol Ann and tell her she couldn't do it.

She slid the letter, now smudged with a drop of her blood, back in the envelope, and tossed it aside.

"Wait." Shasta got up and retrieved the letter. "You're not going to answer it?"

"I'm going to give it to one of the other volunteers."

"How come?"

"I'm not the right person to answer it."

Shasta opened the letter.

"The Cupid letters are confidential." Lace reached for the letter.

"No they're not," Shasta countered, holding it away from her. "They print the letters in the greensheet."

What could she say to that? And why was she suddenly feeling possessive over the letter?

Shasta started reading the letter, moving her lips as she silently sounded the words.

Lace rubbed her fingers together in a "gimme" motion. "I changed my mind. I will answer it."

"Do you believe in soul mates?" Shasta asked, still holding the letter over her shoulder out of Lace's reach.

"No."

"Then how can you answer people's letters to Cupid?"

"I bring my own special skill to the table."

Shasta rubbed a palm across her mouth, clearly giving that some thought. "How is being good with plants gonna help you give this girl love advice?"

"Because I know a little bit about what she is going through."

"Yeah?" Shasta canted her head, studied Lace a long moment.

"Yes."

"How's that?"

She didn't really want to get into it. "Let's just say I've been where that girl has been."

"Loving someone who didn't love you back?"

"That's right."

Shasta's expression changed from skepticism to respect. "Do you still love him?"

"Oh no. I put that crush behind me a long time ago."

"What are you going to tell her?"

"That while the feelings she has for this man are very real, loving him might not be in her best interest."

"If someone had told you that about the guy you were in love with, would you a listened?"

"No," Lace admitted, holding her palm out.

"I don't think you should tell her that." Shasta folded the letter.

"What would you tell her?"

"I'd tell her how she could meet the guy she loves."

"It wouldn't be right to encourage her delusion." Did Shasta herself have a crush on someone?

"What if she's not delusional? What if this guy really is her soul mate?"

"Shasta, it's a nice fantasy, but there really is no such thing as soul mates and hey, even if there were, it's not always possible to be with the one you love."

Her assistant's chin hardened. "If I was in love with someone nothing could keep me away from him."

"What if he was already married?"

"Then he could get a divorce."

"What if he loved his wife and they had kids?"

"It wouldn't matter. Not if I was his soul mate."

"So you'd advocate breaking up a family just so you could have what you wanted?"

Shasta paused, and then shook her head. "My mama always said love conquers all."

"You're still young so you don't understand that life is a lot more complicated than that."

"I may be young, but I bet I seen a whole lot more of life than you." Shasta's eyes glistened in the light, and in that moment, she looked decades older than her young age.

"Since I don't know what you've been through, I can't comment on that."

"You don't know what this girl's been through neither." Shasta tapped the letter.

"You're right."

"Know what I think?"

"What's that?"

Shasta straightened her shoulders, slanted a sideways look down her nose at Lace. "You're full of sour grapes 'cause your love affair didn't turn out the way you wanted it to."

Lace swallowed and her heart skipped a beat. She

had so much and this kid had nothing. Why not let her believe in her fantasies about love? Soon enough she'd learn the truth. "You might be right. I'll take that into consideration when I answer the letter. Could I have it back please?"

"Under one condition."

She tamped down her irritation. While she shouldn't be negotiating with the girl, she couldn't help admiring her spunk. "What's that?"

"Give her some kind of hope."

"Even if it's false hope?"

"You don't know that," Shasta said staunchly. "Besides, false hope is better than no hope."

"Do you really believe that?"

"Hope is the only reason I'm standin' here."

How could she argue with that? "All right, I'll leave her with some hope."

"That's all I ever wanted," Shasta said, and placed the letter in Lace's open palm.

FOUR DAYS HAD passed since Pierce's encounter with Lace in the hospital parking lot, but he couldn't stop thinking about her. Several times, he'd taken the long way home from the hospital to the Triple H, the route that went past the botanical gardens, hoping for a glimpse of Lace, but he hadn't spied her. He was acting like a moony kid, and that was certainly not his style.

What was it about her that stirred this compulsion in him? He dreamed of her every night and woke in the morning horny and drenched in sweat. It was damn unsettling. When was the last time a woman had roused him like this? Hell, had a woman *ever* roused him like this?

The hospital sent his father home without a diagnosis. All the tests had come back clean. The doctor started Abe on a protein supplement drink, gave him a prescription for a drug to improve cognitive functioning, and ordered him to take daily high-potency B vitamins. Pierce had to admit that after his stay at Cupid General, Abe seemed to be getting better. His color had improved and his appetite had returned and his memory was more reliable.

The first thing their father said when the three of them pulled into the driveway was, "Grub up some sweet taters, Malcolm, and have Hildy cook a batch for dinner and see if she's got some of those little colored marshmallows to melt on top."

"The man loves his sweet potatoes," Malcolm muttered. "I can't stand the things."

"I never much cared for them either," Pierce added.

"They're taters and they're sweet." Abe grunted. "What's not to like? If Brussels sprouts came sweet, I'd eat them too."

"You eat so much of them I'm surprised you don't have sugar diabetes," Malcolm grumbled.

"I'm just happy he's hungry," Pierce said. "I'll grub up the potatoes. I noticed you moved the patch."

"Crop rotation. It's a new spot. Nothing has ever been planted there." Malcolm motioned to a patch of ground lying a few yards beyond the split rail fence where an old storage shed had once stood.

"What happened to the shed?"

"Boards were rotted out from desert termites and Dad wanted to plant his precious sweet potatoes closer to the house so he didn't have to walk so far to dig them up."

"Boiled, baked, fried, mashed, grilled, roasted, I like sweet taters any way you cook them, though I like 'em best with Hildy's colored marshmallows on top," Abe expounded.

Pierce went around to help his father get out of the car. He was careful to brace with his good leg. Abe paused and looked out over the field. "This ain't a friendly country, boys. Not for farmers, nor ranchers much neither."

"I've been meaning to ask you about that, Dad." Pierce put out his arm for Abe to lean against, but his father waved him away and took a halting shuffle toward the back door. "How come our relatives stopped here when there's so many greener places in the world?"

Abe met Pierce's eyes. "Free land. Homestead Act of 1862."

"That would do it." Malcolm nodded.

"You gotta suspect anything that's free." Pierce swept his hand at the desert surroundings. "Case in point."

Malcolm pointed at the Davis Mountains to the north. "You look there and tell me that's not beautiful."

"Compared to the Rockies, those are anthills."

Abe lost his balance and both Malcolm and Pierce leaped to stabilize him. Their father pulled away. "I'm all right. Quit yer fawnin'."

Pierce and Malcolm exchanged a look. The doctors in Cupid might not have been able to find anything wrong with Abe, but he was far from well.

"Malcolm," Abe said sharply, his gaze fixed on the sweet potato patch that was looking kind of droopy.

"Yessir."

"Why haven't you planted the pumpkins?"

"I've been pretty busy what with you being in the hospital and all."

"You should have had the hired hands do it."

"The hands work cattle, Dad. They're not farmers."

A sour-pickle look puckered Abe's face. "We gotta get them pumpkins in the ground."

"Would it be the end of the world if we didn't have a pumpkin crop this year?" Malcolm asked.

Abe stared at Malcolm as if he'd just announced he wanted to slaughter all the puppies in Cupid. "Boy, that talk there is almost blasphemy. Hollisters have been supplying Jeff Davis County with pumpkins ever since there was a Halloween. It's tradition. We have an obligation to fulfill."

"I'm behind on vaccinating the cattle and that's a two-week job; by the time I can get around to planting pumpkins, it'll be too late. We're just going to have to let the good people of Cupid go to another pumpkin supplier this year."

Abe made a soft whooshing sound of a man who'd gotten gut-slammed with a medicine ball.

Pierce took hold of his father's elbow. "Don't worry, Dad. I'll plant the pumpkins."

Malcolm let out a whoop of laughter.

"What's so funny?" Pierce glared.

"You?" He hooted. "Mr. Fancy Pants, I-got-a-million-dollar-condo-in-Las-Colinas, planting pumpkins?"

"I was born on this ranch."

Malcolm's nostrils flared. "When did you ever work the land?"

It was true. While Pierce had helped with the cattle a few times, mainly because he enjoyed riding horses and being outdoors, he'd never done any farming. As soon as Abe realized Pierce had a talent for slinging a football, he hadn't wanted him to do any work that could harm his hands—no digging, tilling, planting, or harvesting. Plus, with all the practicing and going to school, it left little time for anything else, especially when he got old enough to start chasing girls.

"I'm perfectly capable of planting a crop of pumpkins."

"Uh-huh." Malcolm was grinning like it was the funniest thing he'd ever heard.

"How hard can it be? Stick seeds in the ground, water and feed them, watch 'em grow."

"You really didn't pay much attention to what goes on around here, did you?"

Pierce shifted his weight, rubbed his achy leg, felt a pearl of sweat bead at his throat. Guilty as charged. Plenty of times he'd come home from football practice to find Abe with the bills scattered over the table, a calculator crunching numbers that didn't add up, a worried frown on his face. Ranching in the Trans-Pecos was hardscrabble, but Pierce had managed to float above that reality. He wasn't about to admit that to Malcolm, however.

"I'm gonna plant those gourds," Pierce promised. "In fact, it's going to be the best damn pumpkin crop ever grown on the Triple H."

"I thought you were off the DL in October. You won't be around to harvest this bumper crop of pumpkins." Malcolm sniggered.

That gave Pierce pause. "The October date is just a ballpark figure. I could push my return back a couple of weeks. Stay to harvest the pumpkins and get them to market."

Malcolm looked surprised. "You? Putting off football? This I gotta see to believe."

"Watch close, 'cause it's happening."

"Care to put your money where your mouth is?" Malcolm challenged.

"You're on."

"Five grand says you're full of shit." Malcolm thrust out a palm.

"Why stop there?" Pierce clasped his brother's hand and squeezed it so tight Malcolm winced. "Let's go double or nothing."

Chapter 5

Habit: the overall appearance of a plant.

PIERCE had shot off his big mouth, and now here he was at ten o'clock on Saturday morning, zipping past the colossally dusty grain silos of Angus Feed and Grain, pulling into a parking lot and feeling like he was doomed to end up ten grand lighter. Malcolm was right. He didn't know the first thing about raising pumpkins, but he'd never let a lack of knowledge stop him from doing what he wanted to do.

He caught a glimpse of himself in the rearview mirror. "C'mon, you lead football teams to victory. You can do this. The paneled van that was parked beside him pulled out, revealing a blue Toyota Corolla in the space on the other side.

His pulse did a strange two-step. Was it Lace's car?

Pierce hopped out of his truck, rushed inside the feed store through the side exit. The desiccated smell of dried grain mingled with the vitaminy scent of the animal care medicine hit him head-on, stirring memories of the time he was courting Jenny Angus. Her uncle owned the business and she'd worked here as a clerk during the summers. The persistent smell had invaded her hair, and every time he kissed her, he'd thought of livestock.

What did Lace's hair smell like? Flowers most likely. And sunshine.

His boots made a shuffling sound against the big-planked hardwood floors that constituted the store area. To the left was a teller's cage. To the right, the wooden flooring ended as cement steps went down to the storage area and loading dock. A hallway to the side of the teller's cage led to the front of the store with an entrance on Main Street.

A haze of perpetual dust—sawdust, deer corn dust, barley dust, hay dust, peanut dust, all kinds of agricultural dust—floated in the air, stirred by the lazy spin of the old-style industrial-grade ceiling fans mounted overhead.

He tasted grit on his tongue and his stomach tightened. He hadn't been in the feed store since he'd gone off to college. Hell, who would've thought he'd feel nostalgic over a friggin' feed store? Except for when he was chasing Jenny, he'd hated coming in here with Abe when he was a kid. Bored out of his skull, he'd spent his time perusing the bulletin board that had pictures of local animals for sale—Australian cattle dogs, donkeys, a llama or two, free barn kittens to anyone who would come and get them.

Pierce scanned the warehouse area through the haze, looking for Lace. One side of the warehouse was stacked almost to the ceiling with sacks of feed, salt for water softeners, pesticides, and potting soil. At the other end of the warehouse a tall, wide door was rolled up all the way and a couple of cowboys stood on the loading dock jawing with the teen-age boys loading feed into the beds of their waiting pickup trucks.

Quickly, Pierce tugged the brim of his hat lower and ducked his head, not wanting the men to recognize him and stroll over for a chat. Constant attention could get tiresome.

"Can I help ya?" asked the blond girl sitting in front of an aged PC at a desk in the rear of the teller cage.

She sent a text message on her cell phone, stuck the phone in her cleavage, jumped up from her rolling swivel chair, and came toward the window. She was all of sixteen, had a tiny diamond stud in her nostril and a hickey on the side of her neck the size of a Krugerrand. She wore a baby doll T-shirt emblazoned with The Band Perry logo and jeans so tight he could make out the denomination of the change in her front pocket— two quarters, a penny, and three dimes.

Still glancing around for any sign of Lace, he saun-tered up to the window. "I'd like to buy some pumpkin seeds."

She pulled down a pad of the same order forms that

Jenny had once used. Apparently, Angus Feed and Grain was going kicking and screaming into the digital age. Kind of nice, actually, that some things never changed. You could count on small towns for that and the fact that most everybody knew who you were.

"How much do you need?" she asked.

Pierce rested his elbow on the thin wooden ledge that extended out from the teller cage, crooked his grin out of habit, not an attempt to seduce. "How much should I need?"

She shrugged. "I dunno. How big is the area you're planting?"

Hell, he didn't know. He turned up the wattage on his smile. Surely she recognized him. "I'm planting for Abe Hollister. He buys his seed here every year. Do you mind looking up how much he buys?"

The girl wrinkled her nose. "I haven't been working here long and I'm from Whistle Stop. Don't know Abe Hollister. He any kin to Malcolm?"

"Malcolm's my brother. Abe's our dad."

Her eyes lit up. "You are so lucky to have such a great brother. Malcolm is the sweetest thing. He brings us doughnuts every time he comes in."

Malcolm? Sweet? Maybe to the women at Angus Feed and Grain. "Yeah, he's a good guy."

"Lemme go ask Toby." She turned around, walked to the back of the teller cage, and knocked on the wall. "Toby!"

"Yeah?" a man's voice called back from the other side of the wall.

"Some old dude wants to know how much seed he'll need to plant Malcolm's pumpkin patch." Her cleavage dinged, letting her know she had a text message. She fished the phone out of her bra and went back to texting.

Pierce blinked, swallowed, and shook his head. Old dude? Wow. Talk about a smack to the ego.

Footsteps sounded to his left and he turned to see one of Malcolm's former classmates, Toby Mercer, emerge from the corridor that led to another part of the building. Lace had to be in there.

Toby was shaped like a drinking straw, long and straight and thin. "Pierce!"

Pierce extended his hand, cast a glance at the corridor, and almost called the pale man by his schoolyard nickname, Casper. "Toby."

Toby ignored his hand and instead clamped him in a back-pounding hug. With one arm slung around Pierce's shoulder, he turned him back to the teller window. "Aimee, you dumb-dumb. This 'old dude' is Pierce Hollister, quarterback for the Dallas Cowboys."

Using her thumbs in rapid texting mode, she never looked up from her phone screen, just shrugged and said, "Whatever."

"She's into swimmers. If you were Michael Phelps she would have known who you were," Toby reassured him.

Aimee glanced up long enough to smile dream-ily and murmured, "I love the way that man moves through the water. Like a dolphin."

Pierce stepped back, waved at the warehouse. "You working here?"

Toby puffed out his chest. "I'm the general manager."

"No kidding?"

"Hey, I saw the Super Bowl." Toby hissed in a breath through his teeth. "Rough break." He paused, laughed. "No pun intended. How's the leg?"

"Healing. Thanks for asking."

"I heard rumors . . ." Toby shook his head. "Never mind."

Pierce widened the smile he wanted to drop. Hell, he could just imagine what kind of spiteful stuff was being said behind his back. That was part and parcel of being famous. You had to take the good with the bad. If you put yourself out there, folks felt free to say any damn thing about you that they wanted whether it was true or not. "No, go ahead. You can tell me what people are saying behind my back."

Toby made a dismissive face. "It's nothing. You know how people like to talk."

"They're saying I'm washed up." Pierce said it so Toby didn't have to.

"It's just the contrary folks that are upset because the Cowboys lost the Super Bowl."

"I wasn't happy about it either."

"No one thinks it was your fault, but with the leg and comparison to Theismann, gossip takes on a life of its own."

"You can tell everyone that you heard it from the horse's mouth. I'm fine. I'll be back on the roster by mid-season. My career is going great guns."

"Why, I sure am glad to hear that and not just because I have a Jackson riding on your return."

"I appreciate that."

Toby clapped him on the back again. "Now, let's get you those pum'kin seeds."

They went down the corridor and into the garden supply part of the building. A green water hose lay snaked over the cement, and trays of young plants were growing in cheap black plastic containers. The big picture windows, with the blinds drawn up, fronted North Main. To the far side of the room was a large carousel of seed packets, and beside the carousel sat big plastic bins like those in the supermarket that held gourmet nuts and candies sold by the pound, but here the bins contained a wide variety of seeds.

But Pierce wasn't really paying much attention to any of that. He was on the lookout for Lace.

Another room opened up off the one they were in. When he'd come to the feed store with his dad, that room had been part of a family-owned hardware store, long put out of business by the big box home improvement stores.

"That's new," Pierce said.

Toby laughed. "You've been away too long. Mr. Angus bought Carter Ivy's building and expanded it over ten years ago. That's where we keep the tillers and lawn mowers and weed eaters and such."

"Mind giving me a tour?"

Toby looked surprised by the request. Hell, Pierce was surprised he asked it, but there was this overwhelming urge to see Lace running through him like a commercial jingle you couldn't get out of your head. It didn't make any sense, but there it was. He'd been thinking about her almost nonstop since Monday and the only thing he'd ever thought about that much was football.

"Sure, this way." Toby ushered him into the other room.

Pierce skimmed his gaze over the John Deere lawn tractors, the Ryobi cultivators, terra-cotta patio chimineas, barbecue grills, and a metal cage of propane bottles, but he didn't see her. The starch went out of his spine and his smile drooped.

"Nice collection," he said lamely.

"It's a tough market with them building a Home Depot in Alpine, but luckily we got a loyal customer base who'd rather spend the pennies right here in Cupid than drive. Isn't that right, Lace?"

Lace.

A right nice tingly sensation spread throughout his body and Pierce went up on tiptoes trying to find her amid the gardening equipment.

"That's right, Toby." Lace stood up from where she'd been facing away from them and crouched down beside a display of hedge trimmers.

She dusted her hands on the seat of her jeans—and what a fine seat it was—and turned around. She wore an agreeable red cotton shirt that clung loosely to munificent breasts the size of ripe grapefruits. The color accented her dark hair and fair skin, giving her an otherworldly appearance. He'd had a girlfriend once who dragged him to art galleries. Hadn't gotten much out of the experience, except now he remembered one of the artists because Lace resembled the heavenly women he painted. Rubens. Like the sandwich.

Pierce tried to draw in a breath, but it felt as if his lungs had been frozen by liquid nitrogen and they could neither expand nor deflate. He sort of just gaped at her, mouth opening, trying to inhale.

For one brief second a look of alarm passed over her face, but she quickly covered it up with neutral nonchalance. The band around his chest tightened. What did that look mean?

"You need anything, Lace?" Toby asked.

"I'm good." She waved a hand. "Go ahead and help your customer."

Your customer.

Like she didn't even know him. She wasn't even going to acknowledge him.

Pierce would have said something to her, should have

said something glib and flirty, but his lungs still weren't cooperating. Even so, he must have been breathing on some level or he would have passed out. Right?

Speechless and confused about it, Pierce followed Toby back into the seed room. Toby got a paper bag from above the bins and started dishing seeds into the bag with a big stainless steel scoop. He paused after a moment to weigh it on a pair of scales.

But Pierce was not paying any attention whatsoever because Lace had followed them into the room, the hedge trimmer in her arms, although she was pointedly trying to make her way to the exit as fast as possible.

However, she did cast a quick glance at him and Toby and smirked. What was that about?

"There you go," Toby announced. "Give this to Aimee." He handed him a piece of paper with his purchase written on it. "You can pay her on the way out."

"Thanks," Pierce said, and grabbed the bag feeling as if he'd been zapped with a stun gun. What was it about Lace that grabbed him so forcefully by the short hairs?

She'd already exited.

He rushed to catch up to her, thought of—and discarded—a hundred different smooth-operator lines. Maybe he should start with an apology for the jerk-off thing he'd said to her in the hospital parking lot. But an apology would put him in a weakened position. Give her the upper hand.

When he got back to the main warehouse, he was relieved to see she was at the teller cage, settling up her bill for the hedge trimmer. She wielded the thing like she knew what she was doing.

"Hi," he said breathlessly. *Brilliant. That line will live in pickup infamy.*

She nodded at him, barely. "Thanks, Aimee," she said, and she turned to leave.

Pierce moved to block her way. "Aren't you going to say something to me?"

"Something."

"Cute."

"May I go now?"

"Listen, about the other day—"

"This hedge trimmer is heavy. Could we have this conversation another day?"

"We sort of got off on the wrong foot—"

One eyebrow shot up on her forehead. "We?"

"Okay, me. It was my fault. I acted like—"

"Hedge trimmer." She held it up. "Heavy."

"Oh, right. Here, let me take it for you." He stuffed the sack of seeds underneath his arm and reached for the trimmer.

She clung to it with a death grip. "I've got it," she said through clenched teeth.

They were drawing a crowd. Toby had come into the room and the cowboys and loading dock workers wandered over, as well as a couple of other customers.

Fine by him. He was used to the limelight. "Let me carry it to the car for you. It's the least I can do."

"You don't owe me a thing."

Man, she wasn't giving an inch. He tugged on the box.

"You want to carry my books for me too?" She hung on to the box like it contained her life's savings.

"C'mon. What's the big deal?"

"You want to carry it to my car for me?"

Damn, she was stronger than she looked. He tugged more firmly. "I do."

She smiled slyly and then let go unexpectedly, sending him stumbling backward. "Okay, carry it to my car for me."

He hustled toward the door.

"Hey, Malcolm's brother," Aimee called from the teller's cage. "You gonna steal those pumpkin seeds?"

"Oh yeah, right." He held one finger up for Lace. "Hang on a minute."

She sighed but motioned him toward the teller cage.

"Be right back." He winked.

She rolled her eyes.

"Don't run off."

"I can't. You have my hedge trimmer."

"I'll get you another one, Lace," Toby said. "Drive around to North Main and I'll take it out to you."

"It's okay, Toby. I'll wait."

Pierce turned back to the teller's cage, saw that ev-

eryone in the place was smirking at him. What the hell
was so damn funny? He smiled big. He wasn't about to
let them know he was ruffled.

Aimee held out her palm even though she was
behind a glass window. "Ticket?"

He juggled the hedge trimmer. The thing was
heavier than you might expect and the shape of the box
threw him off balance. He cocked the box on his hip,
dug in his front shirt pocket, and fished out the ticket
Toby had given him. In the process, he dropped the
sack of seeds.

Someone chuckled.

Pierce bent to scoop up the bag and whacked the end
of the box into Toby's leg.

"You're deadly with that thing, Hollister. Are you
sure that you hold on to a football for a living?"

One of the cowboys snorted. No one was asking him
for an autograph.

"Sorry," Pierce apologized. He was not going to stop
smiling. Was not going to let them see he was flustered. This was all Lace's doing. She turned him into a
tongue-tied idiot.

"That'll be ten dollars and fifty-seven cents."

He dug in his wallet.

The door creaked open.

Pierce darted a glance over his shoulder to make
sure Lace wasn't running out on him, but it was another customer coming in. He pushed the bill through

the slot toward Aimee, all the while keeping his gaze trained on Lace. "Keep the change."

He turned to Lace, being careful not to whack anyone else with the box.

"Hey, big shot," Aimee called.

"Yes?" Distracted, he glanced back.

Aimee was holding up a ten-dollar bill. "You're fifty-seven cents short."

"Sorry." He thought he'd given her a twenty. He did the box-balancing shuffle again, dug another dollar out, and passed it to Aimee.

"Hang on, I'll get your change."

But he was already walking toward Lace, sweat beading on his brow. It was damn hot in there.

Lace gave him a Mona-Lisa-ain't-got-nothing-on-me smile and he followed her out the door. Hell, he'd follow that butt just about anywhere.

She sashayed around to the back of her Corolla and opened the trunk. He rushed over to put the hedge trimmer in for her. Stood there breathing like he'd just run the ball fifty yards into the end zone himself.

The tip of her tongue flicked out to moisten her upper lip. "Pierce?"

Was she going to forgive him? Thank him? "Yes?"

"I think you should know something."

He leaned in closer, getting a deep breath of her deliciously earthy scent. "What's that?"

"That sack of seeds?"

"Uh-huh?"

"Take a look at them."

Confused, but willing to do just about anything she asked, Pierce opened the crumpled paper bag and peered in at the thin, spiny, brittle seeds.

"Do those look like pumpkin seeds to you?"

His mind vapor locked, and for the life of him, he could not remember what pumpkin seeds looked like. He blinked, glanced at her. Talk about pressure. He felt like he was back in calculus class. "Um . . . um . . ."

"Did you ever carve a jack-o'-lantern when you were a kid?"

"Yeah, sure."

"Think back," she said with extravagant patience. "What did the inside of the pumpkin look like?"

"It had this orange yucky crap in it and these big—" He met her eyes. "These aren't pumpkin seeds."

"Very good." She gave a little half clap like he was a puppy who'd managed to hold his bladder until he'd gotten outside.

His eyes met hers. "What are these seeds?"

"*Salsola iberica.*"

"In English," Pierce said. She was getting a kick out of his ignorance.

"Russian thistle."

He frowned. "Russian thistle? What's that?"

"Fancy name for tumbleweed."

His face warmed. "These are tumbleweed seeds?"

She nodded.

"Why would Toby sell me tumbleweed seeds?" he asked.

Lace canted her head. "For one thing, a slick-talking salesman conned Toby into investing a thousand dollars' worth of Joe Angus's money for *Salsola iberica*, convincing him that it was the cattle fodder of the future, and Toby needs to unload it to stay on Joe's good side."

He swore, using one short, stark, succinct word. "Toby thought I was too dumb to know the difference."

Lace shrugged, straightened her head, and raised her brow, but she didn't say what he figured she was thinking. *You did buy them, dumbass.*

"I do know the difference," he said defensively.

Her eyebrows went higher.

"I wasn't paying attention when Toby was scooping up the seeds because I was busy looking at you."

"So it's my fault?" Her lips twitched in amusement.

He grinned back. "Totally. If you knew how hot you looked in those jeans—"

"For another thing," she interrupted, ignoring his compliment, but a pale pinkness tinged her neck and slowly spread up her face to color her cheeks. "Malcolm called before you got here."

"Malcolm called?"

"He told Toby about your bet over the pumpkin crop. They punked you, Pierce. It was a group effort."

"So when Aimee called me 'old dude' and pretended she didn't know who I was—"

"Setup."

"And the part about people saying I'm washed up?"

"Untrue. People are on pins and needles waiting for you to get back on the gridiron."

Well, that was something of a relief. He wasn't a has-been. *Yet.*

Lace motioned toward the door of the store.

He turned to see everyone who'd been in the store standing outside grinning at him. Joke. It had all been a joke. Well, damn. He could take a joke. In spite of the hollow feeling in his gut, he grinned, held up the sack of seeds, and called, "You got me."

The bunch at the door burst out laughing.

Toby waved him back inside. "C'mon. I'll get you the real pumpkin seeds."

"Be right there," he said to Toby, and then turned back to Lace. "You were in on this prank too?"

"I wasn't. I overheard them."

"Why did you tell me the truth instead of letting me get home with the thistle seeds so Malcolm could do a gloaty dance?"

"Because I hate seeing anyone humiliated. Even you."

He looked deep into her soulful blue eyes, and saw the remnants of childhood hurt lingering. She blinked and it went away, but for a brief second, he'd seen it, and while she'd clearly gotten past her teenage crush on him and the shame it had caused her, that public pain was part of who she was.

His throat constricted. Damn. He was so sorry for that. He reached out a hand to touch her, but she stepped back, just out of reach.

"Better go fetch your pumpkin seeds and get them in the ground or they won't be ready in time for Halloween." She slammed the trunk closed. "Then again, smart money says Malcolm's going to win the bet."

"The town is making bets?"

"Uh-huh."

"How much did you put in?"

"Twenty on Malcolm."

Pierce splayed a hand to his chest. "Ouch."

"You might be good at flinging a football, but a farmer?" She shook her head. "You're not."

"I can't believe you backed Malcolm."

"What can I say? For once in your life, Pierce, you're a long shot. Now you finally know how the rest of us feel."

Chapter 6

*Abscission: the natural separation of
flowers, fruit, or leaves from plants.*

SLIGHTLY over forty-eight hours later, Pierce was in
Valley Ranch, on the examination table of Dr. Hank
Travers, the physician for the Dallas Cowboys who over-
saw his care. It was a previously scheduled, six-month
postoperative visit. He'd spent Saturday and Sunday
getting those pumpkins in the ground, and his butt hurt
from riding a tractor. He'd driven to El Paso Sunday
evening and caught a flight to Dallas this morning.

Everything in the office was top-notch, state-of-
the-art, no-expenses-spared in the pursuit of health for
income-generating athletes. While it was nice, sometimes he felt like he was little more than a Thorough-
bred racehorse. Only valued for what he could provide,
interchangeable with the next young hotshot who
strolled through the door.

*Knock it off. You're fine. You haven't had to take Vi-
codin in two months.* Although planting those pumpkin
seeds had stirred up the pain, he was handling it.

Technicians had just run him through X-rays and a CT scan, drawn blood, and taken his vital signs. He was waiting on Dr. Hank to appear and give him a clean bill of health with a firm timeline of when he could return to football.

If it was October, he wouldn't be there to harvest the pumpkins. Why did that make him feel kind of sad? It wasn't the loss of ten grand. That was chump change. But hell, he sort of liked the rhythm of Cupid. Missed it already and he wasn't even gone yet.

Be honest. You'll miss Lace.

That was ridiculous. How could he miss her? He'd seen her exactly twice in a week's time and before that, he hadn't seen or thought much about her in twelve years. Maybe so, but on the first-class flight to Dallas, he kept wishing she was with him so he could show her his world. Then again, she probably wouldn't be all that impressed with his high-rise condo in spite of the killer view of the Dallas sky-line and all the amenities, including a health club and spa, a nine-hole golf course, and a twenty-four-hour concierge. Now, if they had an arboretum, that might impress her.

She was a lot more down-to-earth than the women he usually dated. *Um, you're not dating her.* But he could be. He wanted to be. The only thing getting in his way was Lace. An image of her popped into his mind, those lips, that lush figure, jet black hair, and he started having all kinds of Snow White fantasies—minus the seven dwarfs, of course.

It was a bad idea for a guy wearing a paper gown waiting for a doctor to show up. He closed his eyes, willed away visions of Lace in order to stop the half-boner from becoming full-fledged.

There was a double rap of knuckles on the door and then Dr. Hank entered without waiting to be asked in. Calling him a doctor was a bit of a stretch, since he was younger than Pierce. It could just as easily have been Jay Bettingfield coming through the door.

Dr. Hank's teeth were dental-commercial straight and his thick dark hair, swept back off his face, gave him an Elvis Presley resemblance. He wore a blue polo shirt with the Dallas Cowboys logo on it in silver, pleated khakis, a short white lab jacket thrown over the ensemble, and boat shoes without socks. A black stethoscope dangled around his neck and he carried a chart in his hand and an oversized brown X-ray folder.

Dr. Hank's brow wrinkled in a frown.

Pierce's balls drew up tight and flat and he suddenly felt queasy. "What is it?"

"I'm afraid your leg isn't healing as quickly as we hoped. You've been going to physical therapy, right?"

Pierce swallowed back the bile souring his throat and nodded. "Yeah, sure, three times a week, except for this past week. Not this past week though."

"Why not?"

"My dad's been sick—"

"That's no excuse. Hire a caretaker for your father if you need to, but if you want to have a prayer of getting back to the gridiron you must do your physical therapy, No ifs, ands, or buts about it."

A chill passed through him and he put a hand to his injured leg. "Is it that bad? I mean it doesn't even hurt all that much anymore."

"The bone isn't growing back the way we'd like." Dr. Hank took the X-rays out of the folder and shoved them up on the lighted X-ray thingamajig mounted on the wall. He took a pen from his pocket and pointed out the area of concern.

"Is there a pill or something I can take to speed up bone growth? Steroids? Or those pills old ladies take so they don't break their bones?"

"No, drugs for osteoporosis won't work in your case, and I'm afraid the steroids we had you on right after the surgery to control swelling might have contributed to the problem."

Sweat beaded on his upper lip and he brushed it away. Oh shit, oh shit. He *was* Joe Theismann.

Dr. Hank went on explaining things in medical mumbo-jumbo. Pierce's ears rang and he caught only bits and pieces of what the doctor was saying. "Ligaments, tendons . . . blah, blah . . . support . . . blah, blah . . . but hopefully no permanent limp."

"What—" His voice cracked and he cleared his

throat, started over. "Are you saying that I won't be ready to go back on the field in October?"

Dr. Hank did not meet his gaze or answer his question. He set down the chart, came closer. He had the well-fed look of a man living the high life. Probably owned a Jag. Or two. "Could you lie back and let me examine your leg?"

Pierce sucked in a deep breath. As he lay back, the doctor pulled out the sliding shelf from underneath the top of the examination table to support his legs. Talk about vulnerable. Bare-assed in a paper gown while someone who's younger than you are tells you that your career is all shot to hell.

Dr. Hank poked and prodded his leg with hands that were too cold. The scar was still tender. Pierce flinched.

"Does that hurt?"

"When you poke like that."

"It shouldn't be that tender."

"Normally, it's not."

Dr. Hank looked like he didn't believe him. "Have you been under a lot of stress lately?"

"You mean besides breaking my leg during the Super Bowl with a hundred million people watching?"

"You mentioned something about your father."

"He's been sick and they can't find out what's wrong with him, but he's starting to get better."

"You lost your mother to cancer, didn't you?"

"How do you know that?"

"It's in your chart."

"Oh. Yes, my senior year of college." He didn't like thinking about that. "What's that got to do with anything? You don't think . . ." He sat up abruptly, almost whacking Dr. Hank in the head. If he'd been an older doctor with slower reflexes, Pierce probably would *have* whacked into him.

"You don't have cancer," Dr. Hank assured him and pushed the shelf back in so Pierce could sit all the way up.

"Then why did you ask about it?"

"I was just thinking that you've been through a lot."

"No more than anyone else, less than most. Hell, I'm thinking I've been the most fortunate son of a gun on the planet."

"Until now," Dr. Hank murmured.

A chill passed through him, but he quickly shook it off. No. No. He didn't care how gloomy the good doctor looked. He *was* coming back from this. He was *not* Joe Theismann, no matter how much the media liked to draw that comparison.

"You can get dressed and I'll meet you in the corridor." Dr. Hank picked up the chart and turned to go.

Pierce put out a hand to stop him. "Bottom line it for me, Doc. Will I be able to return by Thanksgiving?"

Dr. Hank's features softened. "I know this is hard to hear, Pierce, but there's not going to be any football for you this year."

WHILE PIERCE WAS in Dallas getting bad news, Lace was in the greenhouse twining young tendrils of *Podranea ricasoliana*, also known as pink trumpet vine, around wooden stakes. In a few weeks, the plants would be large enough to transplant into the garden for an added splash of color along the rock wall behind the Cupid fountain.

Several times she paused in mid-twine to stare out the glass greenhouse at the Davis Mountains rising up from the desert floor just beyond the town limits, but she wasn't seeing the mountains. Instead, she kept picturing Pierce looking humbled and chagrined but sheepishly good-natured over the prank that the crew at Angus Feed and Grain had dished out.

She'd been doing a damn good job of keeping an amused distance until his eyes had met hers, and a heater of empathy stirred something inside. Something she had not wanted to resurrect. Tempting as he was, she was not going mushy over Pierce Hollister.

Resolutely, she focused on the trumpet vines, taking deep breaths, watching her fingers move as if they were detached from her body, and every time the image of Pierce's face popped into her head, she blinked it away.

Lace was doing a lot of blinking.

The door opened and Shasta came rushing in, the weekly greensheet that printed the letters from Cupid clutched in her hand. Tears misted her eyes.

"Shasta?" Lace dropped the tendril she was twining. "What's wrong?"

"You promised!" Her lips quivered and she looked utterly betrayed.

Lace frowned. What was the girl talking about?

Shasta shook the paper underneath Lace's nose. "You promised you'd give her hope."

"You're talking about my reply to Hero Worshipper?"

"Listen, just listen to what you wrote." Shasta unfolded the paper, cleared her throat, and started to read. "Dear Hero Worshipper, take heart. Many have been in your shoes and it's a miserable place to be, sure enough. Longing for someone who doesn't love you back." She raised her head to meet Lace's eyes. "You don't know that. He might love her back. Who are you to say he doesn't love her?"

"You can't make someone love you. In order to heal, Hero Worshipper needs to move on."

"But you crushed all her hopes."

"Keep reading, I told her she would find someone who will love her for who she is."

"Did *you* find someone else?" Shasta asked. "After you got your heart broken?"

"No," Lace admitted. "Not yet."

"What if you never do? What if he was your one great love?"

"He's not."

"How do you know?"

"It was just a foolish schoolgirl crush, just like the one this girl"—Lace waved at the greensheet—"has concocted in her head. Her love for him is just a fantasy. He doesn't love her and it would be unkind to advise her to hold out hope for something that can never be. False hope is worse than no hope at all."

"She doesn't want someone else. She wants *him*."

"Not to sound like a Rolling Stones song or anything, but you can't always get what you want."

"Just because you gave up, doesn't mean she can't keep hoping."

Had she given up? It was a startling thought. "Why do you care so much?"

Instead of answering, Shasta turned the table on her. "How can you be so cold when the same thing happened to you?"

"You have a crush on someone too," Lace guessed. "Someone who doesn't love you back?"

Anger flared in Shasta's eyes and her fingers fisted tight around the paper. She opened her mouth to say something, but at that moment, a man appeared in the doorway.

With the morning sun at his back, Lace couldn't see his face clearly and for one long second, her heart skipped a beat. Pierce?

He stepped over the threshold and she saw it was Pierce's brother, Malcolm. In the three months she'd been back home, she had said nothing more to him than a quick "Hello" if they passed each other on the street. Things had been awkward between them ever since "the incident" and they'd avoided each other as much as possible after that. Silly really. They were grown-ups.

"Good morning," she greeted him.

He took off his cowboy hat, nodded at her. "Lace."

What was he doing here? Did this have anything to do with the joke he'd pulled on his brother? "How can I help you?"

"I was wondering . . ." He paused, twirled his cowboy hat in his hand, but did not meet her gaze.

"Yes?"

He shuffled the tip of his boot against the ground. "Uh . . ."

"Is something wrong?"

"No, no."

"Is this about Pierce?"

Malcolm frowned. "Everything in the world isn't about Pierce. It's got nothing to do with my brother. He's in Dallas hoping to get the all-clear from his doctor so he can get back to playing football."

"Oh. Okay." She waited. What did he want?

"Listen, there's a symposium in El Paso this weekend on desert cultivation and—"

"Are you asking me out?"

He looked appalled, plunked his hat back down on

his head. "Oh no, no. Not asking you out, just wondering if you're going in case you'd like to carpool."

Great. Now she felt like a gigantic idiot for jumping to conclusions. Her cheeks heated and she knew they were strawberry pink. Damn her pale skin.

"Not that I wouldn't love to ask you out," he rushed to smooth things over. "In fact, I often thought about asking you out when we were in high school, but that thing with Pierce—"

"Good grief, Malcolm. That was a hundred years ago. I was a kid. I'm so over it. The only reason it's even a thing is because this town is the size of a mustard seed and people don't have anything better to do than gossip about ancient history and stir the pot in search of some kind of drama."

"You mean you would have gone out with me if I had asked?" Malcolm's eyes met hers.

Oh gosh. This *was* awkward. Was Malcolm interested in her? She couldn't imagine going out with him. Not because he wasn't good-looking, because he was, but because she'd once been so crazy about his older brother that history crushed any chance she might have had with Malcolm if she'd wanted it. Hell, it didn't matter that she was over Pierce. Her stupid high school infatuation still mucked things up for her, at least here in Cupid. Why hadn't she just taken that job at the Smithsonian?

Malcolm raised a hand. "Don't answer that question. I don't want to know."

Lace inclined her head in the direction of Shasta, who was standing in the corner, her arms crossed over her chest, shifting her gaze from Malcolm to Lace and back again along with the conversation, like she was watching a tennis match. "Why don't you take Shasta to the symposium?"

"Me?" Shasta perked up.

"I've been meaning to send you to some courses, this would be a great opportunity for you to learn more about plants of the Trans-Pecos," Lace said, eager to get out of this conversation and get back to work.

"You want to go?" Malcolm asked Shasta.

Shasta nodded brightly.

"It's this coming weekend. You can still register online." Malcolm paused at the door to cast an appraising glance over Shasta.

"I'll take care of getting her registered," Lace said.

"Will your brother be going?" Shasta asked Malcolm.

That earned a glower from Malcolm. "Doubtful. He'll be headed back to Dallas before long."

Shasta looked momentarily crestfallen. "Could you get me his autograph?"

Malcolm's jaw clenched. "I'll see what I can do."

Poor guy. It had to be tough living in Pierce's shadow.

Malcolm left and Shasta seemed to have forgotten her pique at Lace over her response to Hero Worshipper. She mumbled something about opening the botanical gardens gift shop for the visitors and took off just as Carol Ann came to the back door of the greenhouse.

"Grand Central Station," Lace greeted her.

"I come bearing gifts," Carol Ann said, holding out three envelopes—one for Lace, one for Manuel, and one for Shasta.

The botanical gardens were on the city payroll and they normally got paid every Friday, but this week the checks had been delayed.

"What was the holdup?" Lace asked, accepting the checks.

"Small banking error," Carol Ann said, but her face was pinched and her eyes faraway.

An uneasy feeling settled over Lace. "Is there something I should be worried about?"

"No, no." Carol Ann waved a hand. "These things happen. Now that I've taken over the books, hopefully they won't happen again."

"Is Cupid in financial straits?"

"With the economy the way it is"—Carol Ann shrugged—"I'd say we're doing better than most."

"'Cause I know when budgets need cutting, beautification programs are the first to go."

Carol Ann rested a hand on her shoulder. "Honey, you have nothing to worry about. The Cupid legend brings in tourists. The gardens are the heart and soul of the legend."

"I thought the Cupid Caverns were."

"Those too."

Lace couldn't shake the feeling Carol Ann was keeping something from her. "When is Melody coming to visit?"

Her aunt's face brightened. "Next Sunday. I'm going to throw her a welcome home barbecue, so clear your calendar."

"Will do."

Her aunt waved at her over her shoulder, and the door had no more than closed behind her than Lace's cell phone rang. Normally life in Cupid moved at a sloth's pace, but for some reason today was different.

She didn't recognize the number on the caller ID. "Hello?"

"Lace?"

"Yes?"

"This is Maurie Landers." Maurie was the extension agent for Jeff Davis County.

"Hey Maurie, how are you?"

"Not good."

"I'm so sorry to hear that. What's wrong?"

"Listen, Lace, I've just come from my obstetrician and he says I have to go on immediate bed rest or risk losing the baby."

"Oh no!"

"I'm trying my best not to freak out," Maurie said.

"Is there anything I can do?"

"Well, actually, there is. Could you take over my

Tuesday night class for community education? It's starting this week."

Lace took a deep breath. While she loved plants and sharing her knowledge about them, she'd always had trouble getting up and speaking in front of groups.

"The pay is pretty good and I don't know who else to ask."

"Can't they just cancel the class?"

"I hate to disappoint the students. We've had a lot of new people moving into the county who are woefully uneducated about what it takes to farm and ranch the Trans-Pecos."

That was true enough.

"I'll owe you big time," Maurie begged.

She wanted to say no, but how could she refuse when Maurie was so desperate? "Sure, yes. I'll do it."

"You are such a lifesaver! I could kiss you." Then Maurie went on to give her a rundown on the course details.

Lace hung up a few minutes later. What a weird morning. From Shasta getting bent out of shape about her answer to Hero Worshipper, to Malcolm kinda, sorta asking her out, to her suspicions that Carol Ann was hiding something about the town coffers, to Maurie's health issues.

Damn if it didn't feel like abscission, when the growing season of a plant was ending and color changes were taking place. Abscission was the first step in a complex process of renewal involving proteins, enzymes, and hormones. And while the creation of the abscission layer resulted in a high concentration of sugar that caused the leaves to change brilliant colors, it was also a time of great upheaval as the short, sweet splashes of vivid reds, oranges, and yellows flared brightly, only to ultimately give way to death of the old so that rebirth could occur.

In spite of the heat, Lace shivered.

Chapter 7

*Taproot: a plant's primary root, often
descending quite deeply into the ground.*

On Tuesday evening at ten minutes to seven, Lace walked into the adult education class, sponsored by the Cupid ISD and held at the high school. The only thing that could have made it worse was if they held the course in her old homeroom. Stomach jittery, palms soaked in dread, she forced herself inside. Four students were already there.

Just get through the class. It was only two hours. Once she made it through the first class, she'd be okay. She thought about the beta blockers a doctor had prescribed for her when she'd first gone to college so she could handle getting up in front of the class. She wished she had some now. *You don't need medication. You've gotten past that. You're not going to stutter. You're going to be fine. You're not that shy teenager anymore.*

Still, she couldn't help reaching for her ubiquitous comfort, mentally reciting botany terms—*ovate, lanceolate, cordate, oblanceolate.*

At seven, she took roll from the attendance list she'd picked up in the administration office. They'd told her there might be a few more last-minute sign-ups, but everyone on the list was there. She introduced herself, wrote her contact information on the blackboard and had the students introduce themselves and tell the class why they were taking the basic gardening course. That killed ten minutes, only an hour and fifty minutes to go.

Lace turned to the board to start writing down a few basic terms when she heard the door open. Was it one of those last-minute stragglers?

An immediate ripple of murmured whispers went through the class.

Intrigued, Lace peered over her shoulder to see who or what had caused the stir, and there he was, bigger than Dallas. Pierce Hollister.

Her body—the traitorous thing—responded instantly. Her pulse sped up and her womb tightened.

Really? Seriously? One look and she was craving him like a chocolate connoisseur craved Debauve & Gallais truffles? How could that be?

"Sorry, I'm late, Teach," he drawled, removed his Stetson, ran a hand through his hair, and took a seat in the front row.

Her stomach took the express elevator to her throat. Oh good God. What was he doing in her class?

"And you are?" she asked coolly. Okay, she was

being ornery about it, but she was scrambling trying to find some equilibrium.

"He's Pierce Hollister, miss," said one of the younger men in the class. "Quarterback of the Dallas Cowboys."

She locked eyes with Pierce, who was grinning at her like she was the most humorous thing he'd ever seen. Stay calm. Don't panic. Never mind that the look on his face was melting her panties to her skin. "You don't say."

"I'm not playing this year," Pierce said. "Maybe you heard that I injured my leg."

The male students started asking him questions, while the female students batted their eyes at him, even the elderly lady who'd come into the class on a scooter.

Lace cleared her throat. "Class."

No one paid her any attention.

She raised her voice. "Class."

People were out of their seats crowding around Pierce, asking for autographs, pumping him for gridiron stories.

Lace clapped her hands. "Excuse me. I know it's fun to have a celebrity in our midst, but could we get on topic?"

A couple of people glanced over their shoulders at her, but most everyone kept right on talking to Pierce. She pressed her lips together, knotted her hands into fists. *Sepal, calyx, carpel, pistil.*

"So what's it like knowing you'll probably never play ball again?" one of the men asked Pierce.

Pierce absorbed the question with his smile firmly fixed, but Lace spied a quick flicker of pain in his eyes. "Who told you that?" he asked the man.

She marched over and put a hand on Pierce's shoulder. "May I see you out in the hallway please, Mr. Hollister?"

He looked relieved and grateful for the rescue. "Why, it would be my pleasure, Ms. Bettingfield."

Once the door closed behind them and they were in the empty corridor, he leaned one shoulder against the wall, absentmindedly rubbed the outer thigh of his left leg as if the limp he was struggling not to show had caused his muscles to ache.

The high school corridor.

Scene of the crime. Nothing had changed in twelve years. Same big old industrial clock mounted in the hallway that loudly ticked off the seconds. Same dingy gray lockers. Same smell of book glue, rubber erasers, government-subsidized food, and teenage angst. Same trophy case in the hall. The biggest trophy was from the year Pierce quarterbacked Cupid to the state championship.

Before his recent return to Cupid, the last time Lace had seen Pierce—other than occasional brief glimpses on the street—was that day when she'd run away from the taunts of her classmates. Remembering that wretched moment twisted her stomach in knots and she wished she hadn't had that slice of pepperoni pizza before coming to teach the class. Oh, okay, no point stretching the truth. She'd had three slices and enjoyed every bite.

Until now.

"Hey," he said. "Thanks for the rescue—"

"Why are you stalking me?" Lace sank her hands on her hips and glowered, determined to look stern so he couldn't tell exactly how much he turned her on.

He pulled his head back, looked startled. "I'm not stalking you."

She raised one finger. "You were at the hospital—"

"My dad was sick."

She raised two fingers. "You were at the Feed and Grain."

"Buying pumpkin seeds."

Up went her third finger. "And now you show up in my basic gardening class. Are you saying that's a co-incidence?"

"Anyone ever tell you that you've got a paranoid streak a mile wide?"

"Everywhere I go you seem to turn up. That's not paranoia. That's fact. What are you after?"

He raked a hot gaze over her. "What do you think?"

"Aha! So it's true. You are stalking me."

"I didn't know you were teaching the class," he said reasonably. "On the schedule it lists the instructor as Maurie Landers."

So it did. Now she was embarrassed for accusing

him of stalking her. "Why are you taking a class in basic gardening?" she quickly changed the subject.

"Seriously? You need to ask? You were there when I was conned into buying tumbleweed seeds."

"Extenuating circumstances. You were set up."

"Doesn't change the fact that I know precious little about agriculture. Shameful for a rancher's son. I'm determined to change all that."

"You don't have to know anything about it. You're a football player."

"There's more to life than football."

That surprised her. Was he thinking about the future? Was he coming home to Cupid for good? Was he ready to settle down? Her pulse revved at the thought. *Take it easy. No flights of fancy.* "Since when? Last time I checked, jocks rule the world, as evidenced by your following." She waved a hand at the classroom.

"That's all hype and bullshit and you know it. Popularity isn't the measure of a man."

"Yes," she said, "but I didn't realize you were aware of that." Hmm, Pierce Hollister humbled? Something was most definitely off about this. "Malcolm told me you'd gone to see your doctor in Dallas. Did you get bad news?"

"You spoke to Malcolm?"

"Ignoring that last part?"

"When did you see Malcolm?"

"You're ignoring the bad news question? Must be serious."

"It's fine, everything's fine." He winced.

"I'm a good listener," she offered, not knowing why she did so.

"Malcolm?" Pierce prodded.

"He came by the gardens and asked me to go to a symposium with him in El Paso this coming weekend."

Pierce straightened. "He did, huh?"

"Does that bother you?"

"Are you going?"

"Only if it bothers you," she couldn't resist teasing.

"Why would it bother me?"

"You and your brother have a bad case of sibling rivalry. I have a feeling Malcolm was asking me to the symposium just to gig you."

"Alternately, he could have a mad crush on you."

Lace snorted, folded her arms over her chest.

"You don't think that's possible?" Pierce asked.

"I'm not the type of woman that men get mad crushes over."

Pierce's eyes took such a long, leisurely look down her body that it was all she could do not to shiver. "Now where did you ever get an idea like that?"

"I'm too cerebral. It scares men off."

"You got a lot more going for you than just your brains, Lace Bettingfield." His voice rumbled from his chest, dark and thick.

"What's with the full-court press from the Hollister boys?" She threw her arms in the air. "I don't want either one of you."

"Are you sure about that?"

"Positive," she said weakly. That smile of his should come with a skull and crossbones icon. Warning! Deadly!

Pierce lowered his voice, his intelligent eyes sharp. The man didn't miss a thing. "What do *you* want, Lace?"

It was all she could do to meet his seductive eyes. *A kiss. I want you to kiss me!* The crazy thought ran through her brain, unbidden and unwanted. Well, mostly.

His gaze was on her. Not just on her, but searing into her, burning her up.

She notched up her chin. "I want to teach this class before all the students get up and walk out." She put her hand on the doorknob. "I'll let you stay for a while, but if your celebrity status keeps disrupting the class, you're out on your ear."

"Who's going to throw me out?"

"I am," she blustered.

"All by yourself?" He took a step toward her.

Lace tossed her head, held her ground. Every raw, achy cell in her body cried for her to plant a big wet kiss on his lips, but she wasn't about to give him the satisfaction of letting him know how much he affected her. "Sorry, but that alpha male, I'm-gonna-invade-your-personal-space-until-your-knees-crumple-from-the-sheer-force-of-my-masculinity crap doesn't work on me."

"Is that right?" he murmured huskily.

"Absolutely."

He rested his arm on the door facing above her head, leaned in so close she could smell the moneyed scent of his cologne mingling with the fragrance of sandy Cupid soil, underplayed by the smell of high school. "Not even a tiny little bit?"

"Not one iota."

"Not a scintilla?"

"Not even a micro particle."

"What about an atom?"

"Not even a quark."

"Quarks, huh? Now that's an interesting topic. Did you know that there are six quarks but they come in pairs of three. Up/down. Charm/strange. Top/bottom."

"Don't forget the antiquark," she challenged.

"Opposite and equal charges. You looked surprised that I know this."

Lace raised her brows. "The Discovery Channel?"

His grin widened. "Hey, I've been convalescing. Not much else on TV when it's not football season."

"You surprise me. I would never have thought you could flip past late night Cinemax."

"If we were a pair of quarks which one would we

be?" His voice went down another octave. "I vote for top and bottom, although charm and strange does have an intriguing appeal."

"Yes, in that case you'd be the charm, wouldn't you? But you've got it all wrong. We're not quark pairs."

"No?"

"If you're the quark, I'm the antiquark."

He dipped his head so low that his lips were almost touching hers. "You like being the antagonist, don't you?"

"You'll soon find out if you don't step off," she said, far more feisty than she felt.

He raised both arms and took a step back, but as he did, his left leg gave out and he stumbled sideways.

Instinctively, Lace put out a hand to catch him.

Mistake!

Instant heat jumped from his body up her arm. He regained his balance and she quickly dropped her hand, but it was too late to stop the rush of sensation spreading through her. Was she still breathing? Her chest seemed to be moving up and down in the regular way, but if that was the case, why was her head spinning?

She turned away, fumbled frantically for the doorknob, but her palms were so damp that her hands kept slipping on the knob.

His big hand was on hers now, closing over it to keep her from turning the knob. "Stop a minute," he murmured. "Take a deep breath. Collect yourself."

"I'm perfectly collected," she said, her words coming out thin and reedy.

His hand was so big! It swallowed hers right up. But his touch was incredibly gentle. She never suspected he could have such a gentle touch.

"Lace," he said in that tone that sounded like straight-up sex. His back was against hers, his hip brushing her fanny. He had half a hard-on!

She closed her eyes and fought against the impulse to arch her back into his erection. God, she was losing it. All this time she'd told herself he no longer affected her and that she would be completely composed around him. What a liar she was! There was no deception like self-deception, right?

"Please," she begged in a shaky voice. "Get your hand off mine." If he didn't obey, she couldn't be held responsible for what she might do next.

He let go, raised his palms, and stepped back. "As you wish."

Oh great, now she was thinking about Westley from *The Princess Bride*, her all-time favorite romantic movie. Come to think of it, Pierce looked a bit like a more rugged, cowboy version of Westley—same hair color, same cocky attitude.

Do not romanticize him!

Easy to say, but here, trapped by the mesmerizing power of his scent and his big body, she was helpless against the onslaught of female hormones surging through her in response to his total maleness. Was she ovulating? Could that explain the reckless urges rising inside her?

Somehow, she finally got the door opened and stepped across the threshold, only to find the entire class rushing back to their seats with grins on their faces. They'd all been gathered around the door spying on her and Pierce. In a moment of sheer déjà vu, Lace was fourteen again, and instead of her students, she saw her peers sniggering at her for having the audacity to be in love with the quarterback.

The urge to flee gobbled her up, but she was not going to let those memories do her in. She was a grown-up now. She walked to the front of the room, took command of the class, and launched into the lecture.

For the remainder of the workshop, she did her best not to look at Pierce and allowed her love for botany to sweep her away. She talked about growing zones and how to choose a location for a garden. She told them that the ideal growing soil consisted of the right mix of minerals, sand, clay, and organic matter. She touched on composting—they would have an entire lesson on that later—introduced them to irrigation systems, and dug into how to plan a garden.

Her mouth moved, she said the right things, but mentally she was cataloging everything about Pierce without really looking at him—the slight crook of his nose, the nonchalant way he slouched in his chair, long legs extended out in front of him, the fall of honey brown hair over his forehead, the masculine set of his firm jawline. The top two buttons of his blue-and-white-checkered Western-style shirt were unbuttoned, revealing tanned skin and a light tuft of chest hair. She soaked up the details, absorbed him, saturating herself to make up for all the years of not seeing him.

With a sinking heart, she realized that in spite of everything she'd told herself to the contrary, she not only had not gotten over Pierce Hollister, but she wanted him more than ever!

AFTER CLASS A few students came up to ask questions, but most everyone else scattered quickly, including Pierce. Relieved that he had gone, Lace bid the last student good night, picked up her purse and reference material, turned off the lights—Maurie had told her to make sure and turn off the lights so the janitor wouldn't bitch—and headed out the door.

Only to find Pierce waiting in the hallway, his butt resting against the wall, but his shoulders forward, hands tucked into his front pocket, cowboy hat tipped down over his brow, giving him a potent James Dean air. The movie *Giant* had been filmed in Marfa, not far from Cupid, and the area still held on to its reverence of all things Elizabeth Taylor, Rock Hudson, and James Dean. Many of the old-time residents, including Great-aunt Delia, had autographs hanging on their walls to cement the memory.

"Great lecture," he said.

"If you weren't stalking me before, you're bordering on it now." She blew past him. Somewhere in another part of the building a power buffer hummed and the smell of floor wax filled the air.

"Hey, wait up."

From the reflection in the glass door, she saw him push off from the wall, moved fast to catch up with her, limping in the process.

She slowed, turned. "What is it?"

"I'm not stalking you, I just wanted to walk you to your car."

"Why?"

"It's nine o'clock at night and you're alone."

"This is Cupid, not Dallas."

"Things happen here too. I heard about those counterfeiters who used dynamite to implode the bootleggers' cave in the Cupid Caverns."

"You think a mob of counterfeiters are waiting in the parking lot to blow me up?"

A smile jerked at the corner of his mouth. "No, I was merely pointing out that Cupid has its share of illegal activity."

"What's the real reason you want to walk me to my car?"

"I just wanted to talk to you."

"About what?" she asked, trying to ignore the goose bumps spreading over her arms.

He shrugged, sauntered closer. He looked so self-possessed and relaxed. His jeans were Wranglers, just like every other cowboy, but on his left wrist he wore a Rolex and his cowboy boots were handmade. The low tilt of the Stetson hid his eyes, but she could feel the heat radiating out from them. God, he was every woman's fantasy.

"Not really a people person, are you?"

"Is that a rhetorical question?"

"I know it took a lot for you to stand up there in front of the class."

"Was my stress that obvious?" She nibbled on a thumbnail, and then made herself stop.

"I don't think anyone noticed except me." He walked around her, opened the door, stood waiting for her to follow. "You're really good at camouflaging your true feelings."

"Is that a compliment or a complaint?"

"Sweetheart," he drawled. "When it comes to you, there's nothing to complain about."

On anyone else, the line might have come across as corny, but it was all in the delivery, and the way Pierce said "sweetheart" made her heart go pitter-pat. What the hell? She might as well let him walk her to her car. What was the worst that could happen? Fall in love with him all over again? Get her heart broken? It wasn't like she didn't know how to bounce back from that.

The door closed behind them with a soft snick. Moths swirled and fluttered around the security lamps. The scent of honeysuckle, *Lonicera periclymenum*, clung to the night. There were only two cars in the parking lot. Her Corolla and his King Ranch.

"Give me those," he said, and reached for her books.

She held them away from him. "This isn't kindergarten. I can carry my own books."

"You make it pretty damn impossible to do anything nice for you."

"I don't trust nice," she said honestly.

"Why's that?"

"Generally, when people are nice to you, they expect something in return." She stopped beside her car. "What do you expect from me, Pierce?"

He stroked his jaw, produced a soft rasp of beard against his fingers. The goose bumps moved from her arms all the way down her body. Yes, all right. She was one of those women who found guys with a scruffy day's growth of beard sexy, but was she going to allow herself to be entranced by a five o'clock shadow? Yes, the way her stomach was going gooey, apparently she was. Good grief, she was so shallow.

" 'Expect' isn't the right word here," he said.

"What is the right word?"

" 'Hope' springs to mind."

"What are you hoping for?" Why was she asking? Was she really prepared to hear his answer? Great-aunt Delia was fond of saying, "Don't ask questions you don't want to know the answer to."

He cocked his cowboy hat far back on his head and gave her a look so sultry he had to have spent hours in front of a mirror perfecting it. "I think you know."

Her heart did a cartwheel. Determined not to let him know how much he scrambled her brain, she put a mild expression on her face. "I'm afraid I have no idea what you're talking about."

"I like you, Lace." He paused. "A lot."

"Since when?"

"Since forever."

"Couldn't prove it by me."

He was crowding her personal space again. She backed up until her butt bumped against her car door.

"I noticed you."

"When?"

"Back in high school."

She gulped. "You did?"

His gaze drifted over the curve of her breasts and an appreciative light lit his eyes. "Sweetheart, you filled out early. I would have had to be blind not to notice."

She held her books close to her chest. "How . . ." She paused, cleared her throat. "How come you never said anything?"

"You were four years younger than me. Plus you

were Jay's baby sister. Off-limits. Out of bounds. Your brother would have punched my lights out if he'd known what I was thinking. So I kept my mind on football and off you."

"Look, you don't have to try and make me feel better about what happened. It's water under the bridge. I moved past it a long time ago, even though people in this town seem reluctant to let the past die. It's not right to hold people accountable for the silly things they did as kids," she said.

"I never thought you were silly."

"I sure did. Imagine. The two of us." She toggled a finger between the two of them. "Ridiculous."

"How so?"

Lace rolled her eyes. "We are so incompatible that the idea of us being together for anything more than a brief good time is laughable. It's best to keep any of those kinds of feelings to our fantasies."

"So." He grinned. "You do still have fantasies about me."

"Fantasies are fantasies for a reason. In fantasies we can play out scenarios we would never, ever do in real life."

"What if I told you that you've gotten under my skin, Lace?"

"I'm sure this routine works well with the groupies, but I'm immune. Got my Pierce Hollister inoculations when I was fourteen. Now if you'll excuse me."

But he didn't excuse her. He slapped both hands on the roof of her car, pinning her between his arms, the tips of his cowboy boots touching the toes of her sneakers.

Her blood thundered, sending hot spikes of desire stabbing through her veins. The taste of yearning spilled into her mouth, rich and desperately sweet. He lowered his head. His mouth was almost touching hers. His breath warmed her lips. "I want you, Lace."

"You're bored," she retorted. "You've hurt your leg, you have nothing to do but look after your father and watch pumpkins grow until your leg heals. You're looking for a diversion. That's it."

"If that were true I could snap my fingers and call up as many women as I could handle. I don't want to do that because *you're* the one who intrigues me."

"You only want me because I don't want you."

He flashed a cajoling grin. "You want me."

Lace rolled her eyes heavenward.

"Didn't your mother ever tell you that if you keep doing that your eyes would stick that way?"

"God, you are so egotistical that you can't even conceptualize the idea that someone doesn't want to shag you."

"Shag?" His eyes twinkled.

"I like British comedies. So sue me."

Gently, he reached out and traced a knuckle over her cheek.

A shiver started at the base of her tailbone and slowly shimmied up her spine, but Lace forcefully clamped down on that sweet sensation, halting the quiver's rise at hip level. It was like stifling a sneeze. There was only one problem with that; the energy had nowhere else to go. It pooled hot and liquid into her pelvic floor, turning a simple shiver into a red-hot, five-alarm response.

"What else do you like?" he murmured.

"To be in bed by ten."

"I can get behind that."

"Once upon a time this full-court press might have swept me off my feet, but now . . ."

"What?" he prompted.

"I recognize it for what it is."

"And what is that?"

"A man desperate to prove he's still got it and a career-altering injury."

A flicker of hurt passed over his face but it quickly disappeared. "You're just trying to make me back off."

"I'm serious about this, Pierce."

"Uh-huh." He placed his legs on either side of hers. If he came any closer, he'd go through her.

"Your ego can't accept that there's a woman who isn't falling at your feet."

"You did once," he said. "Fall at my feet. Remember when you dropped your books in the hallway and I helped you pick them up and our hands touched?"

Boy howdy, did she remember! She'd thought of

nothing else for months afterward. "When I was a very impressionable teenager. I got over it as I suppose most women do with you."

"Ouch." Playfully, he rubbed his arm. "You can pull in your claws, kitten."

"Does anything about me look kittenish to you?"

He tracked another gaze over her ample body. "Correction. Wildcat."

"This has been real," she said. "And it's been fun, but it hasn't been real fun."

"You see." He breathed. "I really like this fiery new spirit you've developed. Kudos. Sass looks good on you."

"Listen, I'm not going to be just another notch on your belt. Let it go already."

"Oh, really?"

"Really."

"Not even if I did this?" he whispered.

Her body responded instantly, heating up in the center of her belly, liquid lava pooling into her pelvis. How many long lonely nights had she dreamed of this?

One of his hands moved to her shoulder, the other slipped around her waist. Her bones liquefied. It was a miracle her legs held her up.

He tasted of salted caramel. She loved salted caramel.

Her breathing quickened and her glasses fogged. She tried to stay stiff, but her lips softened and she almost relaxed into the kiss and let the moment carry her away. Instead, she pumped steel into her spine. Once upon a time she would have spontaneously combusted if Pierce Hollister had kissed her. Now her control had tempered her reaction, akin to cookies left in the oven too long. Burned to a crisp.

His tongue traced her lips.

She was tempted to haul off and slap him across his smug mug like some spunky heroine from a 1940s movie, but then slapping him would mean that he had affected her. He had *not* affected her. So she held back her hand. Held her tongue. Held back everything inside her. Stood there unmoving. Resisting. Mentally reciting—*connate, adnate, hypogenus, perigenus, epigenus.*

Wait a minute. All those terms had something to do with plant sex. Better knock that off. Except her determination was slipping away. His magnificent mouth was wearing her down.

He was an expert kisser. She'd give him that.

Do not give in.

But her disloyal arms had a mind of their own, they wrapped around his neck and pulled his head down, knocking off his cowboy hat and practically forcing him to deepen the kiss. Her breasts were mashed under his hard chest. She could feel the entire length of him against her. *All* of him.

It was the perfect kiss. Not too dry. Not too moist.

Not too hard, not too easy. It was sweet and soulful and lusty and provocative. If he was that good at kissing, what would he be like in bed?

Someone moaned, loud, needy, and wanton. Mortified, Lace realized that it was she.

Without warning, Pierce abruptly broke the kiss and gently set her aside. He winked and picked up his fallen hat. "There now," he said. "Put that in your fantasies and dream about it."

Chapter 8

Germination: the beginning or resumption of growth.

PIERCE drove home with a raging hard-on, more determined than ever to change Lace's mind about him. Whether she'd intended to or not, she'd issue him a challenge and aroused his take-no-prisoners instincts that made him such a success on the football field. When Pierce put his mind to something, he *always* got what he wanted.

Which was also why he was going to grow the best crop of pumpkins ever seen in Jeff Davis County and be back on the gridiron this year—if not by October, then by Thanksgiving, no matter what Dr. Hank said.

You've a big checklist there, Hollister. Seduce Lace, grow prizewinning pumpkins, get to the bottom of Dad's illness, and fully rehabilitate your leg in three months.

"Piece of cake," he muttered. He was used to juggling things, had in fact felt out of place and out of sorts these last few months with nothing to do but exercise and brood.

So where did he start? After Lace's lecture on gardening—of which he honestly hadn't heard a word since he'd been so focused on that dynamite body of hers—he figured he ought to put the award-winning pumpkins at the bottom of the list, leaving the top three tasks at a neck-and-neck tie. He'd already made an appointment for his father with a well-respected internist in San Antonio, but the doctor couldn't work his father in for an appointment for three weeks, so that goal was at a standstill. Healing his leg was of utmost importance, and as soon as he got back home, he'd join the Cupid gym and hire a trainer.

That left the most pleasant goal on his list—seduce Lace—which was going to be a hell of a lot of fun. She might protest that she wasn't interested in him, but her body's response belied her words.

Pierce licked his lips. He didn't know how, when, or why she'd gotten under his skin. He only knew she was buried down deep and it was damn scary for a guy who for the most part kept his relationships light. It was easier that way. But there was something about Lace that made him want to jump headlong into the deep end.

Watching her teach that class tonight, her face enrapt as she talked about planting beds and zones and timing and preparing the soil and . . . well . . . something had crept up behind him and boxed him the back of the head, reminding him of the big gaping hole right in the middle of his life that he'd managed to fill up with football because he was so terrified that without the sport there was nothing to him.

Lace made him feel substantial in a way he'd never felt before, and that both intrigued and alarmed him. He wanted to feel more of it, but he was afraid she would change him too much. He loved being Pierce Hollister, quarterback for the Dallas Cowboys. It was every dream he'd ever dreamed and every dream his father had dreamed for him.

But now his dreams were starting to shift. The ranch was calling to him in a way it had never called to him before. Whereas Cupid was once the one-horse town he'd run away from, it now beckoned like a shiny jewel tucked into the valley of the Davis Mountains. Called to him with its strong sense of community and family ties.

Most of all there was Lace, compelling him as he'd never been compelled.

Pull out all the stops. He knew how to woo a woman. He was going to pull out all the stops and, come hell or high water, Lace Bettingfield was going to be sharing his bed before the summer was out.

LACE WAS NOT going to pretend she wasn't still buzzing from Pierce's kiss. Nothing lay down that road but bumps and potholes and she was not traveling the unrequited love highway again—no way, no how. So what if he'd given her the most amazing kiss known to womankind? She wasn't going back for seconds.

Besides, she had enough to worry about. Carol Ann had called at six A.M. asking Lace to meet her at La Hacienda Grill for breakfast. That was so out of the ordinary that the hairs on her arms had lifted.

All the parking spots in front of the restaurant were taken, so she had to drive around and park in the back. She'd no sooner gotten out of her car than a brown King Ranch Ford pickup pulled in beside her.

Pierce!

Instantly, her throat constricted and her heart leaped. Frigging Venus flytrap, really?

The temptation to stop and flirt with him was so strong that she ducked her head, pretended she hadn't seen him, and started walking as fast as she could, without breaking into a run, around the side of the building. Wait a minute. If she ran off, that meant he was getting to her. She couldn't let him know he was getting to her, even though, dammit, he was.

"Hey, Lace, wait up."

Not Pierce's voice.

Lace relaxed, while at the same time she felt ridiculously disappointed. She paused and turned to see Malcolm striding toward her.

"Hi," he said breathlessly.

"Good morning."

"I borrowed Pierce's truck," he said.

"I can see that."

"I came to buy breakfast for my dad. He wanted La Hacienda's huevos rancheros and won't eat the eggs our cook Hildy made. He probably still won't eat them, but I've got to try something."

"Your father isn't getting any better?"

"He seemed to be. We thought he was, but he appears to have relapsed."

"I'm really sorry to hear that, Malcolm."

Malcolm massaged the nape of his neck. "Um. Listen."

She canted her head. "Yes."

"Um . . ." He stopped, moistened his lips. "I've got something to ask you."

Yikes, was he going to ask her out again? She better beat him to the punch before this got any more awkward than it already was. "Listen, Malcolm, I like you, I truly do but—"

"You've got me wrong." His face turned the color of borscht and he plastered a palm to the nape of his neck. "I'm not trying to ask you out."

The tips of her ears burned. Ego check! "Oh." Her voice squeaked like a rusty hinge.

He raised an apologetic hand. "It's not that you're not attractive, because damn, let's face it, you're beautiful, but I think I gave you the wrong impression the other day when I asked you to the symposium."

Lace shifted her weight. What a relief that he wasn't interested in her. "Okay."

"I invited you to the symposium because I wanted to ask Shasta out but I was too afraid she'd turn me down."

She smiled softly. "Why didn't you just say so?"

"I'm saying so now. She's quirky and funny and even though she's really young, I like her a lot."

Lace touched Malcolm's upper arm. "I don't know the details, but Shasta's had a hard life. She could do with a steady guy who has his head on his shoulders."

"Does she have a boyfriend?"

"I don't think so, but I do get the impression she likes a guy who doesn't like her back."

Malcolm blew out his breath. "That seems to be the story of my life. Why am I attracted to women who aren't attracted to me?"

"As you say, she's really young. Give her a chance, Malcolm."

"So you think I should ask her out?"

"You never know where it might lead until you do."

"Thanks, Lace." He smiled. "I appreciate it."

She crossed her fingers, held them up for him to see. "Good luck."

"I'm just gonna"—he jerked a thumb at the side door labeled with a "Takeout Only" sign—"pick up Dad's breakfast."

Lace waved good-bye and scooted off to the front entrance. The smell of rich French roast, bacon, and huevos rancheros scented the air as she walked inside the restaurant. Big-bulb, old-fashioned, multicolored Christmas lights were strung in loose loops from the ceiling. At this time of the morning, the garish decorations were annoyingly cheerful. Piñatas hung between the holiday lights—a pink pig, a green toad, a purple horse—Tex-Mex kitsch to the max.

Carol Ann sat in a booth at the far back of the corner. She waved a hand. Lace weaved her way around the tightly packed tables, saying hello to everyone she knew. Sometimes that could be a chore for an introvert, but she had to admit the cocoon of Cupid was more a safe haven than a straitjacket. By the time she reached her aunt, she had a goodwill buzz tamping down the alarm that Carol Ann's early morning call had roused.

"Please have a seat," Carol Ann said tightly.

She took one close-up look at her aunt and her stomach turned over. Not only had Carol Ann neglected to put eye shadow on her right eye, the shadow on the left was haphazardly applied, and she was also wearing mismatched shoes. One black. One brown. Carol Ann was nothing if not a clotheshorse. She never set foot outside her house without looking as if she'd stepped from a bandbox.

Lace wondered if she should call attention to her aunt's disheveled appearance. "Your shoes—"

"I know. I put them on in the dark. I'll go home and change later."

Lace pressed a hand over her heart and her mind

immediately went to dark places. "What is it? What's wrong? Did something happen to Mom and Daddy?"

Her parents were out on the road, attending cutting horse competitions with their prizewinning quarter horses.

"Your parents are fine." Carol Ann placed a finger over her lips. "Sit down. Order. Act like everything is normal."

"You're freaking me out."

"We really shouldn't be doing this here." Carol Ann looked over her shoulder, which was unnecessary because there was a wall behind her.

"Doing what? Having breakfast?"

"I thought about coming over to your house, but honestly, I needed to be around activity to quell my nerves."

Lace didn't understand that at all. Tranquility—and plants—quelled her nerves, not people and activity.

"And I'm suspicious of that girl of yours."

"Shasta?"

"She pops up in the most unexpected places at the most unexpected times like a stray cat."

"I admit that Shasta is different but she's got a good heart."

"Please, sit." Her aunt waved again.

Lace eased down on the edge of the orange vinyl seat. She saw Cousin Natalie and her fiancé Dade canoodling in a corner booth. She waved at them, but they only had eyes for each other. Still, if Carol Ann went completely off her rocker, it was good to know there were reinforcements in the room.

"Spill it," she said.

"Order something first," Carol Ann insisted.

"Don't pussyfoot around, Auntie. I'm a rip-the-Band-Aid-off-quick kind of person."

"You are indeed," Carol Ann mused. "You think that thing in high school had anything to do with that?"

"There's nothing wrong with wanting the bad news up front," Lace said. "Best to just take the dodgeball to the gut and hit the ground because the only place to go from there is up. If you string out the bad news, the imagination goes nuts with anticipation, making it all that much worse. I don't like to wallow. I'm not a wallower. For heaven's sakes, just tell me what's going on."

Carol Ann handed her unopened menu to the waitress who'd strolled over. "I'll have an egg white omelet, hold the toast, black coffee, and a side of fresh berries."

"Lace?" the waitress asked. Her name was Joleen—with a name like that waitressing seemed her destiny—and she was distantly related to Lace by marriage. After "the incident" in high school, Joleen had been among a group of girls who'd teased her mercilessly. They'd spray painted "PATHETIC FATSO LOOSER" on her locker in yellow neon. Yeah, maybe so, but at least she knew how to spell.

Lace smiled to show she didn't hold a grudge. Bygones were bygones, right? And after four kids, Joleen herself was now rocking a size fourteen. "I'll have the breakfast special."

"Sausage or bacon."

"Both," Lace said.

"Whole wheat or white toast?"

"Could I have biscuits and cream gravy?"

"You got it," Joleen offered a tenuous smile and scurried off.

Lace braced, waiting for Carol Ann to lecture her on her food choices. She had a quip ready, but her aunt didn't say anything, giving her even more cause for alarm. She'd ordered all that stuff just to get a rise out of her.

"Let's have it." Lace folded her hands on the table and squarely met Carol Ann's eyes.

Her aunt snatched a napkin from the dispenser on the table and slowly began tearing it into thin strips. "I don't know how to say this."

Lace blew out a little chuff of air. Her mouth was dry and her throat hot. Was she coming down with something?

"I feel so badly about this. I'm the one who talked Winnie Sparks into staying on until you got your doctorate. I lured you back here when you should have taken that job at the Smithsonian."

"I wanted to come home," Lace pointed out, but the sick sensation in her stomach expanded.

"It was selfish of me. I know. But Lord, with Melody

off living in New York, I couldn't help wanting the rest of you girls to stay close to home." Little tufts of paper were flying in the air as she finished off that napkin and reached for another. The nail of her pinky finger had broken off and had not been filed down, further proof of Carol Ann's mental state.

Lace reached across the table, laid her palm on the back of her aunt's hand. "What is it? What's happened? Please tell me."

Joleen set the food down, but neither of them made a move for their plates. "Y'all need sumpthin' else?"

"We're fine," Lace said.

Carol Ann shook her head. Her eyes misted. She hovered on the verge of tears.

Good God, what on earth could it be? Did her aunt have cancer? Was she leaving Uncle Davis? Maybe something bad had happened to Cousin Melody.

"Look, I can't help unless you tell me," Lace said softly.

Carol Ann glanced around like a Navy SEAL on a reconnaissance mission, looking left, right, in front and behind her. Lace half expected her to look underneath the table. Finally, Carol Ann leaned forward, almost dragging her bracelet through her egg white omelet.

At this point it was all Lace could do not to grab her arm, shake her, and yell, *Just tell me already!*

"Remember how your paychecks were late?" Carol Ann whispered.

"Considering it was just this past Friday, yes."

"Shh, keep your voice down." She darted another glance around the room.

"Do we need to go someplace private?"

"This is fine as long as we're careful."

"Okay then, let's have it."

"The paychecks weren't a banking glitch."

"What do you mean?"

Carol Ann slumped back against the seat, folded her arms over her chest, and gazed with glazed eyes over Lace's shoulder. "Sometimes I wish I'd never given up smoking."

"You used to smoke?" That was a new one on her.

"Years ago. When I was a teen. Everyone smoked back then."

"Good thing you quit. Smoking is terrible for the skin."

"Don't I know it?" Carol Ann put a hand to her cheeks as if checking for wrinkles.

"Not to mention the lung cancer thing."

"I know, but sometimes, you just want a long drag of nicotine to calm the nerves, but don't worry, I'm not going to walk across the street to the Zip and Drive to buy a pack of Virginia Slims." Her tone went wistful on "Virginia Slims."

"Only because you know everyone in town would be talking about it."

"True."

"You have to stop stringing me along." Lace picked up her fork and poked at the eggs on her plate.

Carol Ann had stopped shredding napkins and was now shredding the toast that Joleen had brought her even though she'd told her to hold the bread. A pile of carb-heavy crumbs piled up on her plate, dusted her eggs. "I probably shouldn't be telling you this, but I couldn't in good conscience not give you a heads-up."

"About what?"

"The city council held an emergency meeting last night."

"About . . . ?" Talk about harder than pulling hen's teeth! Where was a pair of dental pliers when she needed them?

Carol Ann started to say something, blew out her breath, and eventually inhaled deeply. "You know I took over as Cupid's CPA when Olive Cooksey left town, ostensibly to elope."

"Uh-huh."

"Well, it turns out true love was *not* why she left town."

Lace's skin tingled as creepily as if fire ants were crawling all over her bare skin. She did not like the direction this conversation was headed.

"Olive Cooksey embezzled five hundred thousand dollars from the town of Cupid."

"Five hundred thousand!"

"Shh!" Carol Ann plastered her index finger to her lips.

Lace lowered her voice. "How in the world was she able to embezzle that much?"

"She was very good at cooking the books. The best I've ever seen, but of course it was a house of cards. Once I started looking into why we didn't have enough funds to cover the city payroll . . ." Carol Ann trailed off, shook her head.

The sick feeling settled into the pit of Lace's stomach and pushed against her lungs. "What does this mean?"

"The town is facing drastic cost-cutting measures. We have to keep the schools going, obviously, sanitation, water, fire, police, all the essentials, and even that is going to take some mighty juggling on my part."

"That means all the nonessentials have to be lopped?"

"The library, the visitors' center, after-school programs, the—"

"Botanical gardens."

Solemnly, Carol Ann nodded. "I'm so sorry, Lace."

Lace sat there, staring at the grease congealing on the sausage on her plate, trying to absorb the information. Poof! Just like that she was out of a job. All her plans for the garden up in smoke. "When is the city council going public?"

"We've called outside law enforcement. Once they give us the go-ahead, the mayor will hold a press conference, so you absolutely positively can't tell anyone about this until then."

Lace nibbled her bottom lip. "Maybe we could consider charging admission if it would save the gardens."

Carol Ann was shaking her head. "It won't be enough."

She knew that. She was grasping at straws.

"Where is Shasta going to go?" Lace wasn't worried about herself. Her parents would float her a loan until she found another job, but Shasta had nothing to fall back on.

"Hopefully we can help her find a job or get back to where she belongs."

"What about Manuel?"

"He's old enough to retire."

"What about the plants? Without someone to look after them they'll die."

"I don't know."

Lace thought she just might throw up at the thought of the gardens going untended. "What about the Cupid fountain and the letterbox? It's part of our town history. It brings in tourists. We can't just do away with it."

"The city council recommends moving the fountain and the letterbox to the courthouse square, but try not to despair. As soon as the town recovers from this crisis, they'll open the gardens back up again."

"It will be too late and you know it."

"There is one hope."

Lace squeezed her hands together in her lap. "What's that?"

"We could raise the money through private donations to keep the nonessential services going."

Lace groaned. "That's a daunting task. I don't even know how to go about something like that."

"No, but your cousin Melody does and she's coming in earlier than expected. Her flight is landing in El Paso at nine. She's renting a car and should be home before noon."

Chapter 9

Prickle: a small sharp outgrowth,
usually more slender than a thorn.

"THE solution is simple," Lace's cousin Melody announced that same afternoon, as she and Lace lay buried up to their necks in a mud bath at the Cupid Mineral Springs Resort and Spa. Melody preferred the elegance of the mineral springs to Junie Mae's LaDeDa, which was little more than a couple of massage tables in the back of her hair salon.

"I'm glad you can see it, because I'm blind about how to fix this." Normally, Lace was not much of a spa girl, but the first thing Melody had said when she told her about her troubles was, "Let's hit the spa, I think better when I'm relaxed. My treat." Lace had picked the mud bath over other treatments, because hey, if she had to take time away from the garden, at least she was in dirt.

The lavender that had been added to the bath masked the mineral-heavy smell of volcanic ash. The attendant had wrapped their hair in white towels and placed cucumber slices on their eyes. Lace had already taken off the cucumbers and vaguely considered eating them. She was hungry, since she'd been too distressed after Carol Ann's news to eat breakfast, but now her appetite came roaring back. Nah, if she ate them, it would probably earn a stern look from the attendant and a sigh and an "Oh, Lace, *really*?" from Melody.

One Halloween, when Lace was seven and Melody was nine, Gram had taken all four of her granddaughters trick-or-treating. Natalie went as a policewoman, Zoey as a bandit. Melody had been dressed as a princess, resplendent in pink chiffon. Carol Ann had ordered Melody's costume from a specialty store in Houston. Lace's mother had made her a lacewing costume because they were her favorite insects, mostly due to the fact they shared her name. Unfortunately, no one else had known what she was.

Afterward, the four cousins had sat in Gram's kitchen going through their loot, Melody primly extracting the "good quality" chocolates and leaving behind the "pure poison" like Nerds, Laffy Taffy, and Smarties. Lace had scooped up her cousin's leavings, dumped them in her bag, and then opened a box of Nerds and stuffed the entire contents in her mouth.

"Mmm, I lo . . . lo . . . love . . . poison," she stuttered, spitting Nerds onto Melody's princess costume.

Melody had leveled her a look of utter disgust and said, "Oh, Lace, *really*? You are such a pig."

Lace pushed the memory aside, slapped the limp cucumber slices back over her eyes, and slipped lower into the mud bath.

"All you have to do," Melody said, "is throw a dinner party. A thousand dollars a plate."

"Whoa! That pricing might work in New York City, but this is Cupid."

"Which is why I said a thousand instead of two thousand a plate."

"That's delusional."

"It's not. Five hundred guests at a thousand dollars apiece will net the same amount that Olive Cooksey stole from the coffers."

"Five hundred guests? There's no venue in Cupid that will accommodate a dinner party of five hundred people."

"Sure there is."

"Where?"

"Michael and Mignon's vineyard. They host big wedding parties there all the time."

"Not five hundred people big. Where are we going to get enough tables and chairs?"

"The community center, the library, the high school, churches." Melody ticked off the options on a mud-coated hand.

"Let's say that by some miracle we get five hundred people to show up. How much is it going to cost? A thousand dollars a plate won't be pure profit."

"You get sponsors to pay for the meals," Melody said like it was the easiest thing in the world.

"I'm not an outgoing extrovert who knows how to schmooze," Lace said.

"Lucky for you, I am."

"That's nice of you to offer to help, but what happens when you head back to New York and I'm left trying to pull this off?"

"Didn't Mother tell you? I've taken a six-week vacation." Melody sounded wildly cheerful.

So cheerful in fact that Lace didn't trust her glee. Something was definitely up with her cousin. "How come you're taking six weeks off?"

"I had scads of vacation time built up. I had to take it or lose it."

"As much of a workaholic as you are, I'm surprised you didn't opt to just lose the time."

"Pot. Kettle. Black."

"Which is why I can't imagine you not working for six weeks. I know I couldn't do it," Lace commented

"So see, you'll actually be doing me a favor if you let me put this event on for you."

Lace sat up, the cucumber fell off her eyes, and she stared over at Melody in her pit of mud. "What is going on?"

"Nothing." Melody laughed gaily, but the sound was forced. "Can't I do something nice for you?"

"For the last five years that you've lived in New

York, you've only come home twice a year, at Christmas and on your mother's birthday. Why the sudden Cupid love?"

"It's not sudden. I've just reached the age where I'm revaluating what I want in life."

"The only thing you've ever wanted is to be the Princess of Madison Avenue. You're well on your way, why would you stop now?"

"I'm not stopping. It's just . . ." She paused. "I needed to take some time, okay?"

"Okay." Lace eased back down into the mud.

"So anyway about the event—"

"You do know the entire population of Cupid is just over three thousand, right? I don't know where you expect to round up five hundred people who can afford to pay a thousand dollars a plate."

"Which is why we must cast a wider net. We'll need to draw from all around Texas—Houston, Dallas, El Paso, San Antonio, Austin."

"Why on earth would they come to Cupid?"

"For a Labor Day celebration. We'll make a weekend-long event of it. Organize a stargazing tour at MacDonald Observatory. We've got the caverns and the mineral springs, and the lake and dove season opens September first, so there's something for hunters."

"Who generally aren't the kinds of men who will pay a thousand dollars a plate for dinner even if they have the money."

"Not just dinner," Melody said, "but an event, a celebration. Music, dancing, gourmet food, including exotic game, and a chance to mingle with a big sports celebrity."

"What sports celebrit—" Lace broke off, sat back up. "Oh no. Not Pierce Hollister."

Melody sat up too, plucked the cucumbers from her eyes. She had a swatch of mud across her right cheek. "I know you have a painful history with Pierce, but Lace, he *is* the quarterback for the Dallas Cowboys."

"Who currently happens to be on the disabled list."

"It doesn't matter. He's a big celebrity. In fact, his injury makes him even more desirable. Emotion. Conflict. Suffering. The struggle back. Pathos sells!"

A heavy feeling settled in Lace's stomach. She knew her cousin was right.

"It's the only way you're going to draw a big crowd willing to pay a thousand bucks a plate," Melody went on. "Not only that, but think of all the money an event like this will funnel into the local economy. It's a win-win for everyone."

"Yeah, I get that." Damn that Olive Cooksey's thieving hide.

"I'm willing to do all the legwork. You only have to do two things."

"What's that?"

"Show up at the big dinner with a date and do a little glad-handing."

"What else?"

"Ask Pierce to headline the event, and since he's re-cuperating it shouldn't be that hard to convince him."

No indeed, the hard part was going to be driving up to the Triple H and asking him to do her a favor. She could already see his smug smile and audacious wink.

The big question was why did she suddenly feel so excited about the prospect of seeing him again?

THE NEXT MORNING Lace worked up the courage to call the Triple H and ask for Pierce.

"He and Mr. Malcolm are moving the herd down from the mountains. He'll be gone all day and he's out of cell phone range," the housekeeper told her. "May I ask who is calling?"

"It's not important. I'll call back later." She was half relieved he wasn't there, half nauseated that she wouldn't be able to get this over with.

"Sugar," the housekeeper said. It came out *shooger*, slow as maple syrup and false as artificial sweetener. "Can I give you a word of advice?"

"Sure," Lace said, wondering where this was leading.

"Young ladies call here all the time. He never calls 'em back. A man doesn't respect a woman who throws herself at him."

Lace bit her tongue to keep from telling the house-keeper that she was certainly *not* throwing herself at him.

"Do you have any idea how many women are trying to become Mrs. Pierce Hollister?" the housekeeper went on.

"Couple of dozen?" Lace guessed.

The housekeeper laughed. "*Shooger*, more like a couple of thousand. It's gonna take a one-in-a-billion gal to catch the likes of Mr. Pierce. Are you one in a billion?"

"Rats, I'm only one in nine hundred and ninety-nine million. Damn the luck."

"Well, you do have a sense of humor. I'll grant you that. Go ahead and give me your number. If he's interested, he'll call. If he doesn't call, well, *shooger*, you have to face the truth. He's just not that into you."

Apparently, the woman had been watching too many *Sex and the City* reruns. "How will I ever live?" Lace quipped.

"You'll find a nice man just right for you—"

"Thank you for your time," Lace said, and hung up before she said something snarky she might regret.

She slumped back in the wooden swivel chair. From the window of her office in the botanical gardens, she could see stoop-shouldered Manuel putting fresh mulch around the scarlet *Anisacanthus linearis*. His face was as familiar to her as her grandfather's. He'd worked at the gardens for over twenty-five years. As a child, whenever she'd wandered over to the gardens from her parents' livery stable across the road, Manuel would pluck a pack of Trident cinnamon gum from his front shirt pocket, give her a piece, and take one for himself. They would chew in companionable silence, as he'd tell her the common names of the plants in both English and Spanish. Miss Winnie was the one who'd started teaching her the Latin names and she'd learned there was a method to the nomenclature.

Lace sighed, stretched, and got up to pace. Melody's plan had better work. If the gardens closed, it would be the end of an era.

Yeah, well, before her cousin's grand scheme could work, Lace had to do her part.

It would be so easy to go into the garden, spend her time happily digging in the dirt, put off asking Pierce to headline the fund-raiser for another day, but the sooner she got the ball rolling, the better. Pierce might not be within cell phone reception range, but she knew where the Hollisters pastured their cattle in the grasslands that grew up the gentle slope of the Davis Mountains. When she was a teenager she'd ridden up there often enough, hoping to catch a glimpse of Pierce when he and Jay helped Abe herd cattle to earn date money.

Lace pushed back from her chair, called to Shasta to hold down the fort, and walked across to Bettingfield Stables to saddle her quarter horse, Peony. Twenty minutes later, she was galloping out of town, headed up the mountain.

The temperature was a good ten degrees cooler

up here than it was in town. The late morning breeze
stirred in her face. The skies were clear, the altitude
crisp and dry. Confronted with Peony's hooves, feeding
jackrabbits broke and scattered, their long ears folded
back flat against their heads. A small red-tailed hawk
circled overhead, looking for lizards and rodents easier
to tackle than the big-footed jackrabbits, and finally
came to land in the bare branches of a dead piñon pine
with a soft whapping of his wings. The sound startled
Peony, who sparked and jumped over a prickly pear.

As she rode, Lace scanned the terrain, cataloging
plant life. To her, the sweeping landscape of the Trans-
Pecos was the most beautiful in the world. Any old
plant could grow with unlimited rainfall, but in this
spot only the hardy thrived. When she was a girl, she'd
ride the country, pretending she was a Native American maiden. Once she was out of sight of civilization,
it could have been a hundred and fifty years ago, until
a plane flew overhead and ruined the image. She loved
it here. The place was in her heart, her blood, and her
soul. If she could not save the gardens, she'd have to
leave home in order to make a living.

It took her over an hour to reach the Hollisters' grazing land. Here, there were no fences. Since Pierce's
housekeeper had said they were driving the cattle
down, Lace picked the southwesterly route to the Triple
H. She'd traveled less than a mile when she spied a roll
of dust in the distance and through it, horsemen loping

along behind a herd of longhorns. She spurred Peony faster and when she got nearer, spied three Blue Heeler cattle dogs keeping the herd in line.

One of the horsemen said something she couldn't hear and motioned in her direction. A man broke off from the group, wheeled his horse, and cantered toward her.

It was Pierce, looking like a real cowboy, instead of a Dallas Cowboy. He rode tall in the saddle; wore chaps, straw Stetson, boots, spurs, the works. Her heart swelled, crowded her lungs, making it hard to breathe. *Don't do it. Don't go there. Do not have those fantasies.* Ah, but no one could deny he looked as if he had ridden straight out of a romantic Western movie, and she'd always been a sucker for cowboys.

Her pulse took off at a dead gallop. It was crazy, this . . . this autonomic response to the sight of him.

He was smiling as he rode up. He adjusted his hat, giving it a rakish tilt that revealed more of his face. His brown eyes twinkled. "Why, look who's here."

Lace blew out her breath. Steady, steady. Damn if she was going to let him know how much he'd gotten under her skin. "Morning, Pierce."

He squinted up at the sun beating down directly overhead. "Might be afternoon by now."

Her chest grew tighter by the minute. She didn't know how to start this conversation.

Pierce rested both hands on the horn of the saddle

and shifted forward in his seat. The leather made a creaking noise that punctuated the silence.

She didn't know which was worse, saying something, or sitting here trying to avoid looking into his eyes and not saying anything. "You're working the cattle," she said at last.

He cast a glance over his shoulder. Malcolm and the ranch hands had already driven the herd some distance away. "Looks like it."

"How does that feel?" she surprised herself by asking. "Being back in the saddle again?"

"Feels better than I expected, but it's not really the saddle I want to be back in."

"Football. That's your saddle."

"That's where the best of me is."

"I don't believe that."

He looked taken aback. "What do you mean?"

"Are you seriously saying that the best of you is over? You're just barely thirty. What are you going to do for the next fifty-odd years?"

"My career isn't over," he said adamantly. "Not by a long shot. This is . . ." He waved a hand at his leg. "Very temporary."

She wasn't going to point out that he might not be facing reality about his chances of being what he once was on the football field. She'd heard people compare him to Joe Theismann. She'd been raised in West Texas where football trumped everything. She understood how brutal the sport was. Initially, the Dallas Cowboys might cut him some slack, but it was a money game, and if he didn't soon return to the field at one hundred percent capacity, they'd cut him quicker than she would deadhead a rosebush. Individual roses—even if there was still some bloom left—had to be sacrificed for the health of the plant.

"You're a big deal," she said honestly. "I can appreciate why it would be hard to let go of that."

He cocked his head and shot her a sidelong glance. "You're confusing me."

"How's that?"

"I can't decide if you're actually being nice or sarcastic minus the tone."

She nodded. "I'm stating fact. You are a big deal in this town. You're a big deal all over Texas. Hell, let's be honest, you're a big deal throughout the country. I mean, come on, how many people have ever quarterbacked in the Super Bowl? You're among the elite of the elite."

A suspicious expression crossed his face. "I hear kind words coming from your mouth, but I'm waiting for the other shoe to drop. Let's have it."

Lace shrugged, fighting against her pulse that sped up every time she met his eyes. "No dropping shoe."

"You rode all the way out here to tell me that I'm a big deal? C'mon, let's have the other shoe."

Pierce's stallion walked closer and nuzzled Peony's

neck. Of course Pierce rode a stallion. No mare or gelding for a wild-oats-sowing alpha man. That would be way too tame. Luckily, Peony was not in estrus or there could have been trouble. Lace pulled up on the reins, guided Peony away from his horse.

Undaunted, the stallion approached again and went back to nuzzling Peony.

"Could you handle your steed, please?" she asked.

"He's got a mind of his own." Pierce smirked.

"You're in charge, be in control."

"You're the one who rode up here on a mare in heat."

"She's not in heat."

"A mare's cycle can turn erratic around fall."

"It's the second week of August."

"Autumn is just a few weeks away."

"If she was in heat, your stallion would be going crazy."

"You've got a point."

Lace squirmed in the saddle. She was a scientist. This talk of a mare's reproductive cycle should not be making her uncomfortable, but it was.

"If that's all you need, I've got cattle to drive." He clicked his tongue, turned his mount back toward the herd.

"Wait."

He stopped.

She kneed Peony forward until they were side by side with Pierce and his stallion. "You're right. There's a shoe. I don't want there to be a shoe, but there's a shoe."

"I'm listening." He smelled like home. No cologne today, just the honest fragrance of horse and hay and leather, sun-warmed cotton and musky male.

An unexpected gust of wind lifted a strand of her hair and tossed it in her face. She tucked the strand behind one ear. His gaze tracked her movements, fixed for a moment on her ear, and then he gulped visibly. She wasn't the only one unsettled.

"Ask me, Lace," he murmured. "Ask for what you need."

She rolled her eyes. He sounded so damn seductive.

"You do that as a defense mechanism, you know," he said.

"Do what?"

"Roll your eyes. It gives you away every time. You do it when you feel insecure."

She put a hand to her forehead. Was she really doing that? Gotta stop the eye rolling.

"Well," he prompted.

"Here's the deal," she said. "I need you."

A grin split his face and he cupped a hand around the ear closest to her. "Excuse me. I didn't quite catch that. Did I hear you say that *you* need *me*? Why didn't you say so? Just let me gallop home and get a condom and I'll be at your service."

She suppressed a gigantic eye roll. Do not rise to the

bait. "Allow me to rephrase. The town of Cupid needs your help."

"Ah, I'm disappointed. The other phrasing was so much more provocative."

"Olive Cooksey embezzled five hundred thousand dollars from the town coffers," she said, and then proceeded to tell him what Carol Ann had revealed to her and Melody's solution to the problem. "So you see, you're the only one that can save the town."

"You mean save the botanical gardens, save you."

"Not just the gardens, but the library and the—"

"Yeah, yeah, just admit it. You need my celebrity status to save your hide."

Did he have to look so smug about it? "Yes, yes, fine. The town needs you. Happy now?"

"No."

"Why aren't you happy? I stroked your ego. You're the best thing since sliced bread. Everyone bows down at your feet, yada yada."

"You might want to take a course in diplomacy before you ask someone to do you a favor the next time." He loosened the reins and nudged his stallion gently in the flank. The horse took off.

"Wait!" She couldn't let him get away. She had to smooth this over or good-bye botanical gardens.

He slowed to let her catch up with him. "I'm listening."

"This is hard for me," she said. "Can we start over?"

"All right."

She took a deep breath. "Pierce, would you please headline the fund-raising event to save the nonessential, but very important, city services from going away?"

He turned his head, met her gaze with those brown eyes flecked with green, looked straight into her.

Her heart thumped, stumbled. "Well?"

"No."

No? She wasn't expecting that. "Why not?"

"You didn't say 'please,'" he said, and rode off again.

"Will you stop doing that!" she hollered, and chased after him. "Stay still."

He stopped again as if they were playing some odd equestrian version of Mother May I.

Oh, he was enjoying this to no end. She clutched the reins so tightly that Peony halted in mid-step while Pierce spurred his stallion forward again.

"Please, Pierce. I need your help. Please do this for Cupid."

"Nope," he called over his shoulder.

"Ah, c'mon!" She hurried to catch up with him at once. Peony snorted as if to say, *Make up your mind psycho bitch.*

"I'll only do it if you ask me to please do it for *you.*"

"Fine, fine." She huffed.

"And you have to ask without the attitude."

She smiled forcefully, her jaw aching from gritting her teeth.

"You look like a shark."

Argh! She relaxed her face into a natural smile. "Pretty please with sugar on top, will you do this favor for me, Pierce. Please will you help me save the botanical gardens? I want you. I need you. I have to have you or my life is over. How's that?"

He looked at her like she was the most amusing thing this side of Disney World. "Now was that so hard?"

"A root canal without novocaine would have been easier."

"You still don't get the whole concept of how to ask for a favor, do you?"

"Good God, are you going to do it or not? If not, then just stop torturing me."

He canted his head, and as they trotted side by side he gave her a contemplative look so long she started to get itchy.

"Well?" she nudged.

"I'll do it," he said.

She let out a whoop. "Thank you! I really do appreciate it."

"But only under one condition."

Uh-oh. The torment continued. "What's that?" she asked warily.

"You agree to be my date to this Labor Day dinner—"

"Seriously?"

"It's nonnegotiable. I don't want to have to fend off groupies all day. I need a date. You're elected."

"Okay, fine. I'll be your date, but don't expect me to

enjoy everyone fawning all over His Royal Highness."

"And—"

"You said one thing. You can't go adding a stipulation after you said one thing."

"Then never mind."

"You like seeing me squirm, don't you?"

This time when he looked at her, the light in his eyes was wickedly, unabashedly sexual. "You have no idea."

A shiver of icicles prickled down her back. Her breathing was coming so short and shallow it was a wonder she didn't hyperventilate.

"What is it? What else do you want? Just know up front that if your request is that I spend the night with you it's a total deal breaker. You are not the only hotshot football jock in the world."

"Ah," he said, "but I'm the only hotshot football jock that you know. Relax, sleeping with me is not the stipulation, although if you've got a mind to do that, I'm not the least bit opposed." He gave her a slow, sexy wink and a smile to match.

Goose bumps spread over her skin and she shivered again. The man knew how to seduce. She'd give him that, but she certainly wouldn't tell him to his face. "Spit it out. What further suffering do you have up your sleeve for me?"

"Sweetheart," he drawled, "if you want me to snap this ball, you have to agree to go shopping with me and let me pick out what you're going to wear."

Chapter 10

*Metamorphosis: transformation of one
state to another, as a bud to a bloom.*

THE town of Cupid closed nonessential city services a
week after the mayor's announcement that Olive Cooksey had absconded with half a million dollars of the
town's money. Lace had gotten her parents to temporar-
ily hire Shasta and Manuel to work at the Bettingfield
Stables, so at least they were going to be taken care of.

Even though Lace had been director of the botanical gardens for only a few months, the grief she felt
watching city workers cut off the water and electricity,
move the Cupid fountain—which had been the main-
stay of the gardens since the 1930s—padlock the front
gate and post a "Closed Until Further Notice" sign, was
akin to losing a much beloved pet.

Her cousins stood ringed around her, offering support in their own unique ways. Zoey said, "Drinks at
Chantilly's on me when we're done." Melody pressed
a key to the padlock into her palm and whispered, "I
sweet-talked the mayor's secretary into making a copy

for you." Natalie put a comforting arm around her shoulder. "Dade's bringing the van and we're all going to pitch in to help you move the plants."

"Thanks," Lace whispered. "You guys are awesome."

The majority of the plants in the outside gardens were indigenous to the Trans-Pecos so they would survive months without constant attention, although the more assertive species like *Cylindropuntia imbricata,* the cane cholla, might try to muscle out others, and most of the vegetation would become overgrown and unkempt without Manuel's artful maintenance.

The inside gardens and the greenhouse plants were another matter. They would all have to be transferred to Lace's house. Not that she minded having her home crammed with plants, but it was a daunting task, even though she'd already started moving some of the plants. Thank heaven for her family. You couldn't buy this kind of loyalty and devotion.

If the gardens were closed for only a few weeks, in the grand scheme of things, this was just a minor glitch in the gardens' history—a juicy story for future generations to tell. But if Melody couldn't pull off this fund-raising thing . . .

Heavy pressure weighted Lace's chest and she blinked against the lump forming in her throat. She was putting all her eggs in a basket named Pierce Hollister.

Lace, her cousins, and Dade spent the next hour loading plants she'd already prepared for shipping into Natalie's van and Zoey's Toyota pickup truck. When they'd packed and secured as much as they could into the two vehicles, Lace gave Natalie the key to her house while she stayed behind to wrap and pamper the plants she hadn't yet had time to prepare for the move.

The greenhouse was eerie in its silence and she was trying to keep her thoughts on wrapping maidenhair ferns in newspaper and off her heavy sense of loss, when there was a rap of knuckles against the greenhouse door.

She glanced up from where she was crouching to see the silhouette of a man in a cowboy hat. Before she could get up to answer the door, it opened and Pierce poked his head inside. "Hello, anybody here?"

Instant perspiration sprouted between her breasts and her lips seemed to have a mind of their own as they curled into a smile. "Pierce, hi!" she said breathlessly.

"Hey." He stepped into the greenhouse looking sexier than any man had the legal right to look.

Lace got to her feet, dusted her palms against the seat of her jeans. "If you've come to tell me that it's time to pay up on my part of the bargain, you've caught me at a bad time."

"Now that you mention it, we need to set a date for our shopping spree, but that's not why I'm here."

She tilted her head and her smile grew. Why did the guy have to be so intriguing? "No?"

"I came to help. Look, sleeves rolled up and everything." He tugged at the sleeves of his shirt peeled up into cuffs that banded his biceps.

A rush of gratitude blew through her as swift and surprising as a sandstorm on a windless day. She didn't know why he'd shown up, but she was ridiculously happy that he had. "I don't . . . yes, thank you. I appreciate an extra pair of hands."

"What do you need?" he asked, heavy emphasis on the word "need."

She decided to ignore that part. "We're down to the more delicate plants that require extra care. They need to be wrapped in newspaper and placed carefully in those packing boxes."

Pierce rubbed his palms together. "Let's get to it."

"This way." She showed him how to wrap the plants in newspaper and secure them with twine, nestle them in the boxes, and cover them with packing peanuts.

"Assembly line would make this go faster," he said. "How 'bout you do the wrapping and I'll do the packing."

"Sounds fair." She squatted beside the maidenhair ferns again, finished securing the first one, and passed it on to Pierce. Had any pair of jeans ever fit a butt so perfectly? She rocked back, lost her balance, and ended up sitting on her ass. Seriously, there oughta be a law that a guy who looked like that could not wear tight-fitting jeans.

Pierce turned. "You okay?"

"Fine," she muttered, and forced her attention back to the ferns. This was what mattered to her, after all. Keeping the plants healthy during this upheaval. Getting things back on track as quickly and easily as possible.

So why was she staring at Mr. Hard Body's butt again and thinking about that kiss he'd given her in the parking lot? The kiss that had knocked her socks off and put starch in her underwear? *Maidenhair ferns, Lace.* Adiantum capillus-veneris.

He came back toward her. "This assembly thing doesn't seem to be working, does it?"

"Huh?"

"You don't have another plant wrapped for me to pack."

"Oh." She shook her head. "No."

He squatted beside her, started wrapping a fern, his hands moving fast and sure in bold strokes. She watched him, hypnotized. The quick flick of his tanned, muscular wrists, the way his fingers both expertly and gently tucked the paper around the plants as if he'd been doing this his entire life.

"Wow, you're pretty good at this," she said. Yes. Stay friendly but cool. That's the way to play it. "That little fern looks snug and safe."

"Thanks." He didn't look up from his task.

"I do appreciate your help."

"You're welcome." No lifting of his chin. No meeting of her eyes. Where was the smile? The charm? Why wasn't he pushing her buttons like he loved to do?

"So, this dress-shopping thing, any idea when you want to pull the trigger on it?" Now why had she gone and brought that up? She was half hoping he'd forgotten that part of their deal, although she did need to buy a dress for the event. Mostly she wore jeans, shorts, T-shirt or Western shirt, and shoes appropriate for gardening. It wasn't that she didn't know how to dress the part. She'd done the whole high heels, tight dresses, and plunging necklines when she'd been skinny, but after she'd let go of the partying and sexcapades and settled into being herself, she hadn't bought those kinds of clothes.

He still did not glance up or answer her. She cut a piece of twine from the roll with her Swiss Army knife and passed it to him. The tips of their fingers touched. An immediate fire blazed up her arm, but he didn't even flinch.

"Thanks." He whipped the twine around the newspapered fern quick as a roper hog-tying a downed calf, set the plant aside, and reached for another one.

"Once I get finished with this plant moving, I'll have a lot of time on my hands," she said. "My only obligation at that point is the gardening class so I could go shopping with you anytime. I heard Wayland's Western Wear got in some new dresses."

He was back to not talking.

"Of course, they've got more clothing options in Marfa with that arty bunch, but their offerings tend to be offbeat and funky and that's not really my style."

"We're not going shopping in Marfa."

"So Wayland's Western Wear? What day?"

"Twine."

She cut off another piece for him. "Except I don't think Melody would approve of a Western-style dress. Not for a thousand-dollar-a-plate dinner. She's got a New York frame of mind about such things."

He raised his head and looked at her with a smoldering gaze. No trace of his cocky smile. Was he mad at her for some reason? He stared at her so long and hard that she was missing those earlier moments when he wasn't looking at her.

Intimidated, Lace gulped, but she wasn't going to be the first to glance away. No sir. Why did he have to be so hot?

A heartbeat passed. Then two. Then three. Frigging Venus flytrap, she hadn't been in a stare down this intense since . . . well . . . she'd never been in a stare down this intense.

Lace licked her lips. Was he going to kiss her? He looked like he might kiss her.

He did not make a move.

Okay, fine. Good. She did not want him to kiss her anyway. Nice to see he was behaving himself.

Finally, she couldn't take the staring one second longer. "What?" she asked. "What is it?"

"Clearly." He dragged the word out long and slow. "You weren't paying attention. Our deal was that I take you shopping and I pick out your dress. There will be no Wayland's Western Wear involved."

Why did the thought of him dressing her make her hot? Really, she should be insulted. "You're still insisting on that silly stipulation?"

His jaw tightened. "I am."

"All right. I agreed, so I'll do it, but I want to go on record that it's reluctantly."

"Duly noted."

"So where and when is this shopping trip to occur?"

"My father has an appointment with a specialist in San Antonio a week from next Monday," he said. "Meet us then at the Cupid Airport at nine A.M."

"You're flying instead of driving?"

"Dad's pretty uncomfortable these days, six hours in a car is too long. I have the money to charter a private jet, so I'm doing it," Pierce said. He pulled a palm down his mouth and for the first time, she noticed faint worry lines at the corners of his eyes.

Her stomach dropped. Here she was, being so silly over this sexual chemistry, obsessing over clothes shopping with him and trying to second-guess what he was thinking. Obviously, he'd been worried about his father and she'd been blathering about Wayland's

Western Wear. How could she have been so self-absorbed?

"I'm so sorry that Abe's condition is deteriorating. I can't imagine how difficult this is for you."

He looked at her with woeful eyes. His smile had disappeared and his voice lowered, deepened. "I'm scared of losing him, Lace, and so soon after Mom."

His raw vulnerability cut right through her. Gone was the cocky jock with his hard, driving desire to conquer the world, and in his place was a simple cowboy who was hurting. When he was like this—oh, she was in a field of trouble. She had no intention of touching him, really she did not, but somehow her hand reached out and took his.

They sat on the cement floor of the greenhouse, simply holding hands. Lace raised her eyes to meet Pierce's gaze and in that split second, the earth moved. This was what she had dreamed of twelve years ago, a quiet moment, just the two of them, unified. It was better than she'd imagined it could ever be. The energy was so overwhelming that she gulped.

His pupils dilated. Completely irresistible.

Her pulse kicked. Rattled. She was rattled like devil's claw seedpods.

"Lace." He said her name in that provocative way of his and squeezed her hand.

Her mouth was dry and her stomach felt as if she'd just downed a gallon of seltzer all fizzy and bubbly.

Bliss. Utter bliss. Mixed with a dash of uncertainty, a hop of hope, and a whisper of *Uh-oh, you're in quick-sand*.

"Yes?" she whispered, mesmerized by him, the beauty of the moment, and every amazing thing she was feeling. What was he going to say?

"I can't wait to see that curvy body of yours in something besides T-shirts and jeans."

Seriously? Here she'd been thinking he was going to say something earth-shatteringly romantic and instead he reverted back to swaggering jock. Stupid woman. Hadn't she learned a long time ago not to romanticize him? She dropped his hand, pressed the heel of her palm against his sternum, and shoved him backward.

He rubbed three fingers along his chest. "What did I do?"

"If you don't know, then I'm not going to tell you."

He scratched his head and pondered that. "I seem to have a knack for pissing you off."

"I can take it from here," she said. "My cousins will be back soon to help me load the plants. Thanks for stopping by."

"I'm dismissed?"

"Yes."

"Why is that?"

Because seriously, if you don't leave soon, I am going to kiss you. "I have to spend all day with you on Monday, won't that be suffering enough?" she quipped.

His eyes lit up and he waggled a knowing finger at her. "Protest all you want, Lacy girl, you're not fooling me."

She started to roll her eyes, but thought better of it. She didn't want him thinking that he made her feel insecure, even if he did. "Who, me?"

"No matter how much you try to deny it, you like me."

"Perhaps in the same way I like *Pachypsylla celtidismamma*."

"Dis mama what?"

"Pachypsylla celtidismamma."

"What's that?"

"Nipple galls."

He raised a suggestive eyebrow, flaunted that quirky grin. "Sounds like a sex toy."

"Only in the mind of a pervert. Nipple galls are those bumps you sometimes see on the backs of tree leaves such as the hackberry and—"

"Yeah, I've seen that before."

"The nipple galls are caused by psyllids—"

"What's that?"

"If you'd stop interrupting, I'd tell you. Let's put this a way you can understand." She made a big production of slowing her speech. "Nipple galls are essentially cocoons for tiny little flying insects called pysllids."

"So you like me in the same way as you like—"

"Ugly parasitic bumps on hackberry tree leaves."

"Wow, you sure took the long route to that insult. You could have just said you liked me about as much as a pile of all-natural fertilizer or something along those lines."

"Clichéd. Besides, what would have been the fun in that?"

"You've just proven my point," he crowed.

"How's that?"

"You're having fun. If you didn't like me, you wouldn't be having fun, but don't worry, you don't have to admit it. I know you like me." He winked.

Lace fought the burn heating up her cheeks. Flytrap. He was right. "How come you don't have a girlfriend? Or maybe you do and you're coming onto me anyway."

"I don't have a girlfriend."

"Why not?"

"She left me when I broke my leg."

Her heart gave a strange little tug. "She sounds like a real peach."

"She claimed it was for my own good. Said she wasn't worthy of me."

"Sounds like a peachy bitch. She's not worthy of you." Yes, sometimes he irritated her and yes, she was scared of falling in love with him and getting hurt all over again, but he was a good guy. She knew a lot of the macho playboy crap was for show. That's what had Lace worried. The empathy he stirred in her.

He laughed. "You do have a way with words."

"Even though you're better off without her, that must have been a kick in the teeth to get dumped when you were already flat on your back."

He stroked his thumb against the backs of her knuckles, and Lace's electrical circuit board lit up. "It hurt less than I expected. I wasn't in love with her or anything like that. The low blow came when she took up with the quarterback who replaced me."

"From the sound of it, they deserve each other."

"Forget them. I'd rather talk about you."

"Pretty dull topic."

"That's just what you want everyone to believe."

"And on what do you base that deduction?"

"Still waters run deep."

"Any particular reason you're buttering me up?"

"You are a very suspicious person, you know that?"

"Not at all. I simply realize that everyone's got an angle. What's yours?"

He hesitated a moment, looked like he was going to give her some bullshit answer, but surprised her by saying, "I'm feeling lonely."

She hooted at that.

He grimaced. "Way to mock a guy who's baring his soul."

"Oops," she said. "You were serious?"

"Of course not." His grin hooked from one ear to the other, but the smile did not reach his eyes. In fact, for one brief second he looked so sad it clawed at her heart, but then it was gone so quickly, she wondered if she'd imagined it. "I was just playing on your sympathy to see if I could coax you into bed."

Zip, there he was, back in his cool quarterback hero persona. Damn her for laughing at him just when he was opening up to her. Why had she done that? Was it because she was secretly terrified that if he did open up to her, she'd fall crazy in love all over again, and this time, there would be no getting over him?

Yep. There it was. That was it. What now? Where to go from here?

She tilted her chin up. "Who is the real Pierce Hollister?"

He looked startled for a moment, and then shrugged too nonchalantly. "Hell if I know."

Darn it, the man was just asking to be kissed.

Palms braced against the cement floor, Lace leaned forward and kissed him.

He tasted even better than he had the night he'd kissed her—richly soothing like butterscotch, but with a spicy flair of cinnamon underneath, as if he'd been to Janelle Stuart's cage at Cupid National Bank and hit the candy stash of Hot Tamales and Werther's that Janelle kept in a jar for customers.

It took less than half a second for him to start kissing her in return, but keeping the pressure gentle, letting her know she could back out if she was having second thoughts.

Was she?

Who could have any thoughts whatsoever when kissing Pierce Hollister? Other than *Yum* and *Boy howdy* and *Holy Venus frigging flytrap*. A dozen very nice sensations coursed through her. She felt all wriggly and giggly and warm. And oops, suddenly tongues were involved. Was she the one who started that? Wriggly, hell, she was positively squirming.

He pulled her into his lap and one arm went around her waist. His beard stubble scraped against her skin and all those warm feelings surged and swelled and for one extreme minute she felt as if she had died and gone straight to heaven.

The sound of voices drifted into the greenhouse, followed by footsteps, and they managed to spring apart and get to their feet, hair mussed, lips swollen, just as Natalie, Dade, Melody, and Zoey came through the door.

Chapter 11

Viability: capacity for germination.

THE flight to San Antonio on the following Monday was uneventful, but the visit to the specialist wrecked all that. The internist, Dr. Simon, was alarmed at Abe's condition and concerned that his physician in Cupid hadn't been able to make a diagnosis.

"We need to admit your father to the hospital and do extensive testing," Dr. Simon recommended. "He's seriously malnourished."

"The only thing he'll eat are the sweet potatoes from his garden," Pierce explained. "He asks for other foods, but when we get them for him, he won't eat."

"I love sweet taters!" Abe spoke up.

They spent the next several hours getting Abe settled in the hospital and hiring a private duty nurse to sit with him. Pierce had to admit that Lace was a lot of help in navigating the medical environment. While her doctorate was in plant science, she knew a lot about anatomy and biology and all those Latin terms. She also had a way of looking at nurses to get them to hop to their jobs, especially when they were lavishing more attention on Pierce than on their patient.

He stood in the doorway looking at his dad, a dead weight in his stomach while the private duty nurse plumped Abe's pillow.

Lace reached up and rubbed Pierce's shoulder.

She seemed to have an instinct for when he was feeling low and her touch lightened his load. He might have manipulated her into coming with him, but he was damn grateful to have her here.

"Let's call off the shopping spree," she said. "Spend the day with your dad."

"Oh no," he said. "You're not getting out of it that easily." Truth was, he needed the diversion from worrying about Abe's condition, and being with Lace was the sweetest distraction he could think of.

She grinned. "Had to give it a shot."

"Most women would love to have a man with a full wallet taking them shopping."

"Honey," the private duty nurse interrupted. "Listen to him. Most women would kill to have Dallas Cowboy quarterback Pierce Hollister take them dress shopping. Better get along before some of the gals in the nursing lounge start sharpening their claws. Don't worry about things here. I'll take good care of your father, Mr. Hollister."

Once they were outside the room, Lace said, "Did you pay her to say that?"

"Which part? About taking good care of my father or women killing to go out with me?"

Lace cut her eyes at him. "Let's just get this over with."

"You don't like shopping?"

"Hate it."

"Mostly just catalog order from L.L. Bean, huh?"

She screwed her mouth up. "What's wrong with that?"

"You have too much plaid in your wardrobe." Not that he really minded her in plaid. He liked her in anything. It's just that he wanted to see her in something that would really show off that rocking body of hers. But if he were being honest, what he really wanted to see her in was her birthday suit. "C'mon, let's start with Nordstrom."

PIERCE HAD RENTED a car at the airport when they'd arrived, and thirty minutes later, they were in the "occasions" section of the women's department at Nordstrom. Once the saleswomen recognized him, they were inundated with help, but he'd held up a palm and told the clerks that if they wanted to make a sale they needed to back off and give them some breathing room. The women scattered, but they kept peeking surreptitiously around dress racks at him.

"How do you put up with that constantly?" Lace asked.

He shrugged. "Comes with the territory. You get used to it."

"I never would." Lace crossed her arms over her chest, feeling completely out of her element. "Maybe that's really why your girlfriend dumped you. She hated dealing with all the women who come on to you."

"I seriously doubt that," he said. "She took up with my replacement, remember. She knew that when I'm with a woman, I'm with her. Too bad I couldn't say the same for her."

"Maybe she didn't believe you. I mean, c'mon . . ." Lace gestured to one saleswoman craning her neck from around the mannequin she was ostensibly dressing. The woman lost her balance, stumbled, and fell off her wedge heels. "Who wouldn't be intimidated?"

"You."

Shows what you know. "So tell me, just how many women *have* you dressed?"

"Do you really want to know?"

"I figured undressing women was more your style."

His grin could have lit up the Vegas strip. "You're right about that. You're my first."

"The first woman you've ever bought a dress for?"

"Yep."

"That surprises me. Confident as you are in the ladies' department, seems like you would have outfitted hundreds of women."

"How many women do you think I've been with, Lace?"

"You're a football player. I couldn't even begin to guess. Less than a thousand?"

"Be serious."

"I was."

"Guess again."

"Three hundred?"

"Not even in the ballpark."

"Give me a hint. Higher or lower?"

"Much lower."

"Seventy-five? No wait, don't answer." She clamped her hands over her ears. "I don't want to know."

"Because you wouldn't feel special if it was a lot?"

"Because I don't care."

"It's—"

"Shh! Don't tell me."

"Ah." He shook a finger. "I know why you don't want to know. You don't want to compare numbers. Because if I tell you how many I've been with, you're going to feel—"

"No, really, I do not care."

Pierce picked through the rack of cocktail dresses. "What size?"

"I'm not telling you my size. I can pick out my own clothes, thank you very much."

"I've been to a million of these fund-raisers. When I first joined the Cowboys they hired an image consultant to show me how to present myself for maximum impact. Trust me. I know exactly what you need."

I know what you need.

His words wrapped around Lace, both irritating and enticing. "I do not need you to control my image."

"Do you want those sponsors to open their wallets?"

"I'm not Eliza Doolittle and you're certainly not Professor Henry Higgins," she snapped. Yes, she was being touchy, but she knew she was on the verge of rapidly losing control of the situation.

"Audrey Hepburn was hot in that movie."

Lace rolled her eyes. "I'm talking about *Pygmalion*, not *My Fair Lady*."

"Pig what?"

"*Pygmalion* by George Bernard Shaw. From whence the characters of Eliza Doolittle and Henry Higgins sprang."

"So *My Fair Lady* is a remake?"

"I guess you could call it that in jock-speak. More accurately, *My Fair Lady* is an adaptation."

One eyebrow inched up on his forehead and a smile plucked at the corners of his mouth. "Jock-speak?"

"The language of the *Homo sapiens jockularus*."

"And what do you speak? *Homo sapiens geekularus*?"

She laughed.

The corner of his mouth plucked back as if an invisible harpist played his face, and he sent her an appraising glance. "Size fourteen?" he guessed, shifting back to the topic she'd sought to avoid.

She felt naked under the heat of his appraising gaze. "How did you know?"

He shrugged. "Fourteen is my jersey number."

"So it was just a lucky guess?"

"It was synchronicity."

"What do you know about synchronicity?" she asked.

"What? *Homo sapiens jockularus* is too dumb to know such words?"

"That's not what I said. It just doesn't seem like a word that you would use."

"While you were getting your degree in something useful like plant science, I was trying to skim by with what I thought were easier courses. My BA is in social psychology."

"Synchronicity. That's Jung, right?"

"A series of meaningful coincidences. You're a size fourteen. My jersey number is a fourteen. It's gotta mean something."

"I was fourteen when I wrote that stupid letter to Cupid about you."

"That too. Synchronicity." He smiled mildly and handed her a simple black cocktail dress.

Or she thought it was simple until she turned it around and saw the cutout in the back. "No. I couldn't wear a bra with that."

"I know," he said in a low, throaty voice.

"Put it back on the rack."

"If you're going to be difficult about this, we'll be here all day."

She sighed and took the black dress just to shut him up, but she was not about to buy it. "So what does Jung have to say about synchronicity?"

"There are some things that science just can't explain."

"Psychology isn't a science."

"It's a social science."

"I rest my case. Not real science."

"You're killing my romantic overtures here."

She grinned.

"As was clearly your intention. Here, go try this one on." He handed her a purply blue silk sheath dress the color of *Lupinus texensis*, Texas bluebonnets. "The color matches your eyes."

It was a romantic thing to say and got her to thinking about how good kissing him had felt. "The hem is too short."

"Trust me. Go try it on."

"I'll look like a whale in this."

"Don't put yourself down. You'll look like a goddess."

She seriously doubted that, but if it would shut him up, she'd try it on. She headed for the dressing room, while he took a seat outside near the three-way mirror.

"Want me to hold your purse?" he offered.

"I've got it."

"It will be easier trying on the dress without having to worry about keeping up with your purse."

"I'll hang it over the hook on the back of the door. No big deal. Believe it or not, I've—*gasp*—shopped for clothes on my own before."

"Scared I'll go through your credit cards, steal your identity, buy an ATV under your name, and then use it to take another woman four-wheeling in the desert and run over some rare fragile plant life?"

"As much as that nightmare situation keeps me awake at night, desert plants aren't fragile. That's why they thrive in the desert."

He leaned back against the chair, interlaced his fingers, and cupped the back of his head in his palms. "And that's the part of the crazy scenario you latch on to?"

"Hey, you're the one who came up with the crazy scenario."

"Only because you are acting so paranoid."

Lace screwed her mouth up. "I'm not paranoid."

"Then just leave your purse with me."

"Look here, I'm not one of those girly-girls who enjoys having a guy act like her lapdog. I don't need my door opened or your hat tipped in my direction or for you to hold my purse. Got it?"

"I know that," he said. "That's one of the things I admire about you. Your independence."

Lace gulped.

"But every now and then, all women enjoy a little extra attention. There's nothing helpless or weak in wanting to be taken care of once in a while."

"Not me," she muttered. "I don't want extra attention."

"Why not?"

Why not indeed? Well, for one thing, receiving attention required something of her. Something she might not be able to give, and admitting that would mean she was lacking. She didn't want him to think her lacking, even if she was.

"It's ja . . . just . . . um . . . I . . . I . . ." Frigging flytrap! She was stuttering.

He held out his hand. "Purse."

"Fine. Here. Take it." She thrust the handbag at him.

He chuckled.

Once inside the dressing room, she tried on the black dress. The back was cut all the way down to her hipbone. No freaking way.

"How's it going?" he asked from outside the door.

Lace crossed her arms over her chest. "Why are you in the ladies' dressing room?"

"Relax, there's no other customers in this department."

"Get out of here. Go back to your chair."

"Please don't make me go back out there. Although I can't see them, I can hear the saleswomen breathing down my neck."

"Oh, poor you. I thought you got used to it."

"Everyone has a tipping point. Which dress do you have on?"

"The black one."

"Can I see?"

"No you may not."

"Dips too low in the back?"

"Any lower and I could qualify to repair plumbing."

He laughed out loud.

Lace couldn't help smiling that she'd made him laugh.

"How about the blue one?" he asked.

"I haven't tried it on yet."

"What are you waiting for?"

"For you to go back to your chair."

"I'm going, I'm going."

She wriggled out of the black dress and slipped the blue one over her head. The material was luxurious, refined. Really nice. Hmm, how much did something this comfy cost? She flipped over the tag. $699.99. Holy organic fertilizer! Seven hundred dollars for a dress? Surely it was $69.99 and she'd looked at it wrong. Nope. $699.99. Insanity. She could buy a year's worth of her regular wardrobe for that price, underwear included.

She reached back for the zipper, got it halfway up before it stuck. She contorted her body, struggling to find an angle that would allow her to tug more firmly on the zipper, but the damn thing wouldn't budge. The teeth must have gotten caught on a chunk of material. Her impulse was to yank, but the dress cost seven hundred freaking dollars. If she ripped it . . .

Terrific. Maybe she could slip it off over her head. She grasped the hem, bent at the waist, and wrestled the skirt of the dress up to her rib cage, but there it stopped, and refused to budge an inch farther. The way her arms were crossed created a straitjacketlike effect and she could move neither up nor down. Houdini couldn't have gotten out of this. Don't flip out. Take a deep breath and calm down.

Except that she could not take a deep breath with the material wrapped around her lungs, and with her head upside-down she was starting to feel light-headed.

What to do?

Fighting back the panic pushing into her esophagus, she cleared her throat. If she called for help, would Pierce be able to hear her from the chair where she'd shooed him back to? "Um, hello?"

"Yes?" His voice rumbled from just beyond the door.

If she hadn't been so relieved that he had not gone back to the chair, she would have taken him to task. Instead, she merely said, "Could you call a saleswoman in here?"

"What do you need?"

"Just call the saleswoman," she said and because desperation was closing in, added, "Please."

"I'll be happy to help."

"Then I beg of you, go get a saleswoman." Her breath was coming out in uneven seesaws as if she'd just lugged a two-hundred-and-ten-gallon tree tub loaded with a full-grown Benjamin ficus up three flights of stairs, and the light-headedness swiftly shifted into full-fledged dizziness. Her arms had caught in the material of the skirt of the dress, and the garment had essentially become Chinese handcuffs; the harder she struggled to get out, the tighter the material constricted.

"Lace?" Concern tinged his voice. "Are you okay?"

This upside-down thing wasn't cutting it. She raised her head, but the movement must have been too quick because her head spun like a carousel and she fell heavily against the wall. "Uh."

The next thing she knew a big masculine arm was snaking over the top of the door to unslide the lock from the inside.

"No!" she exclaimed, or at least tried to, but she had so little air left in her lungs that it came out, "Na."

"Hang on." Pierce was inside the cubicle, his hands on her shoulders.

Mortified. She was absolutely mortified. Held prisoner by a seven-hundred-dollar dress in her bra and panties.

"Easy, easy." He steadied her by putting an arm around her waist, his bare hand on her bare flesh.

Kill me now. Just kill me now and end the humiliation.

Somehow, miraculously, he untangled her arms

from the dress and smoothed it down over her body, his hands touching her in the way she'd once dreamed he would touch her, except this seemed to be the nightmare version. His gaze met hers and his eyes twinkled mischievously. "Love the siren red bra and panties. Never would have pegged you for a scarlet woman."

"Isn't that odd, because you're exactly how I pegged you. Full frontal Neanderthal."

"Sweetheart, how do you expect a guy to react under the circumstances? Close proximity with a beautiful, shapely woman." He stepped back as far as he could in the tiny space, tilted his head, and let his gaze graze over her. "That dress . . . well . . . wow! You look like Snow White. The fairest in the land."

Heat pushed up Lace's neck to her face. The mirror was behind her, so she hadn't seen herself in it.

"Turn around," he said, "and I'll get your zipper unstuck."

Not knowing what else to do—she had to get out of the damn dress—she gave him her back and caught sight of her reflection.

The soft silk caressed her curves but did not cling. The color brought out the shades of violet in her blue eyes, and accentuated the creaminess of her complexion against the darkness of her hair. In this dress, she looked like the kind of woman who could hold the attention of a man like Pierce, at least for a couple of minutes.

His head was down, his attention fully focused on

the zipper, his breath warm against the nape of her neck, his nimble, callused fingertips gentle against her skin. He freed the zipper and smoothly slid it up. She closed her eyes to keep from shivering and when she opened them again, he was watching her in the mirror.

"Fits you like a glove. Flaunts those gorgeous curves, and the hem shows off just enough leg to get a guy drooling, but not so much as to give away the mystery." He winked.

Her pulse sped up. Quickly, she glanced away, spied her purse on the floor where he must have dropped it when he'd come in. "You can go now."

"Use me and toss me aside, huh?" he teased. "I feel like a soiled tissue."

"I want out of this dress."

"I want that too," he said, his voice shockingly seductive.

"Stop it." She moved as far away from him as the cubicle would allow.

"Do you want me to unzip you before I go?"

"No! And stop grinning."

He pressed his lips together, compressed his mouth into a straight line, but his eyes were laughing at her.

She pointed a finger. "Go."

He opened the door, stood half in and half out of the stall. "Just in case you're thinking of not getting the dress," he said in an end-of-the-discussion tone, "I've already paid for it."

Lace sank her hands on her hips. "Of all the high-handed—"

He scooted out the door, chuckling and leaving her fuming. She locked it behind him, leaned limply against the door, and blew out a heavy breath. She could deny it all she wanted, but the man got to her, and damn if she didn't love the dress.

Watch out! Slippery slope.

She reached around for the zipper, but couldn't seem to reach it. Darn thing. She didn't want a dress that required having someone around to help her get in and out of. She wriggled and twisted, but every time she had her finger on the zipper tongue, it slipped off. "Harrumph!"

"Need something?" Pierce asked in a sugary sweet voice from the other side of the door.

"I admit it. You win. Now get back in here and unzip me!"

"God," he said in a dreamy voice. "I love a bossy woman who knows her own mind."

WHEN THEY RETURNED to the hospital late that afternoon, Abe was asleep. The private duty nurse gave Pierce an update. "The doctor said he should have preliminary reports on the blood work tomorrow morning," she said. "Will you be here?"

Pierce splayed a hand to the nape of his neck. The shopping trip had been a nice distraction, but there was no escaping his father's illness. Flirting with Lace was a great way to hide from his emotions, but standing here looking at his father's pale face and withered frame told him he couldn't keep running from this. Abe was very sick and no one could tell him why. What was the point in going back to Cupid this afternoon if he only had to turn around and return the following day if the lab tests did indeed reveal a serious illness? He glanced over at Lace, wondering if she would mind staying the night in San Antonio.

"Do we need to stay overnight?" she asked, already two steps ahead of him.

His chest tightened and he tapped a fist against his heart. The woman continually bowled him over. "Would you mind?"

She shrugged like it was no big deal, dropped his gaze. "I no longer have a job to get back to and honestly, Melody is driving me a bit nuts prepping for the fund-raiser. She's such a perfectionist. Now I have a good excuse to take a break."

"Thank you," he said.

"There's several hotel chains just a few blocks from here," the private duty nurse said helpfully.

They stayed at the hospital for a couple of hours, but Abe was so lethargic, the nurse suggested they go ahead and check into the hotel. She promised to call if his father's condition changed.

"Would you like to grab some dinner?" Pierce asked hopefully.

"Thanks for the offer," Lace said. "But I'm kind of tired. I think I'll just go to bed early."

Normally, he might have pressed the issue, but honestly, he wouldn't have been good company. Besides, he needed to call Malcolm and update him on Abe's condition.

At the hotel, he got them side-by-side rooms and said good night. She lingered a moment at the door, something unreadable in her eyes, then smiled softly. "Sleep well."

He called Malcolm and told him what was going on. "What do we do after we get the results?"

"Depends on what the results are. Don't borrow trouble or count chickens," Malcolm said.

"What if it's something bad." Pierce swallowed. *Like cancer?*

"We deal with it as it comes," Malcolm said.

"But we could be in this for the long haul."

"Don't worry, your haul won't be long. Soon as your leg heals you'll be back in Dallas doing your thing and I'll be here playing cleanup as always."

He was used to Malcolm's snipes, but it still hurt, probably because it was true. He had spent his life being the star of the family while Malcolm was the salt of the earth who had kept everything together. Also, he hadn't told his brother what Dr. Hank had relayed to him about his chances of returning to football this year, partly because it had been too painful to think about, and partly because he was determined to prove Dr. Hank wrong. If he said the words out loud, they'd have real meaning. *Go ahead, make like an ostrich.*

"Mal," Pierce said, "I do appreciate you and everything you've done for Dad."

"I don't need any thanks for taking care of my own father."

The backs of Pierce's eyelids burned. He blinked, pinched the bridge of his nose. "I can't figure out why he got so much better when he was in the hospital at Cupid, but after we brought him home he started going downhill again. I thought maybe when I came back to the ranch—"

"That the greatness of your presence would heal him?"

"You know I don't think that."

"Don't you?"

Pierce blew out a breath. He knew Malcolm resented his success. Who could blame him with the way his dad had always put Pierce ahead of his younger brother? "I'm sorry for so many things."

"Yeah," Malcolm said. "Me too."

That gave him hope that something good would come of their father's illness. Mend a few fences.

"If this turns out to be something really serious, we're going to have to pace ourselves—"

"I was there with Mom, I know how it goes."

Meaning Pierce had no idea how a bedside vigil

went because he hadn't been there while their mother lay dying. "I want to be here," he said.

"You're here right now." Malcolm's voice softened. "That means something."

"I know you've sacrificed a lot for our family, delaying starting a family of your own—"

"Please, let's not go into it. Besides, I'm seeing someone."

"Hey, that's good. I'm happy for you and I want to meet her. We need to have a talk. A long one."

"Gotta go. We have a heifer in labor and she's prone to breech births."

"Listen, Malcolm. I lo—"

A dial tone sounded in his ear.

Pierce hung up. He meandered to the window and stared out at the parking lot. Absently, he ran his hand down his left leg.

A car dragging tin cans pulled up in the parking lot underneath the vapor security lamps. "Just Married" was written in white shoe polish on the back window. The fresh-faced groom got out of the driver's seat, sprinted around to the passenger-side door, and yanked it open. He pulled out a laughing young woman and hoisted her into his arms. He dropped kisses on her face and she flung her arms around his neck.

Pierce's throat tightened. He rubbed his dry eyes, and turned away from their happiness.

Chapter 12

Tendril: a slender portion of a leaf or stem, modified for twining.

LACE had just stepped out of the shower, dressed in nothing but the terry-cloth robe provided by the hotel, when a knock sounded on the door. She only knew one person in San Antonio, so she already knew who it was before she squinted through the peephole because she hadn't yet put her glasses on after her shower.

Pierce stood in the corridor, his sleeves rolled up above his elbows, the top two snaps of his shirt undone, revealing just enough hard-muscled chest to be intriguing, his hair crimped from the impression of wearing his Stetson. Who knew hat hair could be so attractive?

She pressed her hand to her mouth and considered not opening the door, but knowing him he would just keep knocking until she answered. Her hair, still damp from the steam of the shower, coiled against her jaw. Feeling foolishly giddy to see him, she undid the lock, and opened the door.

"Hi." His grin was lopsided, boyish, and just a hint forlorn.

The forlorn part was what did her in, despite the fact that his gaze strolled a long trek down the length of her body, taking in her robe, bare legs, and socked feet. Lace never walked barefooted on hotel carpeting—she knew too much about bacteria to be comfortable doing that. By the time he glanced back to her face, forlorn had vanished, replaced by wolfish desire.

A tendril of heat started in her stomach, twined low and deep. *Well, Little Red Riding Hood, you did open the door to him.*

"You got settled in I see."

"I did." She kept her hand firmly on the doorknob.

He nodded. The air thickened between them. She curled her toes inside her socks, painfully aware of how susceptible she was in nothing but a robe, while he was fully dressed. Not so different from the dressing room cubicle. How was it that she found herself in a similar situation twice in one day, nearly naked in front of the one man who had the potential to dismantle her whole life?

"I ordered room service."

"Well then you better get on back to your room." She started to close the door, but she didn't really want to.

He propped the toe of his cowboy boot against the door. "I ordered room service for us. I told them to deliver it to your room."

"That was pretty high-handed."

Pierce narrowed his eyes. "Do you always react negatively when someone tries to do something nice for you?"

"I suppose in your world trying to get inside my panties is considered doing something nice."

"Do you even have any panties on to get into?" He dropped his gaze again.

"Move your foot or get it slammed," she threatened. She wouldn't really slam his foot in the door, but he didn't know that.

He held up his hand in a gesture of surrender, but kept his foot planted firmly against the door. "I'm sorry. That came out wrong. As you've pointed out, I've got a bad habit of reaching for the jock-speak. Plus, I find you sexy as hell, Lacy, and sometimes I spout off before I think about how it sounds. I just wanted to buy you dinner to thank you for being so understanding about my dad. A lot of women wouldn't have agreed to stay."

Her knees wobbled. "I'm not sure having dinner alone with you in my hotel room is such a good idea."

"Why do you keep pushing me away?" he asked.

Why? Because she didn't want to end up a puddle of goo at his feet. The truth was she didn't know how to moderate her feelings. When it came to love, she was either all in as she'd been at fourteen or she was detached, as she'd been in every single romantic encounter she'd ever had. Her aloof independence attracted men,

but in the end, when she broke off the relationships—
and she'd always been the one to break things off—the
men invariably called her cold. But she wasn't cold,
in fact quite the opposite. She felt so deeply that she
couldn't bear the pain of having her love spurned, so
she never allowed herself to get emotionally close to
anyone.

"Pierce," she murmured. "I can't—"

"Please don't send me away, Lace," he said, and drew
in a ragged breath, and for the first time she noticed the
raw exhaustion in his eyes. "I don't want to be alone."

It had been a long dry spell. After her four-year wild
spree when she was a wide-eyed coed set free on the
Texas A&M campus chockful of cowboys, she'd put
herself on a man-free diet. Which, come to think of it,
seemed to be backfiring. The fact that she hadn't been
intimate with anything other than a sex toy since she'd
started graduate school made Pierce that much more
tempting.

Man, she did not want to be that girl. The one, who
when she finally got a chance to sleep with the guy
she'd once had an unrequited crush on, she grabbed
it like a starving hawk moth caterpillar devouring a
tomato plant. That's what her sexual-exploration binge
had been about, getting him out of her system. And
honestly, it had worked like a charm until he'd come
strolling back into town. But now all her best inten-
tions were shriveling up under the heat of his sizzling

stare and she was thinking things she had no business thinking.

Then again, there was a special magic between them that she could not deny. She knew that with Pierce, she was in for the best sex of her life. Wouldn't she be an idiot to walk away from that? She gave in, gave up, surrendered. White flag. The whole works. *Take me prisoner. I'm yours.*

Quietly, she opened the door all the way. "C'mon in."

He stepped inside, bringing his rugged masculinity with him, and touched down on the mattress of the single queen-sized bed. He looked so commanding sitting there like he owned the world.

Goose bumps played up and down her spine. Here she was alone in a hotel room with Dallas Cowboys quarterback Pierce Hollister. Any number of women would kill to be in her socks. She inclined her head in the direction of the bathroom. "I'm just going to get dressed."

"No need to slip into something less comfortable on my account." He gave her a dazzling grin that sucked the air right out of her lungs. "I promise to keep my hands to myself."

A knock sounded on the door. "Room service."

Pierce hopped off the bed. Lace backed out of the way. She could change—but she'd washed out her underwear and left it to dry over the towel bar so she'd have to go commando under her jeans—or she could just stay in the robe, keep her knees firmly pressed together, have dinner with him, and send him on his way as quickly as possible. Considering he'd already signed for the meal and was wheeling the room service cart into the room, blocking her entry into the bathroom, she took the path of least resistance and moved to pull out the desk chair and sit down.

A delicious scent filled the room and Lace's stomach growled.

Pierce maneuvered the cart in front of her, positioning it to create a makeshift table between the two of them as he sank onto the end of the mattress. He lifted the lids, revealing two plates of chicken-fried steak, a pile of mashed potatoes and gravy, yeast rolls, Roma green beans, and chocolate cake for dessert. Two glasses of iced tea flanked the plates.

"Is it sweet tea?" she asked.

"Is there any other kind?"

"Chicken-fried steak is my favorite. How did you know?"

"Whenever I had dinner at your house and your mom served chicken-fried steak, you'd gleefully announce it."

Warmth undulated through her. "You remember that?"

His brown eyes with those intriguing green flecks studied her. "I remember a lot of things, Lace."

"For instance?"

"I remember how you had this big black magnifying glass you'd take with you everywhere and whip out of your back pocket whenever you found a bug or plant that caught your interest. You were brainy even then."

"My girl cousins thought I was weird because I liked spiders and toads and lizards and snakes."

"But you were every little boy's dream girl."

She laughed. "Not yours. You liked the girly-girls who wore pink and cried when they broke a fingernail."

"I've come to realize that might have been a little shortsighted of me."

"What was?"

"Not looking beyond the pretty surface."

"If you were an insect you'd be *Gerris remigis*," Lace commented.

"What's that?"

"A water strider."

"What makes you say that?"

"Water striders have long legs." She couldn't help glancing at his legs that were stretched out on either side of the room service cart. "So they can easily skim the surface. They spend their lives skimming the surface."

"So they're light on their feet."

"Just as you are. Never going deep."

"Well." His gaze flicked to her lap. "I wouldn't say never."

Lace ducked her head and forked a bit of mashed potatoes into her mouth so he couldn't see her blush. Yes, she was embarrassed, so you would have thought she'd leave it alone, but oh no, once she swallowed her potatoes, she had to keep talking. "When the male water striders are looking for a mate they send out ripple frequency across the surface of the water, transmitting sound waves to attract female water striders. If the female is receptive, she will zip on over. If she's not receptive, she'll emit her own ripple frequency that warns him to back off."

Pierce tugged at his collar. "Ripple frequency, huh? So that's what I do? Cause a ripple?"

"Everywhere you go."

"What would you be?" he asked. "If you were an insect."

She paused to consider that. "I was a lacewing once."

"When?" He chuckled. "In another life?"

"In a second grade school play about gardens. I wore the costume for Halloween the same year. It confused everyone. They thought I was supposed to be a character from some animated space movie. I should have gone as a scorpion. No one can mistake a scorpion. With a scorpion, what you see is what you get."

"You always were light-years ahead of everyone else."

"No. I'm just different. It's not an easy thing to be when you're a small-town kid."

"You think like a roadrunner moves," Pierce said. "Lightning quick."

She straightened in her chair. "Thank you for the compliment. *Geococcyx californianus*, also known as the Californian earth-cuckoo or chaparral cock, is my favorite bird and they can run up to twenty-six miles an hour."

The second she said the word "cock," she realized how suggestive it sounded given the circumstance— them alone in a hotel room, she in her robe without any underwear on—but she plowed ahead. Once upon a time she would have stumbled and stuttered over the word "cock." She braced for his snappy comeback.

Pierce grinned, but he didn't go there. "Californian earth-cuckoo, huh?" Somehow the way he said it sounded even more suggestive than if he'd said, "chaparral cock."

"The name doesn't define their range. They're desert birds."

"Your head was always full of the desert. I'm not surprised you came back here instead of taking that job at the Smithsonian."

"Who told you about that?"

He shrugged, put his napkin onto his empty plate. "You know small-town gossip."

"I imagine they're gossiping about us right now."

"No doubt I've sullied your reputation."

She smiled. "Perhaps I've sullied yours."

"It would take a lot to do that."

"You wouldn't believe some of the stories that get passed around about you," she said.

"Such as?"

"You've had group sex with the Dallas Cowboy cheerleaders."

"Sweetheart," he drawled. "I get enough team action on the football field."

Her heart thumped erratically.

"You've generated some gossip of your own," he said.

"You mean besides turning down the Smithsonian?"

"Uh-huh."

"Which is?"

"I heard that you're still a virgin."

Lace's pulse revved. "Did you?"

"I did."

"Cupidites don't have enough to talk about if the question of my virginity is a hot topic of conversation. You'd think Olive Cooksey's criminal activities would have snagged top billing."

"Are you?" he murmured. "Still a virgin?"

She lowered her lashes, gave him a seductive side-long glance meant to put starch in his pants. If he could tease, so could she. "Am I?"

His grinned widened, but his eyes were serious. "You like messing with people's heads."

"Do I?"

"You know that you do."

"So is that why you're pursuing me so relentlessly? You're interested in deflowering me?"

"That has nothing to do with it."

"But the idea of being with a virgin makes you hot."

"The idea of being with *you* makes me hot."

Perspiration beaded between Lace's breasts in spite of the air-conditioner vent blowing cool air on her. "So if you learned I was not a virgin, would you be disappointed?"

"Honestly?"

"By all means."

"I'd be relieved."

"Why? So you wouldn't have to feel bad about popping my cherry and then sneaking out the back door the next morning?"

"Woman, any man who would sneak out the back door after a night with you needs his head examined."

"But you've done it before. Sneaked out on a woman after a hot night of passion."

He looked guilty. "I'm no saint, Lace."

Neither am I. She'd done her share of sneaking out the morning after, but she wasn't about to let him know that. Those were not some of her finer moments.

"And if I were a virgin," she asked, enjoying stringing him along, "could you deal with that?"

He gulped visibly. "Lace, have you been waiting for me—"

She burst out laughing.

"What?" He sounded hurt.

"Don't worry, Pierce, I have not been saving myself for you, in fact, quite the opposite. I completely purged you from my system."

"Oh."

"That's not what you wanted to hear?"

He looked caught off guard. "But you're not . . . involved with anyone right now?"

"You're just now asking?"

"It just now occurred to me that's why you're resisting this thing between us."

"There's no thing."

He looked smug. "Deny it all you want, there's a thing."

"It would serve you right if I said yes, that I was involved with someone else."

"But you're not."

"No."

He nodded. "Good, great."

"Why the affirmative response?"

"Are you finished?" He waved at her plate.

"Yes, I—"

He stood up, shoved the food cart off to one side, reached down, took her hand, and pulled her to her feet.

"What are you doing?"

"What water striders do best, sending out ripples." He grabbed her around the waist and pulled her up tight against his chest.

"Hey!"

He ended her protest by closing his mouth over hers. Lace stiffened and pushed against him with her palms, but he simply tightened his grip. His tongue pressed against her teeth and, dammit, she opened up like a clam in a hot steamer. He tasted like rich dark chocolate, warm and inviting, too deviously delicious to disobey.

Could she do this? Could she have sex with him and not stir up those old feelings? It was dangerous ground. Emotional quicksand. But here was the kicker, if she *could* sleep with him and keep her feelings from getting involved, then she would know she had well and truly moved past her schoolgirl crush. If she could treat Pierce like a tasty bonbon, as she had done with those guys in college, wouldn't that be the ultimate freedom?

Maybe, but what if she couldn't?

What if she had sex with him and fell madly in love all over again? What then? What if she lost her heart and in the end he didn't love her back?

Just the idea of it made her queasy, and in that split second of sweet agony, she relived her teenage angst all over again. Her crush—and the humiliating way it came out—had been a watershed moment. It had taken her a while to get over him and put the past behind her. Yes, it had been horrible, but the experience had made her tougher, stronger, and more resilient. She'd conquered her stutter, lost weight, and then gained it back when she realized that she had not been the problem. Loving him had changed her in irrevocable ways, good ways, healthy ways, even when he had not loved her back.

That's when Lace realized what she was truly scared of. When she'd loved him before, she'd lost sight of who she was. She never wanted to lose herself like that again. Her fear wasn't of loving him and losing him, but rather, in the stranglehold grip of all-consuming love, she was terrified of losing herself.

Fear and craving warred inside her, a vicious battle leaving her wrecked and helpless. No matter which emotion won, she was destined to lose. Give in and she could lose her heart. Run away and she might forever regret this golden opportunity to live out her deepest fantasy.

In the end, Pierce took the decision away from her.

His mouth siphoned all the energy from her body, rendering her too weak to do more than sag against him, powerless to overcome the heavy lust saturating her pelvis, her relish for him all-consuming. Spurred by the influx of estrogen shooting through her body, she lifted her hands and grasped either side of his face, holding him still while she kissed him back as ferociously as he kissed her.

Pierce toppled backward onto the bed, pulling her off her feet and on top of him. His hands slipped beneath the terry-cloth robe, caressing and stroking. Her skin ignited, bursting into flames everywhere his fingers touched. Their grappling lips fused and only a desperate need for air broke them, momentarily, apart.

The second time they came up for air, he reached up a trembling hand to brush a strand of hair from her face. His obvious desire for her was heady stuff and she was doing plenty of trembling of her own. He moved his hand up the nape of her neck, spearing his fingers through her hair and bringing her face down to his for another long, breath-stealing kiss.

In a glib glide, he rolled them over, pinning her beneath his hard body. His fingers plucked at the sash on her robe, sending a shudder of need rocking over her. The robe fell open, revealing to him that she was absolutely naked beneath the terry cloth.

"Beautiful, beautiful, beautiful," he murmured, and rested his cheek against her breast.

Lace was quivering so hard the bed shook. She knotted her hands into fists, tried to quell the tremors, but it was no use.

Pierce turned his head and planted his lips in the valley between her breasts and slowly kissed his way to a nipple, his teeth oh-so-lightly capturing the tight tip. His tongue strummed the pink flesh, and with each stroke of his tongue it felt as if he was plucking a string attached from her nipple to her womb, every wicked flicker winding her tighter and tighter.

A soft moan escaped her lips and he was back to

kiss her lips while his hands slid over her breasts and his dexterous thumbs played with her nipples. His attention dizzied her head until she felt as if she'd drunk a quart of champagne. She clung to him, overwhelmed by the strength of her excitement.

Lace whimpered, wanting more, trying so hard not to beg him to take her even though she wanted him so badly she was blind to everything but her desperation. She needed to think this through but her body was so alive that it numbed her mind and she couldn't think at all, only feel. And oh, how much she felt. It was a symphony of sensation, a hundred erogenous zones she didn't know she possessed—the backs of her knees felt the cotton of bedspread, her kneecaps rubbed against the denim of his jeans, terry cloth tickled her butt.

He skimmed fingers down her belly, soft as a whisper, and her skin responded like the filaments inside a light bulb, illuminating what was previously in the dark. He alternated the pressure, heavy, light, hard, soft, sending urgent messages to her brain—*Mating is imminent!*

Except she was naked and he was not.

She reached for his belt buckle, her hand brushed against his erection, and impossibly, he grew even harder. Her fingers fumbled.

Pierce closed his hand over hers. "No."

"What?" she whimpered through the brain fog.

"Look at me."

She peered up into his eyes and he held her mesmerized as his hand spread like the tendrils of a twining vine, moving over the springy triangle of dark curls.

He dipped his middle finger over her budding cleft but did not plunge past it into her warm moistness. Instead he put the slightest of pressure against her.

Go in. Go in.

He paused there, driving her mad with need. Her muscles tensed and then every nerve ending in her body started tingling as she tried to anticipate his next move.

He stared into her eyes, finger touching her so lightly it hurt. She was ready to beg him to put that finger inside her.

Instead, she sucked air. "Please."

Suddenly, he slipped a finger inside her and he was not gentle, but she was so wet and ready for him that she enjoyed the firm way he handled her. His gaze was a bradawl boring into her as he slid a second finger inside with the first and his gentle thumb searched for, and found, her feminine trigger.

She gasped and all the air left her lungs, leaving her weak and helpless. He knew what he was doing to her. He was fully and completely in control. His knuckles rubbed against her, heightening the mountaintop high. If having sex was like climbing a mountain, he was her Sherpa and they were headed up Everest.

Maddening. It was maddening to be so close. Sheer bliss! Disorienting. Immobilizing. Brilliant insanity.

It fully hit her then, a sledgehammer reality, who she was with—the man she had loved since she was fourteen, a man who had been with many women, a man with a reputation of playing fast and loose with hearts.

Pierce.

She was in bed with Pierce Hollister.

Maybe she was deceiving herself and it was all another one of her sex dreams.

His incredible fingers slew a few million atoms inside her, killing all resistance, leaving her wide open for the fatal wound. He took her to the edge again and again, until she was wrung out and whimpering, unable to do anything more than utter guttural noises.

Her muscles clenched around his fingers with visceral intensity. He made a sound of satisfaction and finished her off with miraculous timing, sending wave after wave of sheer pleasure rippling through her.

As she called out his name, he bent his head, took her mouth, absorbed her cry.

Haunting. This erotic moment would echo throughout her life, a ghostly vision of stunning perfection left like the image on the backs of the eyelids after a bright camera flash.

His face in that moment, looking both tender and self-satisfied, was branded on her retina forever.

He held her in his arms for some time and she slowly stopped trembling. She was too limp and drained to speak or even move.

Finally, he eased her from his embrace, got to his feet, and closed her robe. Her heart pounded wildly as she looked up into his eyes.

"That," he whispered, "is just a small sampling of what you could have." Then he kissed her softly on the forehead, got up, and walked out of the room.

Chapter 13

Escape: a cultivated plant that has gone wild.

PIERCE could not sleep. His leg was bothering him. He sat up and rubbed the scar running down his shin. He'd been sidetracked of late in his pursuit of Lace and he hadn't been doing his rehab therapy with the diligence it deserved, but it wasn't the leg pain keeping him awake.

Rather, he was aflame with desire. Lace's erotic aroma lingered on his skin. The coyly baffling scent of gingersnaps soaked in lavender and browned in melted butter. Gingersnaps had always been his favorite cookie. He loved the crisp sound they made when he bit into them and the surprising sear against his tongue that stimulated his taste buds in exciting ways. She'd been so responsive and wet, her life force dripping nectar—for *him*.

It had been a very long time since a woman had captivated him so thoroughly. He'd drawn on every self-control trick he knew to throttle back the urge to brutally rip off his clothes and plunge into her warm, plush body, but that would have been an offside move. Ten-yard penalty. This had been a long time coming and he'd wanted to do it right. He'd given her a taste of what they could be like together and hopefully gotten her hooked.

Trouble was, he was still hard as a brick.

He thought about taking care of his problem and moved a hand down the covers, his thoughts on the woman in the room next door, but then he stopped himself. No. He was saving it all for her and if that meant he didn't sleep a wink, then so be it.

In the thrill of the chase, delayed gratification meant increased pleasure, for him, for her, for them both. He could wait. Lace was worth the wait. It hit him all at once exactly how much trouble he was in, and his gut twisted. Time out. Step back. Better run some interference here, Hollister. Because he had a feeling that mere sex with her might not ever be enough.

THE NEXT MORNING, Pierce took her to breakfast at a popular pancake house. He couldn't seem to stop touching her. He offered her his arm when she got out of the car, and as he opened the door to the restaurant, he placed a palm at the small of her back. She wanted to drag him back to the hotel, lock him in her room, and have sex with him until neither one of them could walk.

Nice thought, but the minute they stepped inside he

caused a stir. His fans, many of them attractive young women, approached, asking about his leg and chances for recovery, pleading for autographs and asking him to pose for pictures.

Lace bit her lip and studied him. The man was in his milieu, thriving on the limelight. This was how it would be if she was with him all the time. The only place where she could have him all to herself would be behind closed doors. Good thing that this was only temporary. Eventually, his leg would heal, and even if he didn't make a full recovery and was unable to continue playing in the NFL, he was too big for a small town like Cupid.

If it was a good thing, then why did she feel so wistful?

She shook off the mood. She knew this relationship wasn't headed anywhere, but that didn't mean that she couldn't enjoy being on Pierce's arm while it lasted.

Instead of sitting across from her in the booth, he sat beside her, his thigh against hers. She smiled at her menu, felt giddy and girlish. They ate pancakes with blueberry syrup and talked of the pleasantness of the waitress, the brightness of the sun shining through the window, the noisiness of the construction going on across the street, but neither of them mentioned the night before, and that was perfectly okay.

They'd just finished eating when Lace got a text from Melody asking her when she was coming back to Cupid. The president of the Trans-Pecos Historical Society was interested in sponsoring the fund-raiser, but they wanted to meet Lace first.

Melody texted, *They want to meet u this afternoon.*

Lace let out a sigh.

"What is it?" Pierce asked.

She told him.

"I can put you on a plane back to Cupid within the hour."

"But you'll stay here."

"I have to check on Abe."

Lace glanced at the time on her cell phone. It was eight-thirty. "I'll come with you. It's only a forty-five-minute flight. I'll tell Melody to set up the meeting for three."

"Thanks," he said, and lightly rubbed the knuckle of his index finger along the back of her hand. "I'll call and charter the plane right now."

Twenty minutes later, they walked into Abe's hospital room to find him looking a little more alert than he had the day before.

"How's that throwing arm, boy?" Abe greeted his son.

Pierce moved his arm at the shoulder, showing he had full range of motion.

"Ready for tonight's game, son?"

"There's no game tonight, Dad."

Abe looked puzzled. "There's no game tonight?"

"No, Dad."

"But it's Friday."

"It's Tuesday."

"This is my boy," Abe said proudly to the private duty nurse. "He's gonna take Cupid to district."

"You must be very proud of him." The private duty nurse gave Pierce a conspiratorial wink.

"Just as long as he brings home that title," Abe said.

Lace's heart wrenched. The poor man thought his son was still in high school. This had to be so tough for Pierce.

Dr. Simon walked into the room carrying Abe's patient chart. He shook hands with Pierce and Lace, set down the chart, and went over to Abe for a cursory examination.

Lace stepped into the corner, pressed her back against the wall, getting out of the way. This wasn't any of her business.

"He looks better this morning," Pierce said hopefully.

Dr. Simon did not comment, just put the earpieces of a black stethoscope in his ears. He motioned for the nurse to assist him in getting Abe to a sitting position. The doctor leaned over and pressed the other end of the stethoscope to Abe's back.

Abe startled. "Jesus, Doc! Did you put that damn thing in the freezer?"

"Definitely more responsive this morning," Dr.

Simon observed, removing the stethoscope from his ears and easing Abe back down on the pillow.

"Did you get the lab results?" Pierce jammed his hands in his front pockets, hunched his shoulders forward. She wanted so badly to put her arms around him.

The doctor nodded.

"And?"

"Our tests mirrored those done in Cupid."

"Meaning?"

"Nothing conclusive. Most of his lab values were in normal limits and the few that were elevated were only slightly so. Nothing that would cause the symptoms your father has been experiencing."

"So you're saying that you have no clue what's making him lose weight, causing these memory losses?" Inside his pockets, Pierce's hands turned to bulging fists.

"I'm saying we haven't yet gotten to the bottom of it. There are more tests we can run. We'll do an MRI and a couple of other diagnostic scans."

"More pokin' and proddin'," Abe grumbled.

"But he's better today," Pierce insisted.

"Most likely because of the IV fluids. He was a bit dehydrated. Let's keep him a few more days, run those additional tests, and reevaluate then," the doctor suggested.

"You gonna leave me here to these buzzards?" Abe

asked, his woeful voice driving a stake through Pierce's heart.

"I'm not leaving you, Dad."

"I'll take a taxi to the airport," Lace said, hitching her purse up higher on her shoulder.

"I'll drive you."

"No. You need to spend time with your father."

"I don't mind."

She planted a palm on his chest. "Really, Pierce, it's okay. I understand. If I didn't have that meeting this afternoon, I'd stay here with you."

Like a girlfriend would.

She could be his girlfriend. The idea was very appealing, picnics in the park, best seat in the house at the Cowboys games, long nights—and days—in bed. Yum.

"I know," he said. "I appreciate you." His smile was so warm and genuine that it turned her inside out.

She couldn't resist kissing him, but because Abe and the private duty nurse were watching, it was a demure kiss on the cheek. Even so, the feeling that welled up inside her was overwhelming—tenderness, concern, admiration, and barely contained lust. Feelings so strong she feared there wasn't enough room in her chest to hold them all. Good thing he wasn't going to stay in Cupid forever, otherwise, she just might have to fall in love with him all over again.

"C'mon," he said, and took her by the hand. "You've got a plane to catch."

THEY'D NO SOONER stepped into the corridor than quick, barnstorming footsteps came up behind them. Pierce would know that assertive gait anywhere.

Frankie Kowalsky.

His spirits, which had buoyed after Lace's kiss, took the express elevator to the bottom of his boots. If Frankie had tracked him to his father's hospital room in San Antonio and actually shown up here instead of calling, it could mean only one thing.

Bad news.

"Hollister," said a throaty voice as provocative as a nude beach in St. Tropez.

Yep, it was Frankie. No one else walked or talked like that.

He pivoted on his heel, and because he had hold of Lace's elbow, he pivoted her with him.

Frankie Kowalsky was five-foot-eleven and built like a *Playboy* centerfold. She had long blond hair and Queen of Egypt cheekbones. Her legs were long, her arms toned and well-defined. She wore a form-fitting dress the color of chanterelle mushrooms that hugged her ample chest. Sports team owners, managers, and coaches alike trembled when they saw her coming.

"What are you doing here, Frankie?" he asked, but he already knew.

"Called your house," she said. "When your cell kept going to voice mail. Your brother told me about your father, and I knew I had to see you in person. I didn't want to do this by text or e-mail. Besides, I had to come to San Antonio to meet with the Spurs, anyway. Kill two birds with one stone."

Lace must have sensed his mood. She squeezed his hand and he was damn glad to have her with him, even though it meant she was going to witness his downfall.

Pierce cleared his throat. "Frankie, this is my friend Lace Bettingfield. Lace, this is my agent, Frankie Kowalsky."

Frankie nodded, gave Lace a short, quick pump of her extended hand. "I'm glad you're here. Pierce is going to need a friend."

Yep. There was only one reason that Frankie would show up in person. He had to do an end around pass to save face. Take the sting out of the news she was about to deliver by taking control. "The Cowboys have dropped me," he stated flatly.

"You knew it was coming." Frankie nodded, saying it as a statement, not a question.

Actually, he had not seen it was coming. He must have been living in fantasyland to think he had a shot at coming back from this injury. *There's no deception like self-deception, huh?* "Was it because of Dr. Hank's report?"

"That and Kip Kramer who replaced you is smoking hot in preseason. Haven't you been watching TV?"

Honestly, he'd been too busy with the ranch, his dad,

rehab, and pursuing Lace. Maybe he'd avoided the TV because watching Kramer lead his team was too painful. Or maybe all that activity had just been a distraction to keep his mind off what was coming.

The guillotine.

Frankie gave him a look of sympathy and ran her manicured fingers over his upper arm. "Hang in there, champ. I've got my ear to the ground. We'll get you a deal somewhere. Detroit is hurting for a decent quarterback."

Detroit? What a comedown. He'd worked his entire life to become a Dallas Cowboy. He'd achieved his dream, been at the pinnacle of his career, gone to the freaking Super Bowl, and in the end, his fate had been sealed on national TV. If he signed with Detroit, the move would be nothing but the first big, ugly grease spot on a long, painful downhill slide.

"You'd be manna from heaven up there," Frankie went on, and cast an eye at Lace. "Can you take a meeting with me so we can talk details?"

"Right now?"

"If you can," Frankie said.

"I'm on my way to take Lace to the airport," he said.

Lace touched his hand, and her eyes were full of sympathy. "Let me see if Melody can reschedule my meeting until tomorrow so I can be here for you."

Ah, damn, she was feeling sorry for him. He gritted his teeth. He hated to let her go. All he'd have to do was ask her to blow off that meeting and she'd do it in a heartbeat.

For him.

"You have the gardening class to teach tonight."

"I'll call and cancel the class." She whipped out her phone, turned it on. "I'm staying here."

That was a biggie. Realizing she was willing to put her job in jeopardy to stay here and bolster him while his career was falling apart. He couldn't allow her to do that. She was starting to care about him too much. Hell, he was starting to care about her too much, and right now, he couldn't make her any promises. Not with everything up in the air.

He heard his old high school coach, Cab Martinez, holler inside his head, *Are you in it to win it?*

All his life, the answer had been yes, but when it came to Lace, he no longer saw her as something to win. There were consequences here. If he took things to the next level, made love to her, and it turned out to be something more than great sex, and then he couldn't deliver on a long-term commitment, he could hurt her badly, and he'd rather break his leg ten times over than do that.

The only option he had was to play defense. *Say something to make her get on that plane.*

He put a hand to her wrist. "I'll call you a cab. Go to your meeting. Teach your class. You'll just be in the way here."

DURING THE TUESDAY evening gardening class, her gaze kept drifting to his empty seat in the front row, and several times during the lecture, she lost her train of thought because she was thinking of him.

She thought he might at least text her and ask how her meeting with the Trans-Pecos Historical Society went—they became a sponsor and even promised a small endowment once the gardens reopened, *if* the gardens reopened. But apparently he had too much else on his mind to think about her.

She didn't hear from him the next day or the day after that. Lace had to admit her feelings were bruised, even as she realized that he had probably withdrawn to lick his wounds after learning the Dallas Cowboys dropped him. There was also the issue of Abe's mysterious illness. It was a lot for anyone to deal with. Still, she kept hearing his parting words. *You'll just be in the way here.*

Maybe it was for the best, he had his problems to deal with, and she had hers. Now wasn't really the right time to start something, even if that something was only sex.

Her impulse was to leave him be, clear her own head, and stay busy helping Melody get ready for the event—time was slipping up on them fast after all, Labor Day was the upcoming Monday—but she also kept picturing him alone and hurting without anyone there to offer moral support, so despite her fear that he might not want to hear from her, she sent him a text message on Thursday night.

She texted *HIG*, trying to hit a casual note with the abbreviation for *How's it going?* There was a long lapse. She gnawed her bottom lip. Had she made a gaffe? Just as she started to obsess about whether she should have texted him or not, her phone pinged that she had a message.

Lace?

Her heart gave a ridiculous hop of joy. *Yes.*

Hey.

Now what? Before she could compose a carefully worded reply, Pierce sent another text. *So glad you texted. I was thinking of u.*

She caught her breath and typed, *How's yer dad?*

Better.

Diagnosis?

Not yet.

Okay. They'd covered his father's condition. Where did she go from here and why was she feeling so preposterously excited? *R u ok?*

Hanging in there. Thks 4 asking.

Will u b home for gala?

I'd never let you down, but Melody's got me hopping with events all weekend long.

Me too.

So I guess we won't see each other until Labor Day.

Her mouth went dry. How did she answer that? Her fingers trembled as she punched in, *See u Monday.*

Pick u up @ 6 for dinner at the vineyard.

She ached to keep the conversation going, but was afraid she'd make a misstep. How to sign off? She wanted to strike the right balance between cool and anticipation. *Can't wait.*

Lace held her breath, waited for his response, and when it wasn't immediately forthcoming, she started fretting. Had she come across as too eager? Ack!

Seeing u again is the only thing keeping me sane.

Clutching the phone tightly in her hand, she did a little happy dance. *Nite.*

I'll dream of u.

Lace smiled and turned off her phone, so very happy she'd had the courage to make the first move.

Chapter 14

Stamens: the male parts of a flower.

IN spite of all the sexy fantasies dancing in her head when Pierce came to pick her up on Labor Day for the final event of the weekend, the fund-raiser dinner at Mon Amour Vineyard, she was completely unprepared for the overwhelming sight of him in a tuxedo. He'd gotten a haircut, and late afternoon sunlight turned his hair honey gold. The clean, smooth lines of the midnight black tux were in sharp contrast to his rugged good looks. Lava rocks on velvet. The man was craggy luxury.

It was all she could do not to rub both eyes with her fists to make sure she wasn't dreaming, and here she'd believed there was nothing sexier than Pierce in Wranglers and cowboy boots. Learned something new every day.

He had his hands clasped behind his back and he flashed his straight white teeth at her. His gaze honed in on her with pinpoint precision. Uh-oh. Drop her in boiling oil and she wouldn't burn as much as she did from the sizzling heat of his gaze.

She felt like taffy, pulled in so many directions, and the running commentary through her brain wasn't helping matters. *I want him. But am I going to get my heart broken? But how could this be wrong if he makes me feel so good. Wine makes you feel good until you have too much, puke your guts up, and wake up with a raging migraine. So a little taste isn't a bad thing, then. Just don't overdo. A sip. Half a glass at most?*

"What do you have behind your back?" she asked.

"I brought you a little gift."

A gift? For her? A sweet, fizzy sensation, as if she breathed in champagne bubbles, washed over her. "That wasn't necessary."

He took his hands from behind his back. She was expecting flowers. Who wouldn't expect flowers from a dreamboat guy in a tuxedo? But it wasn't flowers, at least not exactly. In his hands he held something that looked like a giant chestnut with a thick squamous stalk in the center, and it was roughly the size of a toddler. The image of this dapper man putting on the Ritz holding the gigantic tuber of *Amorphophallus titanium* was a picture Lace would never forget.

"Omigosh." She put a hand to her mouth. "This is absolutely amazing." She fisted her hands, shivered, did a little dance, and then moved to wrap her arms around the tuber, trying to keep it away from her dress, but the thing did weigh twenty-five pounds.

He held on to it. "Where do you want it? I'll carry it there for you."

She glanced around her living room, which was jam-packed with plants she'd brought home from the botanical gardens. "Could you carry it out back to the greenhouse for me?" she asked. "But I'll need to try and make room for it. I'm maxed out on space since the gardens closed."

"Tell you what," he said. "We're running a little late. How about we just find a handy place to stow Lulu for now, and after the event, I'll take her to the greenhouse for you."

Lace grinned. "Lulu?"

He shrugged. "She comes with a name. Who knew?"

"Lulu," Lace said dreamily, and stroked the tuber as she beckoned for Pierce to follow her into a kitchen strewn with planting tubs, grow lights, seed packets, potting soil, trowels, and other tools of her trade.

"How do you cook in here?"

"I'm not much of a cook."

"Where do you eat?"

She nodded to the only spot at the kitchen table not loaded down with some kind of plant product.

"What if you have guests?" he asked.

"It hasn't come up."

He looked like he didn't believe her. "Not ever?"

"I've only lived here since April." She guided him toward the deep stainless steel sink. "Put Lulu in here."

The tuber wouldn't fit in the sink. Pierce arched his eyebrows. "Next?"

"Okay, just put her on the one empty spot on the table."

Pierce got Lulu settled and washed up at the sink while Lace pushed her glasses up on her nose and studied the tuber intently. "She's magnificent."

"So you like her?"

"I *love* her. In fact, I think it might be the most perfect gift anyone has ever given me. How did you know I've always wanted *Amorphophallus titanium*?"

"You told me once."

Lace scratched her forehead. "I did? When?"

"You were about eight years old. You showed me and Jay a picture of the corpse plant and spoke glowingly of its infamous stink."

"How is it that you remember that when I don't?"

He lowered his eyelids, gave her a sultry look. "I remember a lot of things about you, Lace," he said in a voice so low and seductive that her toes curled inside the high-heeled shoes she did not want to wear. "I remember when you were a kid and you used to keep little orange clay pots of plants in your bedroom window."

"Lima beans," she said. "They were the first things I ever grew. My grandmother Rose bought me this miniature seed kit when I was five. I can still remember that magical feeling I got when I saw the first sprout and watched it grow to produce beans. When I saw the first bean, it felt like Christmas morning. Except as it turns out, I hated lima beans."

"The Christmas morning equivalent of a stocking full of coal?" He chuckled.

She made a "yuck" face. "In spite of the lima beans, the allure of planting seeds and watching them grow had taken root inside me."

"Gardening became the love of your life."

So far. Unnerved, she moved back to the table to run her fingers over Lulu. "Where did you get her? It's not like you can run into your local nursery and pick one up."

"Let's just say that being a star quarterback has its advantages and Frankie knows a lot of people with pull in San Antonio and most of them owe her favors."

"I'm not surprised about that. Your agent is very beautiful," she said.

"She is." His eyes twinkled.

"It must be very distracting having such a beautiful agent. I imagine that can blur the lines." *Shut up! Stop talking.*

"What?" Pierce's grin widened. "Did you think Frankie and I—"

Lace made a sputtering noise. "Na . . . no, of course not."

"You did! You thought Frankie and I were lovers."

"No I didn't," she denied.

"You're jealous."

"I am not!"

"That's why you got all weird at the hospital."

"It didn't get all weird."

"Whatever you say."

"Okay," she admitted. "Maybe I was a little jealous."

"Lace," he said. "You have nothing to be jealous of. You're the whole package: beauty, brains, wit."

She gulped and smoothed her dress even though it wasn't wrinkled. No one had ever sweet-talked her this way. While she craved it, she was simultaneously terrified of it because it made her only crave more. "Let's get this thing over with."

"Is being with me such torture?" he asked, lowering his eyelids to half-mast, looking all bad-boy sultry.

Um, yeah, the best kind of torture. Problem was a girl could get seriously addicted to his brand of tender torment, and where would that leave her if the supply dried up?

Just like any addict, of course, hooked, hung up, and hopeless.

THE SETTING OF Mon Amour Vineyard was picture perfect. Cousin Melody had outdone herself, but the extravagance only made Lace fret about how much of the cost of putting on the event hadn't been picked up by sponsors. Whenever she asked about the financial situation, Melody would wave a hand and say, "You have to spend money to make money. We'll discuss all that after it's over."

Tables and chairs had been set out across the slope of lush green grass achieved through constant watering. Behind the expanse of lawn, the vineyards rolled in a friendly wave of fruit, following the hilly slope that led up to mountains. Twinkle lights draped loosely from the pergola over the dance floor. Men wore suits and tuxedos; women were in cocktail dresses and evening gowns. The owner of a car dealership in Alpine had arranged to have a makeshift stage erected, and a five-piece orchestra played chamber music.

And Lace was on the arm of the hottest quarterback in the NFL.

It was something straight out of a movie where the nerdy girl in high school gets revenge on those who treated her shabbily by ending up with the high school quarterback.

How many times had she imagined such a scene? Briefly, she closed her eyes and allowed herself to savor the beautiful, fragile moment. How many times did a schoolgirl fantasy come true?

And as much as she'd kicked up a fuss about the dress, she had to admit it looked gorgeous on her. As soon as they were spotted, handlers took hold of Pierce and whisked him away, leaving Lace alone feeling foolish and out of place, a swift kick of reality. She might be on the arm of the quarterback, but she'd never be in his league.

"Wait!" Pierce said, shook off the handlers, pivoted,

and strode back to her. He leaned down to plant a big kiss on her lips right in front of everyone. Cameras and cell phones snapped pictures. He was not hiding the fact that he was with her.

"Find out where we're sitting," he whispered. "I'll come find you when the dog-and-pony show is over."

Her heart gave a crazy pitter-pat and she placed her palms over her chest. Easy. Calm down. Good advice, but she couldn't help tilting her head to watch him walk away. The man was pure sex on two legs.

Immediately, Melody, Natalie, and Zoey grabbed her by the elbow and pulled her off to the side to grill her about her relationship with Pierce. She tried to play it cool but she didn't know if she pulled it off or not. She didn't want people to start defining their relationship before they had. She kept searching the crowd for Pierce, spotted him glad-handing sponsors. Women were all over him like honeybees to clover.

Her joy evaporated. *Don't be jealous. He came with you. He kissed you in front of everyone.* Lace smiled, fingered her lips.

"You're looking mighty smug," Zoey said. "Have you two done it yet?"

"Zoey!" Natalie chided as she rested her head on Dade's shoulder. He mussed her hair and drew her closer, nuzzled her ear.

"Oh, you're one to talk." Zoey snorted. "You and Dade have barely gotten out of bed all summer."

"You're just jealous." Natalie patted Dade's flat stomach.

"Hells to the yeah! Where's my man?" Zoey bemoaned. "I want *my* Prince Charming."

Dade murmured something to Natalie and cupped her fanny in his palm. Natalie giggled, and Dade guided her off toward the winery.

"Ten bucks says they're going off to do it right now," Zoey said, moving in time to the music, which had shifted from the elegant classical music to the haunting "You're Beautiful."

"No way. I'm not losing ten dollars," Melody said.

Lace couldn't stop herself from searching the crowd for a glimpse of Pierce.

"Seriously, where is my guy?" Zoey whined. "Natalie's got Dade, Lace has got Pierce. Monumental score, I might add." Zoey raised a palm to Lace. "High five on that one, cuz."

"Pierce isn't mine," Lace said, not wanting to jinx what was developing between them. If she dared to want it too much, it could evaporate under the strength of so much desire.

"That kiss he just planted on your lips says differently."

"I'm just his escort for this event."

Zoey folded her arms. "I'm not buying it. The dude is your high school crush and you lassoed him! Be proud. Puff out your chest and strut!"

"I didn't lasso him, Zoey."

"But you could. He's ripe for the plucking."

"Yes, and see all those women ready to pluck him?" Lace nodded to where a couple of female reporters were hanging on Pierce. Jealousy delivered a swift kick to her abdomen. "Who wants to contend with that?"

"If you let Pierce Hollister slip through your fingers, Lace Bettingfield, you're not half as smart as I thought you were," Zoey scolded. "He's within grabbing distance. Grab him!"

"Zoey, life isn't like some fairy tale. Where you gaze into a guy's eyes and it's bam! bap! a lightning strike."

"Tell that to Natalie and Dade." Her cousin waved in the direction her sister had departed.

Melody threw Lace a look of sympathy and took Zoey by the arm. "Come with me, cousin, there's someone I want to introduce you to."

"A cute guy?"

"We'll see about that." Melody guided her away, leaving Lace feeling like she'd just gotten caught in a tornado's updraft.

Before Lace had a chance to sneak off for a little peace and quiet, Carol Ann swooped down on her. "You weren't thinking of running off, were you?"

"Actually—"

"Because as the director of the botanical gardens it's your duty to come meet the sponsors and distinguished guests."

"Everyone is here to see Pierce. No one cares about me."

"Honey, you're the heart and soul of this fund-raiser. Pierce is the flash, but you're the substance."

"No, that would be Melody. She deserves all the credit for this," Lace said.

Carol Ann pinched Lace's cheek. "Stop underestimating yourself. Without you, there are no gardens. Now come on."

Mignon, looking impeccable in a vampishly cardinal, sequined dress, pressed a glass of red wine into Lace's hand. "Fortification."

For the next half hour she smiled, sipped wine, shook hands, made small talk, and watched Pierce do the same on the opposite side of the pavilion. He must have been telling football stories because he kept making throwing motions with his right arm. Her heart twisted. It must be so hard for him to put on a happy face knowing that he'd gotten dropped. So far, the Cowboys hadn't announced it yet, so for now, no one here knew his secret except her.

Once, their eyes met through a break in the crowd of people. He smiled and winked and she couldn't help feeling desperately special. Dangerous. It was a dangerous feeling and yet she couldn't stop it from lodging deep inside the center of her chest.

At one point, Melody returned.

"Get Zoey squared away?" Lace asked.

"I found her someone to flirt with."

Lace shifted her weight. "Did we get enough sponsors to cover the cost of this shindig?"

Melody grimaced. "Not quite."

"How much are the expenses going to cut into the take?"

Her cousin blew out her breath. "We'll probably get to keep six hundred of the thousand dollars a plate."

"So we're still not going to have enough to reopen the nonessential city services."

"All is not lost. I've been talking to people about endowments after the Trans-Pecos Historical Society asked about granting one to the gardens. I'm also looking into state grants. We'll get there."

Lace met her cousin's eyes. "But when?"

"I'm doing the best I can."

"I know you are. I deeply appreciate all you're doing for me and Cupid."

Melody tucked a blond curl around her ear. "Hey, it's my hometown too."

"Since when have you claimed Cupid? You were always so anxious to get out of here."

Melody gazed off in the distance, a contemplative expression on her face. "When you turned down that job offer from the Smithsonian." She shook her head. "I was so shocked. But lately . . ."

"What?" Lace prodded when her cousin trailed off. She shook her head. "I don't know. Sometimes when you get your dream, you realize it's not what you thought it would be."

The skin on the nape of her neck wriggled. She looked for Pierce, found him posing for more photographs. A jittery sensation lodged in the pit of her stomach. "Is something going on, Melody?"

"No, no." Melody forced a smile. "I guess being back home has made me sentimental. Look, there's Guy Grover." Guy ran the biggest car dealership in Cupid. "Let's go talk to him about giving an endowment."

After the welcome reception, the guests took their seats in the rows of folding chairs set up before the stage and the ceremony began. There were speeches and toasts. Melody got up to thank the sponsors for their support. Pierce was honored in a big way. There were jokes and gridiron stories. And when he took the podium to talk about the importance of the botanical gardens, the library, and the after-school programs, the crowd hung on his every word. The man could command an audience. No question about it.

When dinner service began as the sun was setting over the winery, and the guests wandered from the row seating to the outdoor tables, they finally made their way back to each other.

"Did you find our table?" Pierce asked.

"I didn't get a chance. I was too busy listening to your speech. You were mesmerizing."

He blushed at her compliment. "I've had a lot of practice."

"Don't minimize your natural charisma. People are drawn to you."

He shrugged that off, took her hand, and led her on a weaving path around the tables, looking for their names on the placards. He stopped at a table positioned at the far edge of the expansive lawn. "Here's your name."

"Good, we're out of the way." Lace sat down.

Pierce plunked down beside her.

"That's not your name," she said, pointing at the placard.

"Marvin Yates," he read. "I'm sure Marvin won't mind."

"Pierce!" the mayor called out, and came over to clamp Pierce on his shoulder. "C'mon, son, you're sitting up front at our table."

"Let's go," Pierce said, reaching for Lace's hand.

The mayor turned to her. "I'm sorry, Lace, but there's not an extra space at our table for you. I'm sure you understand. Sponsors want to sit with the man of the hour."

"If there's no room for Lace," Pierce said, "then there's no room for me."

The mayor looked flabbergasted, splayed a hand to the back of his head, and looked from Pierce to a table up front where his wife was waving at him. "I . . . um . . . well."

"It's okay, Pierce." Lace motioned for him to go. "I'll be fine right here with Marvin."

Pierce refused to let go of her hand. "It's a package deal, Mayor. If you want me, Lace comes along too."

The mayor looked flustered. "Well, you see, some of the movers and shakers of Cupid are at our table and—"

"Lace moves and shakes with the best of them, don't you, sweetheart." Pierce lifted her hand to his lips, kissed her knuckles. A wave of tingly shivers swept up her spine. "So we *will* find a place for her at our table."

Lace's face flushed. It was really sweet and kind of him to insist that she be seated at his table.

"But most of all"—Pierce slung his arm around her shoulder and drew her closer—"Lace is my date."

"Yes, of course, I'm so sorry for the mix-up," the mayor sputtered. "This way."

The service staff did their thing, shifting everyone at the table and bringing in an extra chair to sandwich Lace in between Pierce and a socialite from Houston who'd recently moved to Cupid. She looked put out to be sitting next to Lace and not the football star she'd expected to sit beside.

It was a tight squeeze and Lace had to keep her arms tucked at her side while eating to keep from bumping elbows with the socialite, who was left-handed. When the filet mignon was served, Lace tried to cut her meat without spreading her arms and ended up knocking her knife on the ground.

"Clumsy," the woman muttered.

"I'm so sorry," she apologized.

"It's not your fault, dear," the woman said, fumbling for a forced smile. "It's difficult to navigate elegant social functions when you're not accustomed to them."

Lace's stomach churned and she felt as if she were four inches tall. It wasn't that she didn't know proper etiquette. Carol Ann was her aunt, after all. No way you could get away with not knowing all that malarkey when you were kin to Carol Ann. Okay, she might be a little clumsy, yes, but that was because her mind was usually on plants and not something silly like which fork did you use to stab a piece of meat. Tonight, however, she was nervous. She wasn't much for crowds or fancy dinners or eating in a seven-hundred-dollar dress with her fantasy man in a tuxedo.

More than anything in the world, she wanted to flee, but she refused to give the socialite the satisfaction of running her off. She raised her chin, met the woman's gaze. Normally, she didn't toot the family tree horn, but if there was ever a time to do it, the time was now. "Do you know that I'm the great-granddaughter of Millie Greenwood Fant? The woman who started the whole letters to Cupid legend that spurred tourism to our town?"

"Um, no, I wasn't aware of that." The woman said it so coolly that butter wouldn't have melted in her mouth. "But now that you mention it, I see the resemblance. Millie was a silver miner's daughter, isn't that right? A common girl who somehow managed to bewitch the richest man in town? Isn't that how the story goes?"

The band started playing again and a few couples drifted out onto the dance floor. Pierce set his napkin over his plate and stood up. "If you'll excuse us, I'm going to dance with my date."

Lace startled. While she was uncomfortable sitting there with this crowd, she was about as graceful on the dance floor as a three-legged step stool. Dancing wasn't the lesser of two evils.

He held out his hand.

She looked around the table. Everyone was staring at her. Left without a choice, she put her hand in his and got to her feet. "Way to put a woman on the spot," she mumbled.

He led her toward the pavilion.

She resisted, literally digging her heels into the earth. "Do we really have to do this?"

"You don't know how to accept rescue gracefully."

"I'm not accustomed to having to be rescued."

"That's a shame."

"What? That I'm independent? Don't tell me you like those clinging women who don't know how to do anything for themselves."

"It's a shame you don't have any rescue fantasies."

"Why would I want to be rescued?"

"Not in real life, but in your fantasies. I have rescue fantasies."

"Sexual rescue fantasies?" she dared, her interest piqued.

"Are there any other kind?"

"So what's your rescue fantasy?"

"I'm not telling until you share yours with me."

"I don't have rescue fantasies," she insisted.

"Ah, and here I thought I was fulfilling your fantasy by headlining this fund-raiser so you could keep the botanical gardens open."

Touché. She opened her mouth to protest, but she couldn't think of anything to say.

"It's a good thing everyone isn't like you," he said.

"In what way?" she bristled.

"If everyone were like you, knights in shining armor would be put out of business."

Lace hooted. "You? A knight in shining armor? You've been listening to your own press."

"And you're trying to start an argument just so you don't have to dance."

"That transparent?"

"Like a gossamer veil, baby."

"Gossamer? Where you'd hear that word?"

"Mignon. She said this time of year the gossamer morning mist makes the grapes sweeter."

"You had to ask her what 'gossamer' meant, didn't you?"

"Yep." He grinned unabashedly. "I'm a cowboy at heart, darling. We're not known to have an expansive vocabulary. C'mon now." He tugged her toward the dance floor where people were two-stepping to "Little Love Letters."

She pulled away, shook her head vigorously, and held up both palms. "Seriously Pierce, I do not dance."

"Can't or don't?"

"Which answer would get me out of this?"

"Neither." He manacled her wrist between a thumb and index finger strong as a steel trap.

Every eye in the place was on them. Lace squirmed. She hated being the center of attention.

"You're courting investors and sponsors. Let's show them what you're made of and give them a reason to put their money in you."

"The garden is my résumé. I don't need to add dancing."

"Shows what you know about marketing."

"And you're Mr. Marketing Guru?"

"Sweetheart, I'm in professional football. It's all about marketing and branding, and the more ways you can slant perception in your favor, the better. They'll be buzzing with 'She's an ace botanist *and* she can dance.' Why do you think *Dancing with the Stars* is so popular?"

"Because there is dancing with *stars*."

"Exactly."

"You're the star, not me. It doesn't matter who your dance partner is."

"PhD in botany. Magna cum laude from Texas A&M, offered a job at the Smithsonian. That's a star any way you slice it."

"Who told you all that? Jay?"

"Nope." His grin widened. "I've been asking around about you."

Her chest tightened and her pulse quickened. Why was she feeling so panicky? It was just one dance. Granted, she wasn't a great dancer, but she did know how. Her mother insisted that both her children learn ballroom dancing to be more "well-rounded."

He didn't give her a chance to offer further protest. Pierce placed a hand to her back and ushered her out onto the dance floor. The band was playing a cover of the Eli Young Band's "Mystery in the Making."

Well, if she had to dance, a slow song was the one to dance to. Couples moved closer together. A canopy of stars shone down, mingled with the glow of the twinkle lights, creating an intimate, romantic atmosphere.

Pierce leaned into her, pressed his mouth against her ear. "Is it really that bad?"

Flustered, she drew back as far as she could with his arm wrapped around her waist. The heat of his palm burned through the thin material of her dress. "Is what that bad?"

"Dancing with me."

On the contrary, dancing with him was magnificent. Which was precisely the problem. She didn't know where this thing was going, especially after he'd been cut from the Dallas Cowboys. Before that, she'd assumed it was going to be just a fling, but now? Dammit, now she had serious hope that this could grow into something meaningful, and hope was a scary thing. She'd spent years toughening her hide, getting strong so she could resist men like Pierce, and now here she was feeling as off balance as a top-heavy plant desperately in need of pruning, because she no longer wanted to resist. She wanted to dive headfirst into this thing and damn the consequences.

"You're not a bad dancer," she said grudgingly.

"Not bad? You sure know how to wound a guy. I was actually approached to be on *Dancing with the Stars*."

"Seems right up your alley. Why didn't you do it?"

"Actually, I had accepted and then—"

"Your leg got broken."

"On television, in front of a hundred million viewers. It's what happens when you're on the bottom of a dog pile."

"I'm having a hard time imagining you on the bottom of anything. You've always been top dog." It dawned on her how humiliating that must have been for him as well as horribly painful. A lot more humiliating than having the entire high school laughing at you because they'd found out you were crushing on a guy you had no chance with.

"Mmm," he said, a sultry light sparking in his eyes.

"I concede your point, but there are times when being on the bottom is definitely worthwhile."

"In the right kind of dog pile?" she asked, impishly lobbing the sexual innuendo back into his corner.

He chuckled. "Love that razor wit, Lace Bettingfield, but believe it or not, I'm not that enthusiastic about having more than one woman at a time in my bed."

"Afraid of being shown up?" she deviled.

"No." His arm tightened around her possessively. "Too selfish. I don't like to share."

She didn't know what to say to that, so she didn't say anything at all. He was surprisingly light on his feet considering his size and the leg injury. She also noticed he'd been subtly drawing her closer until there was no longer a gap between their bodies. His cummerbund was pressed against her belly, his chest cozied up against her breasts, and the zipper of his slacks bulged against her thigh. There was no denying what was on his mind.

Sex.

If she was being honest it was on her mind too. Had been since that night in the hotel in San Antonio.

As if reading her thoughts, he asked huskily, "How long before we can get out of here?"

"Hey, I'm ready right now," she said. "But you're the one who knows how to navigate this hoity-toity stuff. You tell me. We certainly don't want to disappoint the folks who shelled out a thousand dollars to hang out with you, and Melody says we're short funds so I also have to curry more donations."

"I guess that means we have to stay."

"Yes." She sighed, resigned. "But can we go sit back down?"

"In a minute," he said. "After this."

"After wha—"

His mouth crushed hers. Right there on the dance floor for everyone to see. There was no denying this now. They had over five hundred witnesses. A happy flame lit inside her. She'd been aching to kiss him all evening. She relaxed into the kiss, sank against him.

He cupped her face in his hands, deepening the kiss, his tongue slipping between the teeth she so readily parted.

The entire audience burst into applause and she realized they were clapping for her and Pierce. In that glorious moment, she was the belle of the ball.

Chapter 15

*Dioecious: male and female reproductive
structures on separate plants.*

FINALLY, finally, the endless evening came to an end and they were back in his truck headed for Lace's house. Pierce gripped the steering wheel tightly in an attempt to keep his hands from shaking. Excitement—as visceral as what he'd felt the day he'd stood in the stadium before the Super Bowl and heard the roar of the crowd chanting his name—filled his veins with a potent mixture of adrenaline and testosterone. He wanted her so badly he was practically panting.

He peeked over at Lace.

She was full-on staring at him, her blue eyes smoldering. Blue eyes were supposed to be cool, right, ice and all those other clichés? But Lace's blue eyes were hot as a gas flame.

He ran the tip of his tongue over his lips; the flavor of her—like champagne and strawberries—lingered on his taste buds. He couldn't wait to taste her again.

Her small foot was tapping restlessly, those sensational

high heels pattering against the floor mat of his King Ranch. She was as amped up as he was, her hands balled into tight fists against her thighs. His heart knocked hard against his chest and his throat felt scratchy, tight, and dry. He reached up with one hand, yanked at his bow tie.

God, why was it taking so long to drive the five miles to her house? It felt like five million. He'd waited so long for her, and now it was about to happen, he was terrified he'd ruin everything by coming too soon. He hadn't had a problem with premature ejaculation since high school, but then again, he'd never been with Lace.

He ran a hand over his mouth, goosed the truck a few miles over the speed limit. He couldn't remember the last time he'd felt so nervous, not when it came to being with a woman. He'd never had to work for female attention and Lace had really put him through his paces, to the point where he was terrified that she was going to change her mind at the last minute and turn him out. She was so different from any women he'd ever been with—levelheaded, self-contained, even-keeled, and smart as a whip. No drama. No overblown expectations. Independent.

It was her independence that challenged him the most. He was so accustomed to women wanting, needing, demanding things from him, that he didn't know what to do with someone who didn't.

"Slow down," she said. "Kids live in this neighborhood."

"Sorry." He had to force himself to let off the accelerator.

"Your heart is pounding ninety miles an hour."

He jerked his head to meet her hot gaze again. "How do you know that?"

"The pulse at your temple is throbbing."

He put a hand to his left temple. That wasn't the only thing that was throbbing. "And yours isn't?"

She reached over, took his left hand off the wheel, and placed it over her heart. He could feel the *boom-boom-boom* tempo that matched his own crazy rhythm. Touching her only made it worse. Her heartbeat quickened in time with his.

"Much as I hate to take my hand back, I need to concentrate on getting us there," he said, reluctantly returning his hand to the wheel.

She gave a little laugh.

"What's so funny?"

"I'm surprised."

"About what?"

"That you're so excited."

"Dammit, Lace, don't you have any idea what you do to me?"

"More so than any other woman?"

"Yes," he said through gritted teeth. It was true. No woman had ever inflamed him the way she did. "You're special."

She crossed her legs. "Sure I am."

"I'm serious."

"It's only because I made you wait for it."

Was it? He'd never had to wait before and he had to admit the anticipation pushed him to the limit of his endurance. "That's not the only reason," he insisted doggedly.

"No?" She folded her arms over her chest. "In what way am I special?"

"You're unique. For one thing, you're a woman who likes spiders and snakes," he said.

She laughed and shifted in her seat. The hem of her dress inched up, exposing a sweet expanse of dynamite thighs. He couldn't wait until those lush thighs were wrapped around him. Pierce squirmed, bit down on his bottom lip, trying to hold back the shudder that passed through him at that erotic image.

"If I had known that turned you on," she murmured. "I would have put bugs down your pants back in high school."

He had ants in his pants right now and he couldn't wait to peel them off. Right after he stripped her panties off her. Up ahead lay her house. His breath was slipping past his teeth in quick, shallow pants. In her driveway, he jammed on the brakes.

"Whoa there, big boy."

"Sorry," he apologized, killing the engine. *Slow down. Take a deep breath. You've got all night.*

She reached across the seat and touched his thigh.

Hell's bells, he almost creamed his pants.

"We're going to have to do something about that hair-trigger response," she whispered.

"Wh-what do you mean?" His lungs were pumping up and down but he couldn't seem to draw in any air.

Mysterious as a sphinx, she unbuckled her seat belt, opened the door, and moved to get out.

"Lace, what did you mean?"

She tossed a sly smile over her shoulder. "Why don't you come inside and find out?"

MAYBE IT WASN'T nice to tease, but Lace couldn't resist, and while it might not be nice, teasing was a lot of fun. She led the way through to her back door.

He followed, hurrying up the path to catch her as she unlocked the door. He came up behind her, wrapped his arms around her waist. She paused a second, closed her eyes, took a deep breath. *Enjoy the moment.*

Fumbling around, she flicked on the light and they tumbled over the threshold into the kitchen. He turned her around to face him, planted a long, slow, lingering kiss on her lips. Her pulse was going crazy, shooting hot blood surfing her veins. She wove her arms around his neck, entangled her fingers in his hair, and pulled his head down. He bent her backward as his tongue explored her, sent her arousal off the charts.

When they finally came up for air, they were both panting and trembling.

Pierce blinked, released her, and stepped back. "Before we get carried away," he said. "I promised to take Lulu out to the greenhouse for you."

"We can do that later." She reached for him.

He danced out of her grasp. "I'm a man of my word. I'll move the tuber and then there's nothing getting in the way of us."

Us.

As in the two of them. Lace and Pierce. Pierce and Lace. How many times had she doodled that in her notebook? Couple of hundred? At least. It sounded so good. Too good. It made her start spinning happily-ever-after fantasies again. *Take it one step at a time. Right here. Right now. Enjoy this experience and don't think past that.*

"All right," she said. "Let's dispense with Lulu so we can get down to it."

He took off his jacket, tossed it over the back of a kitchen chair, and then turned to hoist the tuber off the table. Tucked it into the crook of his arm as if it was the world's heaviest football. "Lead the way."

Stomach aflutter, she headed toward the greenhouse, barely noticing that the light was still on in the garage apartment where Shasta lived. All her focus was on the man behind her. She could feel the heat radiating off his body.

Various types of grow lights—each tailored to suit the plants and growth stages they serviced—were on an automatic timer, so she didn't bother flipping the main switch for the overhead fluorescent lighting. Different parts of the greenhouse were cast in different colors. Metal halide illuminated blue and promoted leaf creation along with keeping the plants compact. Red LED lights encouraged plants to grow tall. High-pressure sodium lights produced a yellowish glow that stimulated hormone production to increase budding and flowering in the reproductive phase.

Pierce let out an audible breath. "It smells like fertile earth in here."

"You're more of a farmer than you give yourself credit for," Lace said, and shut the greenhouse door behind him.

They stood there in the quiet hum and glow of the lights, the rich aroma of plant sex and potting soil in the air. Pierce cleared his throat. "Uh, Lulu?"

Lace blinked, snapped out of the bewitching spell he'd woven over her, and moved toward the long wooden worktable. "Oh yes. Just put her here."

He sat down the heavy tuber, and then dusted his hands together, the blue shine of the metal halide lights casting his face in dusky shadows.

Not a word passed between them. They stared into each other's eyes and simultaneously moved together. His hands cupped her face, her arms twined around her waist, and their lips merged in hungry desperation.

His fingers caressed twin spots behind her ears,

spots that made her wriggle and squirm. She had no idea the backs of her ears were so sensitive to touch. Her knees dissolved into pudding. At this point if he asked her to be his sex slave and live in his closet, ready for his beck and call, she'd do it. He tore his lips from hers, moved down to catch her chin between his teeth.

Restlessly, she tossed back her head and he planted hot, sucking kisses down the length of her neck. His hands tightened around her as if he planned on never letting her go. Closet sex slave was looking more and more like a viable career option.

Goose bumps prickled up and down the length of her body; her desire was an inferno, his mouth the accelerant. Her body remembered what that mouth had done to her that night in the San Antonio hotel room and her nipples beaded, strained against her bra. She was already aching for him to tease her nipples between those wicked lips but then she remembered her vow to solve his problem of a hair-trigger response. This moment was special. She had waited twelve years for this—the moment when the man whom she'd crushed on was finally crushing on her—and she was determined to make it last all through the night.

Resolutely, she wrenched away, left them both breathing hard.

"What?" he gasped.

"I have a promise to keep," she said, kicking off her high heels and sinking down onto her knees on the hard-packed earth.

PIERCE COULD NOT take his eyes off her. His heart hammered so hard that he could hear it pounding inside his brain. Was he having a heart attack? A stroke? He certainly hoped not, because he'd been anticipating this moment from the minute he'd stepped onto the elevator with Lace at Cupid General Hospital.

She tilted her head back. He looked down into her eyes and every rational thought evaporated. Lace smiled up at him with a seductive, heavily lidded gaze and he knew he was in for the ride of his life. After this, nothing would ever be the same. He caught his breath and the world hung suspended, dark and mysterious, filled with a sweet magic he'd never before encountered.

The musky, loam scent of verdant soil intoxicated him. The aroma swelling and surging in the muggy greenhouse warmth like the cheering of fans in the stands, a heady rush of exuberant noise.

He blasted her with the easy smile that had charmed many a woman into his bed. Her answering grin was just as lethal, a stab straight through into his soul.

Man alive, what a woman. Sexy. Hot. Complicated. Exciting.

He loved how she blew his mind. Time after time. He thought he'd pretty well seen it all. He'd met presidents and royalty, dined in five-star restaurants, and traveled the globe. The extraordinary had become ordinary. He'd grown inured to wealth and success and the trappings that came with it. He'd begun to think there were no surprises left and then he'd come home to Cupid and found the most unexpected treasure of them all in the place he least expected.

Home.

When he looked at her he saw all the things he had not realized he needed. A woman who called him on his bullshit and refused to fall for the charming exterior he'd perfected. A woman who saw past the polished image to the regular guy he was beneath all the hoopla. A woman who stirred in him a sense of joy and wonder about the world that he hadn't felt since Abe had turned his love of football into a goal Pierce must achieve for him.

How she energized his world when he hadn't even known it was dull.

And that expression on her face! Full of wise feminine knowing. As if she held the key to the secrets of the universe.

"Brace yourself," she said.

"What?"

"Against the table," she directed.

He did as she requested, backing his butt up to the table, bracing his hands on either side of him. The table was solid, sturdy. Good thing because he wasn't sure he could rely on his knees to hold him up. Not when her sly hands were already plucking at the zipper of his tuxedo trousers.

She made quick work of shucking his pants and underwear to his ankles and then . . .

Flying f—

He couldn't even finish the thought, he was so
aroused and impressed and crazy for her. It was completely selfish of him to go first, but she seemed to be
taking explicit glee in making him squirm. Once he
had this raging hard-on dispensed with he vowed to
take his time pleasing her.

Pierce hadn't known it was possible to get this hard,
but when her soft mouth touched his skin, his shaft
turned to marble. Air leaked from his lungs in a long
hiss.

When her mouth engulfed him, he came completely
undone. All thoughts flew from his brain and he knew
nothing except the feel of her velvet tongue. Unable to
believe his great good fortune, he closed his eyes. What
a lucky bastard he was. How in the hell had he gotten
so lucky? He didn't deserve this. Did not deserve her.
He opened his eyes, glanced down at her, and his pulse
stammered.

Even braced against the table, he was knocked off
balance. The smell of the greenhouse filled his nose
and his body throbbed. He wanted her out of that dress,
wanted to see her beautiful naked body. He touched her
hair, rubbed the silky dark strands between his fingers.
Such beautiful hair!

She spread her palms over the backs of his thighs

to steady them both, and when she gently kneaded his balls, Pierce's eyes rolled back in his head. She was licking him like he was a snow cone melting on a hot summer day.

He certainly could not get enough of *her*.

His muscles went both rigid and weak at the same time. She flicked her tongue over him in the most erotic way and Pierce groaned loudly.

Her mouth was that incredible.

Lace was that incredible.

Systemically, she dismantled him with her tongue, leaving him wrecked, wasted, immobile. Heat surged through him. An out-of-control wildfire. Pierce groaned again.

So good. So damn good.

Her hands seemed to be everywhere—his back, his butt, his balls. It felt as if she possessed a hundred fingers and ten tongues, all working at once, expertly pushing him to the top of a peak encounter. Climbing Mount Everest couldn't be this awe-inspiring.

His chest expanded, tightened. It was unlike anything he'd ever experienced. Blow job, hell. She was blowing all his circuits. She must have sensed he was close, because she quickened her pace.

"Yes," he hissed. "Yes, yes, yes."

Lace worked her magic, with her fingers and her tongue, leading him into uncharted territory, and she seemed to be having a damn fine time doing it. He'd been with his share of women, but none had ever made him feel this way. He was on sensory overload. Consumed. Overtaken. It felt like the best wet dream in the world.

But this wasn't a dream.

This was really happening!

She was beyond beauty. She was pure life, pure joy. He'd foolishly thought he could teach her a few things, when he was the one being seriously schooled. She pushed him past his knowledge of himself. He had never before been so physically possessed. She rocked his world.

In the haze, Pierce heard the soft buzzing of the grow lights and then realized the buzzing was coming from inside his own head. Relentlessly, Lace pushed him beyond the boundaries of his endurance. He was aching, gushing, throbbing. He threw back his head and let loose with a primal cry, pleading for release from this sweet torture, for the ecstasy he could almost touch.

Sweat poured down his face, rolled between his shoulder blades. He gritted his teeth, dug his heels into the floor, and twined his fingers through her hair. Soon. Please, please let it happen soon. If he didn't come soon, he feared his heart would explode.

He couldn't contain himself. He started thrusting. She took it with a deep-throated chuckle.

A ball of fire rolled down his nerve endings to lodge

in the dead center of his aching shaft and then he left the earth, orbited straight into outer space. He gasped, tumbled, fell jerking and trembling into the delicious darkness. Lost. He was completely lost.

She swallowed him up.

A guttural shout ripped from his throat. His vision blurred. He blinked, looked down. Finally, he saw her through the fog.

Lace was sitting at his feet looking like Snow White in that beautiful dress, smiling coyly, her lips glistening with his essence.

Pierce dropped to his knees, toppled over onto his side. He shuddered, panted for air, and tried to process what had just happened. Lace tugged his head into her lap and humming softly, stroked his hair.

In that exalted moment Pierce knew that there was no going back. He was forever changed.

Chapter 16

Simple: not divided into parts.

LACE looked over to find Pierce's eyes on hers as his breathing returned to normal. It was clear that he did not think any less of her for her boldness, and in fact, he looked quite happy. She smiled at him. She loved the weight of his head in her lap, could barely believe that he was there.

"I've got an idea," he said.

"Should I alert the media?"

"Love your wit, but the time has come." He grinned.

"Time for what?"

"To get down to serious foreplay."

"Aren't we a little late for that? I think we just zoomed past foreplay."

"It's never too late for foreplay." He sat up, shucked the pants and underwear from around his ankles, and tossed them over his shoulder. He was already half hard again. Talk about an excellent recovery record.

"What do you have in mind?" she asked, her pulse slipping fast and quick like water rushing over a falls.

He pulled her into the curve of his arm, kissed her softly while his fingers went to the zipper at the back of her dress. "You say the most provocative plant words you can think of and I'll say the most provocative football term in response."

"This is very strange foreplay."

"Ah, but can you think of a more arousing way for us to get to know each other's worlds?"

She wrinkled her nose, in spite of the tightness in her chest. He wanted to know about her world and he wanted her to know more about his. What did that mean for the future? Hope flared, but it was scary, so she strangled it.

"Really," she said, giving him an out if he wanted to take it. "That's not necessary."

"What's not necessary? Foreplay? 'Cause in my playbook it's absolutely essential."

"Getting to know each other's worlds."

"C'mon. Indulge me." He tugged the zipper on her dress, slowly inching down.

Warm air touched her bare skin. "All right," she agreed, removing his cummerbund.

"I'll go first. Naked."

"Not yet, but we're working on it." She reached up to unbutton his tuxedo shirt.

"It's my word."

"What word?"

"The football word."

"That's not a legitimate football term." She undid the second button and got a peek at that muscled chest.

"Is too." He slipped his hand up her back, his finger expertly unhooking her bra in under five seconds flat.

Impressive. Clearly, he'd had lots of practice. "What does it mean?"

"A naked play is where the quarterback runs the ball outside the belly path and he is not accompanied by a blocker."

She finished undoing the last button on his shirt. "I'm assuming that's a different belly path than this gorgeous trail of golden hair you've got tracking from your navel to your pubes."

He laughed. "You would be correct. When you run a belly path, you travel slightly backward and away from the line of scrimmage before returning to the scrimmage line in a swing pass route."

"It sounds very complicated."

"No more than plant sex. Your turn. Let's see you trump 'naked.'"

"Football has an unfair advantage, the terminology is clearly much more literal than plant science," she said, reaching for his left wrist so she could work the monogrammed cuff links from the French cuff.

"Can't do it, huh? That's what I thought. Plants are too brainy to be sexy."

"Shows what you know about plants. They are sex machines."

"So dazzle me."

"Corneus," she said.

"What does it mean?"

"Horny."

"Ah, the seduction is in the definition."

"Your turn."

"Hot pass." He untied his shoelaces, slipped off his shoes and socks.

"Dare I ask what that means?"

"It's a very quick pass to an offensive pass receiver who is running a replacement route vacated by the defensive pass receiver."

"No wonder you're so good at making hot passes." She uncuffed his other sleeve, and reached up to put the cuff links on the table.

"Now you," he said, pulling her into his lap and pressing a hot kiss to the nape of her neck.

Lace pressed her lips together and whispered, "Succulent."

"Good one. Official definition?"

"Fleshy, juicy." She slipped his shirt from his shoulders and let it fall to the ground behind him.

"Seductive in both sound and meaning. Two points for you." He kissed her lips. "You have a succulent mouth."

"Is that all you've got? Can't top 'succulent'?"

"Sweetheart, we're just getting started. Box."

"That's pretty generic and not necessarily suggestive. Is the comparison supposed to be the vagina? Because 'box' is not really an apt assessment. 'Tunnel' might be a better fit. Any tunnels in football?"

"No."

"That's too bad."

"I suppose you can do better?"

"Is 'bush' too obvious?" she asked.

"Much."

"But it qualifies, at least as innuendo, and more accurate than 'box.'"

"Hmm," he said, slipping his hand up her dress to peel off her panties. "I appreciate your bushiness. It's sexy. Too many women these days opt for the minimalist manicure. I prefer au naturel."

"I'm too busy manicuring real bushes," she said, "to go in for waxing."

"I like you just the way you are." He shifted her off his lap, inched her dress up over her thighs. "Arms up."

"I'm having déjà vu to Nordstrom's dressing room," she said as he peeled the dress over her head.

"That was fun." He flung the dress onto the table. It landed on top of Lulu. "Now where were we? Whose turn was it?"

"Yours."

"Tight end."

She lowered her lashes. "You do have one of those."

"Not so bad yourself. What else do you have?"

"Head."

"You led with that one." He grinned. "In a clear case of show don't tell."

"Are you tapped out of terms?"

"There's 'goose and go,' " he said, and squeezed her fanny. "But I'm going to leave off the 'go' part."

"With all these provocative terms is it any wonder that football players have such reputations as sex machines?" she observed.

"Are you ready to find out firsthand whether the rumors are true?"

They were both fully naked now, staring at each other in the crazy colored lighting.

"So ready," she said.

He laid her down on her back, kneed her thighs apart, and knelt between them. She stilled at the sight of his washboard abs. He was glorious. She'd never had such a well-built lover.

And what a handsome face!

Right now, he was staring at her with those stormy brown-green eyes that sent goose bumps fleeing up her arm and fresh shivers slithering down her spine.

His jaw was chiseled, his cheekbones sharp, his golden-brown hair cut in an utterly masculine but still sexy style.

The setting was her idea of perfection, plants in various stages of reproduction, emitting come-have-your-way-with-me-messages into the night air.

"Before this goes any further," she said, "we need to establish some kind of boundaries."

He stopped kissing her and looked up. "I hear you. I don't like anything going on at my back door, so if that's a concern for you then you don't have anything to worry about it. I—"

"I'm talking about emotional boundaries."

"Oh." He straightened. "I'm listening."

"I don't know where this is going."

"Where do you want it to go?"

Happily-ever-after her heart cried. "Where do *you* want it to go?"

"I asked first."

She blew out a breath. "I need to know if it's just sex. I can handle that." Hopefully! "Actually, I'm quite fine with that, but I need to know up front that's all this is so I can keep my emotions out of it."

"Can you do that?" he asked huskily.

Did that mean he wanted to keep emotions out of it? "I don't want to get hurt."

"Me either."

Did that mean she had the potential to hurt him? If so, that meant he cared. Her throat constricted. "So it's just sex."

Pierce gulped, his Adam's apple moving up and back down. "Is that what you want?"

She nodded, too terrified to say what she really wanted.

He looked . . . *hurt*.

She wanted to say, *I changed my mind, do over!* but she didn't. "Pierce?"

"I guess I'm just a little disappointed," he said. "I thought we were working on something special."

We are! "Maybe we could just take it one day at a time. See how that goes?"

"Yeah. Uh-huh. We can do that." He shrugged. "One day at a time."

Great. Now she'd killed all the sexy energy they'd built up with the word games and she suddenly felt exposed. She crossed her arms over her chest, all her earlier sexual confidence evaporating.

"I made a misstep," he said.

"No, no, not at all."

He got to his feet, reached out a hand to help her up.

"Is this it? Is it over?" she asked, a hard pressure pushed against her chest.

"No," he said, "but the mood has changed. You need tenderness. In a bed. Not here on the hard ground."

She blinked, touched by his sensitivity to her frame of mind change. He gathered up their clothes and, giggling, they tiptoed naked from the greenhouse and sprinted across the lawn. Lace was relieved to see that the light in Shasta's apartment had gone out.

"Where's your bedroom?" he asked once they were inside the house.

She took his hand and led him there. They didn't

turn on the lights because the full moon was shining through the open curtains. He fished something from the pocket of his trousers and then dropped them, along with the rest of their garments, to the floor. Square packets. Condoms. He'd come prepared.

He put a hand to her waist, and she could feel his breath on her face, but she was too afraid to meet his gaze so she stared at his chest. Too scared of the expression she might spot in his eyes, too nervous about what he might see in hers.

He said nothing. Neither did she. The digital clock on her bedside table clicked off a minute.

Do something! Kiss me! Touch me! Make love to me!

Finally, she could not stand the suspense any longer and shifted her gaze from his chest to his face. Pierce was looking at her like a man who'd just stumbled over a treasure trove. His lips locked on hers.

She wriggled, threaded her fingers through his hair.

They kissed for what seemed like forever and then finally they exhaled at the same time, breathing out each other's air.

He burned hot kisses from her throat to her breasts, his beard stubble rubbing her skin in a scandalously erotic rasp. He was smooth and accomplished, no doubt about it. He knew exactly where to linger, tease, and cajole. While his mouth had a field day with her nipples, his hand moved between her legs.

She whimpered, shivered.

"Lace," he growled low in his throat. "You taste so good."

He waltzed her toward the bed, stopped long enough to peel back the covers, and then eased her down onto the mattress. He crawled beside her, straddled her body, and began a slow slide from the tender flesh of her breasts on down to where she most wanted him to go, staggering kisses over her rib cage to the full, rounded flesh of her belly.

When he finally veered down to lick the warm, damp patch of skin between her legs, Lace came unhinged. "Oh!" she gasped. "Oh my!"

"You like that?"

"Very much."

He surprised her by reaching up to skim his fingers over her face, outlining the plane of her cheeks with the pads of his fingertips like a blind man learning Braille.

"Lace." He breathed.

She rode the flow of emotions, navigating the swell of pleasure and desire and discovery. His warmth enveloped her and she experienced a sense of safety with him that she'd rarely felt before. He lifted her to a place she'd never known existed.

She moaned and pushed her pelvis against his hand, arching her back above the mattress. She drifted on the edge of a dark peak, engulfed by his mouth and the beauty of this night. Lace wanted him too much. The passion was consuming her. She'd slipped too far.

Melancholia seized her. This moment when they first made love would never come again.

She shuddered as his lips skipped over the last firm curve of her thigh, stopping just short of her feminine cave. Her body was on fire for him. Blood pulsed through her, hot and frustrated. Pierce moved his head closer, slightly grazing his lips over her moist folds. He showered her with rich, tender kisses.

Her senses swam. She saw music. Tasted colors. Heard smells.

His hot mouth found her eager core. She stabbed her fingernails into her palms, cried out in the darkness. She was writhing and begging him to come inside her.

He did not. He took her to the edge of the cliff and then stopped abruptly.

"No, no," she said. "Don't you dare torture me!"

"Turnabout is fair play. You tortured me first."

She fisted her hair in his hands and gave an impatient tug.

Chuckling, he plied his tongue to her most sensitive spot and it was like switching on a light in a darkened room.

"Yes, yes," she cried. "You know exactly where and how to touch me. How do you know that?"

"You're very responsive," he said. "Your body lets me know what you need."

He laved her with his tongue, cupped her buttocks in his palm, and raised her hips higher to give him deeper access. She arched against his mouth in reflexive savagery.

"Don't stop, don't stop!" she beseeched. "Don't you dare stop."

Pierce gave her everything she yearned for.

Moaning loudly, she clasped her thighs around his head, capturing him between her legs. His tongue obliterated everything. She could do nothing except focus on that one sensitive spot as he took her somewhere she had never been before. Her ears rang. Her eyes could not see. Her blood ran simultaneously hot and cold.

Unbearable. How sweet this perfect torture was. She thrashed against him. "Please! Please!"

Slowly, he released the suction, but kept his tongue playing across her rigid cleft. He toyed with her. Waggling his tongue nimbly around and around until she cried out his name over and over. He owned every inch of her body. She was putty in the palm of his hand. She would crawl across hot coals on her hands and knees if he asked her.

She made a strangled noise. Close. She was so very close.

"Hold on, baby. The wait will be worth it," he promised.

It happened in an explosive bomb. Irrepressible spasms gripped her body and she shattered into a million pieces.

Lace lay naked and perspiring, molten with sexuality, her veins feverish, muscles melted soft, skin blistered, tendons stretched loose, body sore and liquid.

Who knew a man could do such incredible things with a tongue? Pierce's legs intertwined with hers. She pinched the skin between her thumb and index finger, curled her toes, and smiled into the darkness.

Nothing could have prepared her for the depth of emotions tightening her stomach. It had been so easy to get caught up in the vortex of their attraction, but once ensnared, she realized how hard it was going to be to get out of this unscathed.

Sex was just sex. Right?

That's what some people said and maybe sometimes it was true, but when you had this kind of chemistry, this intense connection with another person . . . well . . . it was as if her heart had split open wide and the sun was pouring both into her and out of her, bathing everything in an impossibly bright light.

She reached up to touch his face in the darkness, traced his nose with her index finger; such a masculine nose, so vital, so virile. She bit her bottom lip. Floated in the drunken embrace of lovemaking's afterglow, and this after just oral sex.

Pierce growled low in his throat and rolled over on top of her. Her belly was pressed against his flat, rippled abdomen and his hard erection pulsed against her outer thigh.

Erotic voltage zapped through her entire system. His mouth claimed hers while his hand strayed to explore. His fingers made circles at her navel while his mouth teased hers. She closed her eyes, savoring everything.

Then his tongue went traveling south to the peaks of her breasts. His tongue flicked out to lick over one nipple, while his thumb rubbed the other aching bud.

Her eyes flew open and she lifted her head up off the mattress. She had to see what he was doing to make her feel so good. Her gaze latched on to his lips as she watched him drawing her nipple in and out of his mouth.

His tongue stroked her sensitive skin. She writhed against him, trying to push her body into his, needing more. Glossy streamers of delirious sensation expanded inside her throbbing sex. Her inner muscles contracted.

"I want to feel you inside me, Pierce. I need you now!" she insisted.

He ripped open the condom with his teeth, rolled it on.

She opened her legs, inviting him in.

He moaned low in his throat, an adroitly masculine sound of pleasure, and lowered his body down over hers. He was kissing her again, her mouth, her nose, her eyelids, and her ears. He was over her and around her and at last, at long last, he was inside her.

"Lace," he whispered her name, caressed her ears as he rotated his hips from side to side maintaining highly focused friction. His eyes glowed in the moonlight, his thrusts long and slow. He captured her lips, roughly but lovingly, and their mouths clung as he increased the tempo of their mating.

"More," she begged. "Please more."

He pushed harder, quickened the pace. Lace raised her hips, spurring him on. Infused, she could not tell where he began and she ended. No separation. Their connection was absolute and it filled them in every sense. There was no space for anything else. They were quite simply, breakably whole.

She brimmed with joy, felt strong and resilient, both enslaved and emancipated.

His body stiffened and she wrapped her legs around his waist, pulling him in as deep as he could go. Release claimed them both and he called out her name in a rough cry.

LACE AWAKENED SOMETIME later to the persistent nudge of his erection against her backside. He slid his arm around her waist and pulled her up tight against him.

"Are you awake," he murmured.

"No."

"Ah, that's too bad. I had something for you."

She chuckled and turned in his arms to face him. They kissed a long moment. Lace ran her fingers through his hair. "I might have been wrong about you."

"How's that?"

"Maybe you're not a water strider after all."

"Because I know how to go deep?" he teased.

"Physically, oh yes. You excel at that."

"But not mentally?"

"You're a doer, not a thinker. That's *Geococcyx cali-fornianus* for you."

"The chaparral cock."

"Yes." Was it weird that she was pleased that he remembered the Latin name? "You focus on the task at hand and you're exceptionally committed."

"Well," he murmured, running a finger up her spine, "I wouldn't call this a task but it seems my new position as chaparral cock is a step up from water strider."

"I'm glad you approve of the promotion."

"That's not all I approve of," he said, and lightly sank his teeth into her shoulder.

"No?"

"Hang on." He got up off the bed to retrieve another condom.

A nanosecond later he was back in bed with the condom on, cradling her in the crook of his arm. Her head was nestled against his chest and she could hear the steady thumping of his heart.

Home. It felt like home in his arms.

No. She must not think like that. Could not afford to think like that. It was simply too dangerous. The urgency of their previous mating had died down and in its place was a gentle softness. His fingers massaged her scalp. His lips touched her temple and he nibbled at her skin.

Immediately, her body responded.

"Relax," he whispered, smoothing his palm over her shoulder, moving his mouth from her temple to her earlobe.

But how could she relax when he was running his other hand over her breasts, lightly playing with her nipples? He shifted and his mouth followed his hands, his tongue suckling gently on her beaded peaks. And there went those exploring fingers, tracing down her midriff and sliding between her thighs, his masculine fingers finding her feminine moistness and tenderly slipping inside her.

He didn't make a misstep. Every stroke took the intensity up a notch. He kissed the underside of her chin, his lips wickedly hot. Then he turned her on her side and bumped his hip against her butt. He bent her right leg and edged in closer, positioning himself to sink into her feminine center from behind.

Now, with him deep in her moist wetness, she felt every twitch of his muscle. He lit her up, a match to gasoline. She had no thoughts beyond wanting him deeper, thrusting inside her as far as he could go.

"Ah, my Lace," he whispered. "My beautiful, beautiful Lace."

In that moment, something monumental inside her

moved. It was an emotion unlike anything she'd ever before experienced. She couldn't name it, but she felt it to her soul.

He moved purposefully, the rhythm easy and languid. He was, after all, a purposeful man. She whimpered and pressed against him, urging him to pick up the pace, but he only laughed and went even slower.

The pressure built, tight and heavy. She was acutely aware of every breath, every pulse beat. He cupped her buttocks as he slid in and out, building momentum, working toward something grand.

His hands pulled her helplessly against him. Rocking. Rocking. Soft mewling sounds escaped her throat, slipped into the darkened room to mingle with his pleasure-induced groans. His mouth burned the back of her neck, hot and erotic, tender and loving, but he never lost the rhythm. Their bodies were joined, fused, perfectly matched. Each movement elicited more delight, more surprise.

He rolled onto his back, took her with him, turning her around until she was astride him. Their gazes met and Lace dropped into the exciting comfort of his eyes. He locked his hands around her waist, helping her move up and down on his hard, long shaft.

Swept away, she quickened the pace. Pierce met her challenge, raising his hips up, digging his heels into the mattress, giving her a ride to end all rides. He kept at it, chasing her pleasure with a devotion that dizzied her.

Higher and higher he drove her toward climax. She smiled at him and he laughed with delight. At the peak, she cried out his name over and over.

He followed right behind her, and together they flew high, soared the wind currents, and touched the stars.

He held on to her waist as she buried her face in his neck. She drew in the scent of him. This was the smell of their lovemaking. They clung to each other, quivering and spent.

Pierce stroked her, murmured sweet nothings until her heart rate returned to normal and her body had stilled.

"I've never felt so special," she whispered.

"That's because you *are* special." He lifted her chin, looked deeply into her eyes again. "Lace Bettingfield, you're one in a billion."

Chapter 17

Anthesis: time of flowering.

SUNLIGHT pouring through the window nudged
Pierce awake. He groaned, reached for the covers, and
pulled them over his head before he remembered where
he was. Smiling, he snaked a hand out from under the
bedspread, searching for Lace's warm round body,
only to come up empty-handed.

He ripped the covers off, sat up to find himself alone
in her bed. An ache of disappointment settled in his
gut. He'd planned on getting up before she did and
making her one of his special omelets. Where had she
gone? He got out of bed, picked his trousers up off the
floor, and stepped into them. Feeling like a giant dork,
he went in search of her.

"Lace?" he called, moving from room to room. Her
entire house was an arboretum. There were plants everywhere, including the bathroom. He smiled.

He found her in the kitchen, sitting in the one clear
spot, eating mini shredded wheat and strawberries and
reading a three-inch-thick botany book.

"Good morning," he said.

"Cereal on the bar." She waved a hand without looking up.

He'd never had a morning-after moment where the woman wasn't hanging all over him. Usually, he was trying to think of a graceful way to move on, but Lace seemed as if she barely noticed he was even still in her house. Last night had been amazing and he'd thought they were working on something monumental, but now he wondered if he'd been deceiving himself.

"Coffee?" he asked hopefully.

"Sorry, I don't drink it. Want me to go see if Shasta has any?"

"No, that's okay."

"Bowls are in the cabinet, silverware in the drawer underneath."

Pierce poured himself a bowl of cereal, and since there wasn't any other place to sit that wasn't occupied by a plant of some kind, he stood while he ate, bracing his butt against the kitchen counter.

Lace snaked a brief glance over at him, her gaze resting on his bare chest before sliding down the length of his trousers to take in his bare feet. Was it his hopeful imagination or did she just shiver with sexual delight?

"You have a PhD, didn't you already learn all that stuff?" he teased.

"Learning never stops. Don't you learn new football plays or whatever they're called?"

"I do."

She turned back to the textbook.

He felt richly dismissed. "Is this how you usually spend your mornings?"

"What you see is what you get," she said.

"You read at the breakfast table?"

"No reason not to." She spooned a bite of cereal in her mouth. "Other than the half-naked man in my kitchen, this is a totally normal morning."

"You have a guest, isn't that reason enough to change your routine?"

"I wasn't put on earth to entertain you."

He chuckled. She crossed her legs and stared so hard at the textbook in front of her, he knew she couldn't be seeing a single word she was reading. He padded across the terra-cotta floor to stand behind her. Her shoulders tightened and she curled her hands around the textbook.

"What's so fascinating?" He leaned over her shoulder.

"Meiosis," she said.

"What's that?"

"In jock-speak?"

"English will do."

She couldn't help laughing. "Plant sex."

"Nice," he said, clearing off the chair next to her by moving the flowering plant in the seat to the floor and plunking down beside her. "Plant porn. Read me something."

She snorted, rolled her eyes.

Ah, the eye roll. She was feeling insecure. "No, no, I'm serious. I'm taking an interest in things you like."

"You're just interested because I used the word 'sex.'"

He grinned. "And that's bad because?"

"It's not bad."

He propped his elbows on the table, then cupped his chin in his open palms. "I'm all ears. Read to me, baby."

"Ha, you'll fall asleep in five minutes."

"This is sex we're talking about," he said, wrapping his legs around hers underneath the table. "Sex is never boring."

"Fine. Here goes." She cleared her throat. "Meiosis is two-part cell division in an organism that reproduce sexually."

"Encouraging beginning. Keep going," he urged, and filched a strawberry off her plate.

"You don't want to hear this." She closed the book.

"Ah, but I do." He opened it back up. "Honestly."

She looked skeptical but said, "There's meiosis one."

"Is that like the missionary position or something?"

"It's nothing like the missionary position. They're plants."

"This is more complicated than you might think."

"No, it's more complicated than *you* might think."

"That's what I just said." He leaned in to nibble her ear. "What's meiosis two?"

"Meiosis two is . . . is . . ." she stalled out.

"Uh-huh?"

"Stop doing that. I can't think."

"That's the general idea. You think too much. Let go and just feel."

She pulled back, pushed her glasses up on her nose. He loved those glasses. They made her look so studious, but they did get in the way of kissing. He lifted them off her face, set them aside.

"What are you doing?"

"This." He kissed her substantially, drawing it out.

She responded, but just barely. He stopped. She blinked at him, owl-eyed. "Really, the breakfast tête-à-tête isn't necessary. You're free to go about your day."

Okay, that was a stab to the ego. Last night had been special for him. Apparently, it hadn't been as special for her. "You don't want me here?"

"It's not that." She curled the edge of the textbook page.

"What is it?" He laid his hand on hers so she'd stop curling the page and look at him.

Her eyes were unreadable. "I don't have any expectations, Pierce."

"Why not? Last night . . . well . . . I'm just going to admit it. You were . . . Together we were . . . It was like winning the Super Bowl. That kind of thing only comes around once in a lifetime."

"What are you saying, Pierce, that you want to start dating?"

"Yeah," he said. "I'm saying exactly that."

Slowly, she shook her head, and his heart sank to his shoes. "I don't know about that."

"What are your doubts about taking the next step?"

"You were dropped by the Dallas Cowboys. Your father is sick. You still don't have full use of your leg back. It hasn't been all that long since you were dumped by your girlfriend—"

"Six months," he interrupted, "and it wasn't a big loss. I knew she was not a long-term kind of woman."

"Your head is not in a good place to make a long-lasting decision. Let's just enjoy this thing for what it is."

"Which means?"

"Sex." She smiled impishly. "And often."

"Isn't that the same thing as dating?"

"There's no need to label it."

He should be happy that she was proposing a sex-only relationship. Normally, he would be over the moon at such a proposition. Why then did he feel so disappointed? "All right. I agree." *For now.* "When can I see you again?"

She put her glasses back on, tilted her head. "The gardens are reopening, so I'll be busy with that most of the week."

"I thought that in spite of the fund-raiser you were still short money."

Her eyes met his. "Melody called this morning. A

donor who wants to remain anonymous has pledged a million-dollar endowment to the botanical gardens."

"You don't say."

"What do you know about that?"

He shrugged. "Why would you think I would know anything about it?"

"The name on the caller ID that came through on Melody's phone this morning was Frankie Kowalsky." Her eyes misted. "Pierce, I do so appreciate the donation, but it's far too generous. You're out of a job, you need to save your money."

"Sweetheart, I'm worth thirty times that. It's a tax deduction for me. Don't even try to turn down the money."

"I wouldn't," she said. "I want this too much."

"I just wanted to make you happy."

She gulped visibly and for a moment, he thought she was going to cry. "You did," she whispered. "You have no idea how much."

"Lace," he whispered.

"For you to give that much money to save the gardens for me—" She broke off, tears spilling from her eyes.

And then she was in his arms, showering him with grateful kisses, and he realized why she'd stuck her nose in a book the morning after they'd finally made love. It was because her emotions had so overwhelmed her that she hadn't known how to express them. She'd fallen back on her security blanket—books and plants. She was scared. He got that. He was scared too, but you couldn't get a touchdown if you didn't go for it.

He captured her lips, and things took off from there. They made love on the kitchen floor, hot, quick, and savage, and then they went back to bed and did it all over again.

"SO," ZOEY SAID to Lace at the Wednesday meeting of the Cupid letter committee meeting. "What's going on between you and Pierce Hollister?"

Aunt Delia had been discharged from the rehab hospital and today they were meeting at their great-aunt's house. Framed autographed photos of Elizabeth Taylor, James Dean, and Rock Hudson looked down at them from the paneled wall of Delia's living room. Delia was dressed in a gloriously fuchsia robe and sitting in a straight-backed chair with her legs propped up on a hassock, her walker nearby. Everyone else ringed around her.

Lace shrugged. She was hesitant to admit anything because she knew her family and friends would jump to conclusions, but honestly, this was Cupid. She knew the rumors had already been swirling.

"Well?" Zoey prodded.

It was time she came off the fence. Until she stopped trying to protect herself from getting hurt, she had no chance of developing something meaningful with

Pierce. That left her with two choices. Either break it off clean, no more sex, or dive headfirst into this thing and let the chips fall where they may. She decided to dive.

"We're seeing each other," Lace confessed.

The whole room erupted in a whoop of enthusiasm. The volunteers hugged her and asked a million questions and laughed and hugged her some more. For better or worse, she'd publicly made it official. She and Pierce were an item.

And in the end, she wound up grinning and believing that maybe, just maybe she and Pierce had a shot at something special. If great sex equated to long-term bliss, they were destined to be together for two hundred years.

After things calmed down, the group finally got down to business.

"Lace," Carol Ann said, passing a pink envelope over to her. "Here's another one from Hero Worshipper."

Lace suppressed a groan and opened the letter.

Dear Cupid,

I did what you sugguested and tried to forget about my soulmate, but now he's dating someone else! If I hadn't listenned to you, I could be the one he is goin out with!! I should be the one he is goin' out with. How do I know if I have a chance with him or not if I don't ever try? I'm gonna stop

*sitting on the sidelines and make a move. What
do you have to say about that?*

—Hero Worshipper

"Do you want to give your answer some thought and
take it home?" Carol Ann asked.

Lace shook her head. "No. I'll answer her right now
so it can be printed in the Friday edition of the greensheet."

While everyone else went through the remaining letters, Lace composed an answer to Hero Worshipper on
her notebook computer and answered her as if she were
writing to her fourteen-year-old self.

Dear Hero Worshipper,

*You are right. Who am I to tell you how to run
your life? I have recently come to realize that
you can't find love if you refuse to play the game.
Yes, go ahead. Make a move. If he spurns you,
it may hurt, but at least you will have seized the
moment. Many people let love slip through their
fingers because they are simply too afraid to take
a chance. Be bold. Be brave. Good luck. I wish
you all the best.*

—Cupid

Lace e-mailed the letter to Carol Ann. She and Pierce
had made a date for Saturday and she was going to take

her own advice and tell Pierce what was really in her heart. She wanted more than sex. More than dating. She wanted him. Wanted to build a future together.

She was all in.

ON SATURDAY, PIERCE picked Lace up at the botanical gardens at five. He'd been counting the hours until he could see her again. He had a grand seduction planned. He and Lace would be completely alone, just the two of them.

Steaks were marinating in the refrigerator, charcoal lined the bottom of the barbecue ready to light, asparagus sat trimmed and cleaned for the grill and drizzled with the balsamic reduction he'd made earlier that day, foil-wrapped baked potatoes were in the oven, and there were Parker House rolls he'd picked up from the local bakery. He'd also bought a bouquet of seasonal flowers, and they were in a vase on the kitchen table. A trip to Mon Amour Vineyard yielded a bottle of pinot noir that he'd already opened so it could breathe. He could scarcely wait to show off his culinary skills for a woman who appreciated food.

He opened the passenger door of the King Ranch and held out a hand to help her inside. She was wearing jeans and a light blue blouse than made her eyes stand out. He could not stop staring at her.

"What?" she asked, and suddenly looked shy. "Do I have dirt on my face?"

"I just can't get over how beautiful you are."

"I'm sure you've been with plenty of women much more beautiful than I am. You've dated actresses and models."

"Maybe so, but you're beautiful both inside and out."

She ducked her head. "You keep sweet-talking me like that and you'll never get rid of me."

"That's the plan," he said, and closed the door.

LACE SAT THERE so excited she could hardly breathe as Pierce ran around to the driver's side. Could she do it? Could she take the plunge and tell him she loved him? A rock drummer couldn't beat any faster than her heart knocking against her ribs. It was so scary, this vulnerability. Was she going out on a limb only to saw herself off?

"Before we go to dinner," he said, starting the engine. I need your expert opinion."

"About what?"

"The pumpkins I planted and my father's sweet potatoes too. The plants have a funny color to them and they're not growing the way they should. I appreciate any advice you could give."

"Sure," she said. "I'd be happy to help."

He drove one-handed to the Triple H, his right hand resting on Lace's thigh. Twelve years ago she would have killed to be here with her big brother's best friend, and now she was close to having her long-cherished dream come true. A dream she thought would never be possible. Scarcely able to believe this was really happening, she smiled a little smile.

"How's your dad?" she asked.

"He's doing a whole lot better, even though the specialists still haven't been able to figure out what's wrong with him. He's being dismissed in the morning. Malcolm's gone to San Antonio to pick him up. He took Dad a big pan of those candied sweet potatoes he loves. That man can eat sweet potatoes morning, noon, and night."

"Tell me about the ground you've planted the pumpkins and sweet potatoes in. Is this a spot that's been overplanted?"

"Actually, it's a new rotation. We haven't planted any crops in that patch of ground before."

"Hmm," she mused. "So much for depleted soil theory."

Pierce put his arm around her shoulder and tugged her as close to him as he could with their seat belts on. Occasionally, he leaned over to steal quick kisses. By the time they pulled into the driveway, they were hot and wet and crazy for each other and she wasn't sure they were even going to make it into the house. She took her glasses off and stuck them in her purse stuffed with condoms. She was prepared for some long-term lovemaking.

"You know," Pierce said. "It's the housekeeper's day off. We have the house to ourselves."

"Are you saying the sickly plants were all a ploy to get me over here?" Lace teased.

"No, but there's plenty of time to look at plants later. It's been days since I've been inside you and I don't think I can last one second longer." He was already unbuttoning her shirt.

Lace was equally blinded by lust. "What about your ranch hands?"

"The bunkhouse is half a mile from here." He plucked her shirt from her jeans. "Besides, this time of day they're out feeding the cattle. No one around but me and you, sweetheart."

They kissed nonstop on the way over to the back door. Pierce got the door open and dragged her inside. He waltzed her through the kitchen. She went to work on his buttons. By the time they reached his bedroom, they were topless.

The head of his bed was positioned next to a window. At the foot of the bed lay a closet with a bifold door. The room was decidedly masculine—brown comforter, suede curtains, wagon wheel headboard—but she barely noticed. Her attention was on Pierce one hundred percent.

He held up a finger, broke away, and rushed to the dresser to light scented candles—lemon. And to turn on some music—"Sixty Minute Man."

Grinning, he came back to kiss her.

"Cocky," she whispered.

He pressed his lips to her ear. "It's not cocky if you can back it up."

She fell backward onto the mattress, pulling him down on top of her. Lace looked into his eyes and he stared down at her like she was the most bewitching thing he'd ever seen. He made her feel like a queen.

A rusty hinge creaked behind them.

Simultaneously, they lifted their heads and looked around.

The closet door burst open and a naked woman jumped out yelling, "Surprise!"

Lace let out a shriek and grabbed for a pillow to cover her naked breasts. Pierce bounced off the mattress, his jeans unbuttoned, and his hands instinctively doubling into fists, ready for a fight.

From down the hallway came the sound of running footsteps slapping against the hardwood floor. "What's going on in there?" a male voice boomed.

Everyone shifted their gazes to the door.

Malcolm burst into the room at the same moment the naked woman tackled Pierce, wrapping her legs around his waist.

Shocked, Lace realized the naked female was Shasta Green.

"I love you!" Shasta exclaimed. "Lace told me to be brave and bold and declare my feelings for you. She only wants you for sex, but I want to have your babies!"

"What the hell!" Malcolm and Pierce yelled in unison.

Pierce was trying to pry a naked Shasta off him while Malcolm's nostrils flared and his face flushed the color of sugar beets.

"Shasta, what are you doing?" Lace exclaimed.

Pierce whipped his head around to Lace. "You told her to ambush me?"

"No, no!" Lace blinked at Shasta. "*You're* Hero Worshipper!"

"I thought you knew," Shasta said.

This situation was so ludicrous it was almost funny. Almost. Lace gulped. "How would I know?"

Shasta raised her chin. "I told you I didn't like your answer to Hero Worshipper."

"I was supposed to piece that together? You could have mentioned who it was that you had a crush on."

"The letter-writing rules say you can't mention names."

True enough.

"Dammit, Shasta," Malcolm muttered. "All this time we've been dating you were only using me to get to Pierce?"

"Sorry." Shasta shrugged.

"You." Malcolm spat out the word at Pierce. "Being the king of the heap wasn't enough for you. You had to go and steal the woman I'm crazy about."

"I didn't steal her. I don't even know her."

Shasta untwined her naked legs from around Pierce's waist, moved toward Malcolm. "You're crazy about me?"

"I was." Malcolm snorted. "When I thought you liked me."

"I do like you."

"Then why are you naked in his bedroom?" Malcolm glowered. "I haven't even seen you naked."

Shasta looked confused and conflicted. "You have now."

"Not quite the way I was imagining it."

"I didn't realize," Shasta said.

"This is ridiculous." Pierce yanked open a drawer, took out a T-shirt, and shoved it at Shasta. "Put some clothes on."

"You're what's ridiculous." Malcolm snorted. "You're not satisfied with just one woman, you have to have them all."

Pierce hardened his jaw. "I did not ask her to hide naked in my closet."

"No, but you love strutting your stuff. I have to stay here and work the ranch while you go off and be a star. All my life I've had to live in your shadow. You've got the golden arm. Dad thinks the sun rises and sets out of your ass."

"You think it was easy for me, always expected to win, win, win? I never got to be a regular guy. I always had to produce something in order to get Dad to love me."

"Boo-hoo. Poor you."

"I'm not asking for your sympathy, just understanding that my path has rocks in it too."

"And how did you handle the biggest rock of all? Where were you when Mom died? Oh yes, right. Throwing a fucking football!" Malcolm growled.

"Mom told me to play. She asked me to win the game for her. I played that game for her. I did what I do best. I produced on command." Pierce's face turned the color of a ballistic blister. Indigo veins popped out on his temple and his jaw muscles twitched turbulently.

"Yeah? Well, while you were throwing that ball, I was holding her hand while she stopped breathing."

Shasta had slipped on the T-shirt and came to perch on the edge of the bed beside Lace, looking as fragile as a foolish olive warbler.

Pierce toed off with his brother, stuck out his chin. "Go ahead. I know you've been stewing for years. Get it all off your chest."

Malcolm took off his Stetson, rolled up his sleeves, drew back his fist, popped Pierce squarely in the jaw, and the fight was on.

Chapter 18

*Scar: mark left by the natural
separation of two structures.*

PIERCE and Malcolm punched and shoved, a lifetime's worth of brotherly jealousy and resentment. They wrestled and grunted, bit and gouged. They knocked each other backward, crashed into walls. They cursed each other with every dirty word in the book. The brawl spilled from the bedroom, into the hallway, through the kitchen, and out the back door.

Shasta was screaming and jumping up and down. "You're killing him! You're killing him!"

Pierce didn't know if she meant him or Malcolm.

"Stop it!" Lace hollered. "That's enough!"

Her concerned voice finally soaked through his angry brain. He tried to shove Malcolm off, but his brother clung on, fingers and teeth digging in. Pierce remembered when they were kids and Malcolm would come at him. He would just put a firm palm on Malcolm's forehead and the kid would windmill the air, his short arms unable to reach him. Hell, his brother was reaching him now. Making up for lost time.

"You're brothers, you love each other! Stop this nonsense!" Lace demanded.

Pierce was ready to quit, but Malcolm just kept pounding. If being a punching bag allowed his brother to get rid of his hurt feelings and resentment, okay, he'd let him punch until he ran out of steam. Pierce stopped fighting.

"Malcolm, stop hitting Pierce or I swear to God I'll kick you so hard you'll never have children," Lace threatened.

His brother smacked him a couple more times and then he quit too. They both lay on the ground, breathing hard, covered in dirt and grass burrs.

Pierce tasted blood, cough, spat. His left eye was quickly swelling shut. Who knew little brother could pack such a punch? He peered over at Lace with his one good eye. At some point during the melee, she'd managed to find her shirt and Shasta had located some pants. It suddenly occurred to him that Malcolm had come home early and alone.

"Where's Dad?" Pierce asked, fear winnowing through him.

"Still in San Antonio." Malcolm wheezed. "I think you broke my nose."

"Why didn't you bring him home?"

"Soon as he ate those sweet potatoes, he started throwing up again."

"What the hell is going on? Why can't the doctors find out what's wrong with him? This is crazy. I'm taking him to Houston. New York if I have to. I'll take him to the Mayo Clinic. There's got to be someone somewhere who can find out what's wrong with him."

"Pierce?" Lace's voice drifted over to them.

He sat up, squinted into the setting sun. She'd climbed over the fence and was crounched over the sweet potato and pumpkin patch. "Yeah?"

"I know what's wrong with your father."

SINCE PIERCE'S LEFT eye had swollen shut, he stayed behind while Malcolm drove Shasta home and took Lace by the botanical gardens to pick up her soil testing kit. None of them spoke for the entire trip. It was the most uncomfortable ride of Lace's life.

"Don't be too hard on her," Lace said, after they dropped Shasta off at Lace's house and then went on to the botanical gardens. "She's just a kid with stars in her eyes."

"I know," Malcolm said. "It was my fault for thinking someone could like me for *me* when I've got Pierce for a brother. He'll always be the star and I'll always be chump change."

"I'm sure he was just as shocked by Shasta's little stunt as you and I were."

Malcolm snorted. "You think that's the first time something like that happened to him?"

"It's happened before?"

"More times than you can count. I know you got your feelings pounded in high school when Mary Alice printed your letter in the school paper, but there were just as many other girls crushing on him as you. The ones who bullied you the most were the ones who were after him the hardest. You know Joleen from La Hacienda Grill?"

"Yes."

"My mother found her hiding under Pierce's bed one night."

"Really?" Lace squirmed in her seat.

"And Kara—"

"Please," she said miserably. "I don't want to hear any more."

"I'm just warning you because I know you're getting serious about him. Pierce is a player. Always has been, always will be."

Shasta, she could forgive. The girl was young and naive, but herself? She should have known better than to go falling in love with Pierce Hollister. She'd known what he was all along but she'd allowed herself to believe that he'd changed. Now here was Malcolm confirming every fear she'd ever had about Pierce.

"I'm not serious about him," she lied.

"Good," Malcolm said. "Because I'd hate to see you get hurt. You deserve so much better."

"I can take care of myself," she replied. "Don't worry about me."

At the gardens, she collected her kit and her Corolla and followed Malcolm back to the ranch.

Pierce came out to greet them when they arrived at the Triple H. He had a bag of frozen green peas held over his left eye. "Hey," he said to Malcolm.

"Hey," Malcolm grunted back.

They gave each other an awkward hug and simultaneously winced. Pierce touched his jaw. "Where did you learn to pack such a punch, little brother?"

"Whaling on the punching bag I named Pierce."

"We need to sit down and have a long talk," Pierce said. "Clear the air. With words this time."

"Yeah." Malcolm nodded. "Your hard head split my knuckles open. We can't keep doing this."

They hugged again.

Lace wanted nothing more than to get the hell out of there and leave them to their family issues, but she needed to collect a soil sample to confirm her suspicions that Abe was suffering from a mineral toxicity caused by eating sweet potatoes grown in tainted earth. She batted back her worries and her tendency to withdraw when things got heavy and went to collect samples of the suspect soil.

She thought about how she'd felt when Shasta popped out of the closet, initially terrified, then shocked, and finally disgusted when Malcolm confirmed that it wasn't the first time a woman had shown up uninvited in Pierce's bedroom. Nausea settled in the bottom of her stomach.

It didn't matter that Pierce was no longer playing professional ball. Women would always be throwing themselves at him and having crazy crushes on him. Could she handle that? Always wondering. He was a charming man with a reputation for loving the ladies. It was too much. How could she expect any man to be monogamous when naked women literally threw themselves at him?

"What do you think it is?" Pierce came over to the garden.

Lace studiously collected the soil samples. As long as they were talking about plants, and steering clear of what else had gone on here tonight, she was on solid ground. "From the looks of the plants, right off the bat I can tell there's copper toxicity, but there could be other contaminants as well. For instance, lead. Lead in the soil is toxic to humans and produces a lot of the symptoms your father has, but it doesn't affect the plants themselves like an overabundance of copper does."

"I see."

"You said this is the first time this ground has been used for planting?"

"Yes."

"Why hasn't it ever been used before?"

"We used to have an old shed here until the termites ate it up," Malcolm said.

"What was stored in the shed?"

Malcolm rubbed his bruised jaw. "Pesticides, fertilizers, lawn equipment."

"That's probably where the contaminants came from. Over the years chemicals can leach into the soil. It's a wonder you all didn't get sick."

"Dad's the only one who likes sweet potatoes," Pierce said.

"Does this mean the pumpkin crop is worthless?" Malcolm asked.

"Unfortunately, yes. This whole area will need to be plowed up and measures taken to remove or mediate the contaminants in the soil."

"Brother," Malcolm crowed. "Looks like you owe me ten grand."

"I'll happily pay," Pierce said, "if this gets us to the bottom of what's making Dad sick."

Lace stood up. "I'll put a rush on it. Hopefully, we'll have the results by tomorrow. Until then, you might want to go ahead and call Abe's doctor and tell him what we suspect."

"I'll do it," Malcolm said, and disappeared into the house.

A silence passed between them.

"I'm sorry about tonight," Pierce said finally.

Lace tensed. "Me too."

"I had a great dinner planned. Steaks and everything."

"I'm sure it would have been lovely."

"Rain check until my bruises heal a little?" Pierce asked.

She paused, the collection kit filled with soil samples clutched in her hand, and slowly shook her head. "I don't think that's such a good idea."

"Okay, we don't wait, but you'll have to put up with a lot of yelping." He grinned, looking boyishly ragtag with his eye swollen shut.

She put steel in her spine, refused to let herself be charmed, and backed up. "That's not what I mean."

His smile disappeared. "Lace, is something wrong?"

"Look in the mirror and then you tell me."

"This fight between me and Malcolm has been brewing a long time. I'm sorry you had to see that, but I think we sorted some things out. I'm not normally the kind to solve matters with my fists, but—"

"You're a lover not a fighter," she said dryly.

The cocky grin was back. "Exactly."

She held up a palm. "I can't do this, Pierce. I thought I could, but I can't."

"I don't understand." He blinked like he totally didn't get it. "Do what?"

"Be with you."

He grasped her wrist. "What is it? What's wrong?"

She twisted her arm away. "Do you really have to ask?"

His face fell. "Yes, I do. I thought things were going great."

She could barely meet his gaze. It hurt so much to break off with him, but better now than later. At least she'd never told him she loved him. That was some small consolation. "If you are that obtuse, spelling it out for you isn't going to change a thing."

"How can I fix it if you won't talk to me?"

"That's just the thing. I don't want to fix it."

"What do you mean?"

"I don't want to take this any further."

His Adam's apple bobbed frantically as he gulped. "You don't mean that."

"Pierce, we're not compatible. You're accustomed to the jet set life and I'm a simple country girl. I thought when the Cowboys let you go that, well, we had a chance."

"We do."

She shook her head. "Just because you're not in a Dallas Cowboy uniform doesn't mean the women are going to stop throwing themselves at you."

"They can throw, I'm not going to catch them. You're the one I want to be with, Lace. No one but you."

This was so hard, but she could not cave. She had to get out while she still could. "I'm sorry. It's better this way. And once your father gets better, and if he has what I think he has, he has an excellent chance for a full recovery, you're free to go back to your life in Dallas. There won't be anything holding you here."

"We're done? You're done? Just like that?"

"I'm done," she said. "Now if you'll excuse me, I need to get these samples to the lab."

FLABBERGASTED, PIERCE WATCHED her drive away, the taillights of her Corolla disappearing in the night. Did Lace blame him for Shasta showing up naked in his closet? How was that his fault?

Um, maybe because you've courted the playboy image for quite some time now. You fed it. You let fame go to your head. You became the cock of the walk.

Initially, he'd sought the limelight to earn Abe's love and respect, but at some point he'd bought into his own hype. His fame, fortune, and cocky strut had attracted certain kind of women. He'd had a good time so he'd just kept strutting long after he grew tired of the show.

Guilty. He was guilty as charged. A cold shiver ran through him and a sick feeling settled in the pit of his stomach.

Malcolm came back outside and walked over to put a hand on Pierce's shoulder.

"Ow."

"Sorry." Malcolm dropped his hand.

"You are much stronger than you look." Pierce rubbed the spot where Malcolm had touched.

"And you're not looking so good with only one eye."

Pierce turned to face his brother. "I'm sorry if I've ever done anything to make you feel less than."

"Wow, if I'd known all it took to humble you was a fistfight, I would have punched your lights out a long time ago."

"You probably should have."

"And risk the wrath of Abe for smacking his golden boy?"

"I'm sorry about that too. It wasn't fair of Dad to treat you so differently."

"Don't worry about it. I'm used to it."

They stood there for a long moment not saying anything.

"I'm sorry the Cowboys dropped you. That sucks. Kicking a man when he's down," Malcolm said.

"Where did you hear that?"

"It was on the six o'clock news."

"So they finally announced it." Made it official.

"Why didn't you tell me?" His brother's brow knitted in a frown.

"So you could gloat?"

"So I could buy you a beer. Wanna go to Chantilly's?"

"Looking like this?"

Malcolm stuck his hands in his front pockets. "You got a point."

Pierce blew out his breath. Two hours ago, he'd had the world by the tail. How had everything gone to shit so quickly?

"Whatcha gonna do now?" Malcolm asked.

"Frankie's scouting for me."

"What if no one picks you up?"

Pierce kicked the dirt with the tip of his boot. "Is there a place for me here?"

"I always hoped you'd come home."

Another long silence passed. A bobwhite called from the brush. The scent of the rockroses their mother had planted years ago drifted on the breeze.

"Do you really like that girl?" Pierce asked.

"Shasta?"

"Yes."

Malcolm sighed. "I like her quirkiness."

"She's certainly quirky. I'll give her that."

"Plus I've always had a thing for redheads, you know that." His brother cast him a sideways look. "Are you in love with Lace?"

"Yep."

"Thought so. You gonna tell her?"

"I don't know if it would do any good."

"Are you nuts? That woman has been in love with you since eighth grade."

"That was a crush. I'm pretty well sure she got over me."

"Are you seriously going to take no for an answer? The great Pierce Hollister who doesn't let anything stop him?"

Pierce grinned. "Hell no."

AT SEVEN A.M. on Sunday, there was a knock at her back door as she sat at the kitchen table eating shredded wheat and remembering the morning after Pierce had spent the night.

Her heart leaped. Pierce! She ran to the door and flung it open to find Shasta standing there.

"Are you going to fire me?" she asked.

"Are you going to pull any more crazy stunts like that?" Lace couldn't be too mad at the poor girl. Shasta was unschooled, unsophisticated, and she clearly did not have a good role model in her life.

Solemnly, Shasta shook her head. "No." Her bottom lip trembled. "It hurts so bad when someone you love doesn't love you back."

Lace's heart went out to her. She knew exactly what that felt like. "You don't really love Pierce. You love the image of who he is. I know. I fell for that image too." *Twice.*

"How come you wrote that letter to Hero Worshipper, telling her . . . that is me . . . to go for it?" Shasta asked.

"Because," she said, "it is better to go for it than forever be left wondering. Now you can move on. It's painful, yes, but at least you know where you stand. You're no longer in limbo."

Shasta nodded, wiped away a tear.

"Oh, and next time, don't show up at the guy's place and hide naked in his closet. It's too easy for men to take advantage of a woman under those circumstances."

Shasta hung her head. "I just wanted to show him that I could be a lot of fun."

"There's ways to do that without putting yourself in a compromising position."

The girl cocked her head. "Like how?"

"I'll get my cousin Zoey to talk to you. She's better at spontaneous fun than I am."

"I like Zoey. She's cool."

"She is."

Shasta nibbled her bottom lip. "Do you think I blew it with Malcolm?"

"I don't know. Why don't you ask him?"

"Maybe I will. 'Course, it's probably no good since I got naked for his brother."

"That might take some doing to overcome," Lace agreed.

"Pierce was the guy, wasn't he? The one you told me about. The one you had a crush on when you were young?"

Lace nodded.

"And you still love him."

"I . . ." She couldn't bring herself to answer her one way or the other.

"You don't have to say it. I can see it on your face." Shasta looked sad but resigned. "If he's *your* soul mate, he can't be mine."

"He's not my soul mate."

"Just because you don't believe in soul mates don't mean it's not true."

Lace didn't point out that scientifically the burden of proof was on the believer. If pressed, Shasta would dig up anecdotes that did not qualify as scientific proof but suited the girl's beliefs. That's how confirmation bias worked. "It doesn't matter if he's my soul mate or not. We're not a good match."

"Of course it matters. Love is the only thing that does matter," Shasta insisted. For an uneducated girl who hid naked in strange men's closets, she made a lot of sense. "You should take your own advice. Many people let love slip through their fingers 'cause they are simply too scared to take a chance. Be bold. Be brave."

"You memorized my reply?"

"I was clinging hard to any hope." Shasta pressed a knuckle against her eye and blinked hard.

Lace's heart went out to the girl. "You're an original, Shasta Green. You're gorgeous and fearless. Somewhere out there the perfect guy is waiting for you."

"Thanks for not firing me."

"We all make mistakes."

"You won't regret giving me a second chance," Shasta said staunchly, and gave a little wave as she headed out the door.

Lace let loose a heavy sigh and went about tending her plants. The routine soothed her like nothing else could.

Several times over the next few days Pierce tried to call her, but Lace refused to pick up. He left voice messages, pleading for her to call him, but she wasn't going to let him charm his way back into her heart. He was a good guy, a great guy, but she simply couldn't deal with his celebrity status. He might have come home to Cupid, but his world—the world of groupies and celebrity stalkers—had followed him. It always would.

She got the soil tests on Monday and as she suspected, both the copper and lead levels were off the charts. Unable to face talking to Pierce, she had the lab call both him and the hospital in San Antonio with the results.

When he didn't show up for the last gardening class on Tuesday evening, she relaxed, thinking that yes, maybe he had accepted her at face value and he was going to stop pursuing her, but then she immediately started worrying that something bad had happened to Abe and that was why he hadn't shown up. Had his father's condition been too far gone to reverse? Or was there something else wrong with him entirely? She discreetly asked around town, but no one seemed to have an update on Abe's condition.

On Thursday, her parents called and told her they'd be coming home in a few days and they would stay put until the cutting horse futurity in Fort Worth in November and December. It would be good to see them again.

"How are things with Pierce?" her mother asked.

"He gave a million-dollar endowment to the gardens."

"You told me that the last time I called."

"Did I?"

"Oh dear," her mother said. "It didn't work out between you, did it?"

"How do you know?"

"I can hear it in my children's voices when they're in distress. I am so sorry, honey. Would it help to talk about it?"

"Not right now. Maybe when you get home."

"I heard the Dallas Cowboys dropped Pierce. Did that have something to do with it? You know how men's identities are wrapped up in their jobs. You might consider giving him the benefit of the doubt until he's had time to process this. He's been through a lot lately."

She let that go. "Oh, I found out what was wrong with Abe. Jay's not the only one in the family who can make a diagnosis."

"Really? What happened?"

She told her mother about the contaminated soil and that sidetracked Mom from the topic of her relationship with Pierce.

"You are so smart! I'm blessed with brilliant children. See you soon, honey." Her mother blew phone kisses and hung up.

Lace had no sooner put her phone on the charger than the doorbell rang. Her foolish pulse sped up. Pierce!

Stop it! You can't keep hoping and wishing and praying he'll show up.

She opened the door to find a young local boy standing on her front porch holding a small box. "Hello, Tim. Are you selling band candy again?"

"Nope. A guy gave me ten bucks to deliver this to you."

"What guy?"

"He said not to say his name." Tim thrust the box at her and took off toward his bike parked at the curb.

Lace took the package inside, her heart doing cartwheels in her chest. With trembling fingers, she untied the wrapping to find a black velvet box. She caught her breath and opened the lid.

Nestled inside was a pair of silver and turquoise earrings of *Geococcyx californianus,* the greater roadrunner. Along with it was a folded strip of paper.

She unfolded it.

Did some research. You're right. I'm a roadrunner. They mate for life.

Spontaneous tears poured from her eyes. Oh God, this was a hundred times worse than that silly incident in high school. This was exactly why she had not wanted to let down her guard. She knew this would happen. Knew in her heart that she had never really stopped loving him.

Pierce had fully lobbed the ball into her court. The question was did she dare to lob it back?

Chapter 19

Graft: the joining of two plants.

"THAT girl of yours is pretty special," Abe said.

"She is at that." Pierce smiled at his father, who was sitting at the kitchen table heartily enjoying his lunch. His color was good, his mind sharp, he was slowly getting back to his old self.

"If she hadn't figured out those sweet taters was causin' me to get sick, the doc said I might have been a goner. Funny, a plant gal figured out what a bunch of high-powered doctors couldn't."

"Lace is a doctor," Pierce said, pride swelling his chest. "She has a PhD in plant biology."

"She's sumpthin' else."

Yes, she was.

"You should marry her." Abe waved his fork.

"She broke up with me," Pierce said, but secretly, he couldn't help hoping that the chaparral earrings and the note he'd included would touch Lace's heart. Sending messages instead of showing up in person was not his normal modus operandi, but with Lace, the same old, same old wasn't going to cut it. Normally, if he wanted to get back together with a woman—which, granted, was rare in itself—he'd show up at her door, flash his patented smile and two tickets for her favorite event. It has been a never-fail scheme.

Lace was different. For one thing, she was sharp as barbwire and would see through that tactic in a nanosecond. For another thing, she wasn't like any other woman. When it came to Lace Bettingfield, he had to throw away the rulebook. She was one in a billion.

"Still can't believe the Cowboys dropped you." Abe shook his head.

"Me either," Pierce confessed. He'd been blindsided, but he shouldn't have been. He'd allowed his ego to get out of control.

"Another team will pick you up."

It was a long shot. Pierce understood that now. He would not have one last victory touchdown. His career had ended on a down note. It couldn't be helped. That's just the way things were. He was thirty, not young for a ballplayer, and weakened from his injury. Even if another team picked him up, the chances of him doing anything spectacular were tiny. His career was over. He needed to face that.

Just like his affair with Lace might be over. It had been more than twenty-four hours since he'd sent the earrings and he hadn't heard from her. He had one last Hail Mary pass to throw in his effort to win her back. If that didn't work, he would have lost everything.

No, not all. He still had his father and Malcolm and the ranch. That was a long sight more than many people had. He was a lucky man. Why then did he feel so shattered?

"I appreciate you being here for me, son," Abe said. "I know I was real hard on you growing up, but I was just pushin' you to be the best ballplayer you could be."

"I know that, Dad."

"I'm proud of you, but not just because you played football. You're a good son."

"That means a lot, but Malcolm's a good son too. You need to tell him that once in a while."

Abe nodded.

Pierce's cell phone rang. He fished it from his pocket. Frankie Kowalsky. "What's up, Frankie?"

"Hold on to your Stetson, Hollister. I've got some major news. The Detroit Lions want you."

"OMIGOD!" SHASTA CAME running into Lace's office in the botanical gardens, a copy of the Cupid greensheet in her hands. "Did you see this?"

"See what?" Lace glanced up from the budget that was balancing quite nicely with money from Pierce's generous endowment. Just thinking about him had her reaching up to touch the earring nestled in her earlobe. She'd spent the last two days trying to figure out if she fit into Pierce's life.

"Listen to this." Shasta cleared her throat and read, "Dear Tongue-Tied."

Tongue-Tied? The name she'd used in her embarrassing letter to Cupid about Pierce? Lace's hand froze on the computer mouse. "What? Give me that." She snatched the greensheet from Shasta's hand.

Dear Tongue-Tied,

I apologize that it has taken me twelve years to answer your letter. You are most certainly not a nobody. Never forget that you are very special. There is no one else like you. You are unique. A woman who can love with such stark intensity is a woman to be treasured. Have you ever considered that Pierce Hollister is pining for you as much as you're pining for him? Try telling him how you feel. You just might be surprised.

Yours in love,
Cupid

Lace's heart hammered. The words blurred on the page. She got up and marched from the botanical gardens to City Hall. Inside, she blew past the secretary and stormed into Carol Ann's office.

"Who wrote this?" she demanded, shoving the greensheet across the desk of her startled aunt.

"I don't know."

"Was it Zoey?"

"Honestly, Lace, I don't know."

"Mignon?"

"She didn't say anything to me about it."

"Was it you?"

"I might be a lot of things, Lace Bettingfield, but I am not a liar."

"Who is meddling in my love life?"

Carol Ann held up both palms. "Truly, I don't know anything about this. Do you think . . ."

"What?"

"Well, that *Pierce* could have written it?"

She had not considered that, but the minute she did, her heart pounded all the harder and she just knew that it had been he. On trembling legs, she went back to the gardens, got into her Corolla, and headed for the Triple H, all the while absentmindedly fingering the chaparral earrings.

Ten minutes later, she pulled into the driveway and got out, her knees no sturdier than water. She climbed the back porch steps, knocked on the screen door, and held her breath.

Pierce answered, opened the inner door, and peered at her through the screen.

The sight of him made her head swirl and she realized she wasn't breathing. *Take a deep breath.* "May I come in?"

He held open the screen, stepped aside for her to enter.

She walked past him, stopped, turned. Her throat was dry. How did she start? How to admit she had overreacted about Shasta—it wasn't his fault the girl had a crush on him—and the other groupies? If she wanted to be with him, she'd have to learn how to take his fame in stride.

"You have every right to be mad," he said.

She met his gaze. *He* was apologizing?

"I was cocky. Even after life took me down a peg or two." He rubbed his left leg. "I still put up that cock-of-the-walk strut pretending that's who I really am. It wasn't until I was back in Cupid, until I met *you* again that I started to realize how much the persona I'd perfected had hobbled me. But you . . ." He shook his head. "You saw past all the bullshit. You saw me for who I really was."

"Humble and lovable?"

"I don't blame you for being upset over the incident with Shasta. If a naked man jumped out of your closet, I'd be pretty damn steamed."

That made her giggle. "There will never be a naked man jumping out of my closet."

He wriggled his eyebrows. "You never know. But it's because of you, and the change I've made because of you, that's allowed me to walk away from football."

"What do you mean? The Cowboys dropped you."

"Yes, but the Detroit Lions picked me up."

"And you're not taking their offer?"

"No."

That stunned her. "Why not?"

"Because there are other things that are more important to me now. Dad, Malcolm, the ranch . . . *you*."

"Pierce," she whispered.

"What did you come here to tell me?" He stepped closer to her, his eyes latched on to hers.

"I surrender," she said.

"Surrender?"

"Wave the white flag."

He canted his head. "Okay."

"I give up. You win. You made me fall in love with you all over again—Lulu, the endowment to the gardens, the earrings, the note, the Cupid letter in the greensheet. Who can resist an onslaught like that? I fought it. I resisted. I lost. So here I am, bare and raw and aching for you. Just as crazy in love as when I was fourteen. What do you have to say about that?"

"I say it's about damn time you realized it." Pierce pulled her into his arms and said the words she'd waited twelve long years to hear. "Because I love you too, Lace Bettingfield. I love you too."

Following is a tasty morsel of
New York Times bestselling author
Lori Wilde's
next book in the Cupid, Texas, series

SOMEBODY TO LOVE
Coming in Early 2014
only from Avon Books

And don't miss *The Christmas Cookie Chronicles*
On sale November 2013!

Prologue

Archaeology: The scientific study of material evidence to find out about human cultures of the past.

Dear Cupid,

I've gone and ruined everything by falling in love with my best friend. Now, not only have I lost my lover, I've lost the one person in the world that I could tell anything to. But that's not the half of it. I've also alienated my family, friends, and turned the entire community against me. I thought I was doing a good thing by searching for something meaningful. People accused me of being frivolous and shallow, so I was determined to earn a little respect, prove I could commit, dig deep, find my roots, and discover who and what I am. Guess what? I did and that's what started all the trouble. The things I have uncovered could destroy people I love. I've become a target and I'm condemnably alone. I'm scared, damn scared and at my wit's end. I don't know how much longer I can hang on. Help!

—Spontaneous to a Fault

Zoey McCleary quivered atop Widow's Peak on private land, directly across from Mount Livermore, the very spot where her parents had died over twenty years earlier in an airplane crash that had also severely wounded her older sister, Natalie. Zoey had come out of the accident without a scrape.

Not so lucky now, huh, McCleary. Looks like you've used up the last of your nine lives.

In her hand she crushed the crumpled letter she'd written to Cupid the previous evening. Last night, she thought she'd smacked rock bottom, now she fully understood how much farther she had to fall.

She stared down the sixty-five-hundred feet to the town of Cupid, Texas, nestled in the valley of the Davis Mountains. It was the only home she'd ever known. The town had been named after an impressive seven-foot stalagmite found in the local caverns that bore an uncanny resemblance to the Roman god of love. Local legend had it that if you wrote a letter, begging for divine intervention, Cupid would grant your wish. Her family on the Greenwood-Fant side was steeped neck deep in the lore, the lot of them avid beseechers of Cupid's goodwill.

It was total romantic bullshit and Zoey knew it. Writing that letter spoke to precisely how desperate she was. Forgone conclusion—when a girl turned to a mythological cherub for Hail Mary help, she was seriously screwed.

However, it was the other side of the family that had driven her up the mountain, McClearys and their dark, ancestral secret.

Her pulse beat a hot stampede across her eardrums; she was exposed and vulnerable, stiff with fear, tension-strained muscles, sweat-slicked skin; nicks and scratches oozed blood, lungs flapped with the excruciating pain of trying to draw in air after a dead run up the mountain.

Heat from the setting August sun warmed her cheeks. Desert wind whipped through the Davis Mountains blowing sandy topsoil over her face. She licked her dry lips, tasted grit. On three sides of her yawned sheer drop-off. Overhead, a dozen buzzards circled.

Waiting.

Something tickled her cheek, feather soft and startling as the sweet sensation of an unexpected midnight kiss. She gasped and brushed at her face, her work-roughened fingertips scratching her skin and for one crazy moment she thought, *Jericho*.

But of course it wasn't Jericho—she'd already chased him away by daring to declare her love—it was merely the caress of a passing cloud. She couldn't regret telling him though, could she? Considering the very real possibility that she was about to die. He might not love her the way she loved him, but at least now he knew how she felt.

She put her palm to her lips, kissed it, whispered

"Jericho" and blew the kiss into the gathering mist.

From behind her, she heard her pursuers crashing through the aspen and madrone trees, cursing black ugly threats. They were coming for her. This was it, the end of the trail, the end of the world, the end of *her*, and nowhere left to go but down.

The thundering footsteps were nearer now, closing in. Soon, her trackers would immerge from the forest and join her on the skinned, igneous peak.

Her heart took flight, faster than a hummingbird and thudding with jumpy brutality. Panic shuddered her bones. She could not stop trembling no matter how hard she willed it.

Teeth chattered. Knees wobbled. Nostrils flared.

Don't just stand there. Do something! Do something!

But what?

There was only one solution, only one clear way out.

Zoey gathered her courage, took her last deep breath and jumped.

Chapter 1

Flake: to remove a stone fragment from a core or tool.

Six weeks earlier . . .

THE mewling was so soft that Zoey almost didn't hear it. She had just slung her backpack onto the passenger seat of the Cupid's Rest Bed and Breakfast van parked in the student lot at Sul Ross University, anthropology and archaeology textbooks spilling out, and stuck the keys into the ignition when something caused her to stop, cock her head and listen.

"Mew."

Faint. Helpless.

Freaked out that she had almost started the van with a cat hiding inside the engine, Zoey popped the hood latch, unbuckled her seatbelt and got out. She raised the hood, peered into the engine. No cat. That was good, right?

"Mew."

She muscled closer, angling her neck to get a good

look at nooks and crannies hidden amidst hoses and gears and whatnot. "C'mon little sucker, where are you?"

"Mew."

Hmm. Sounded like it could be coming from underneath the van. Zoey bent over to take a look, her brown-sugar colored ponytail flopping down over her head and brushing the ground. She spied a tiny kitten with bluish-white body fur and a slate-gray face, curled up tight against the back tire. A blue-point Siamese. "Ooh, look at you pretty baby. Where did you come from little guy? Or gal, whatev."

The kitten narrowed its eyes as if to say, "I'll never tell *you* my secrets."

"Kitty, kitty, kitty." She moved to the rear of the van, crouched down and rubbed her fingertips together as if she had a tasty treat she was willing to share. "You gotta come out from under there so I can go home."

The trembling Siamese boldly met her stare. It might be scared, but it was scrappy. Gently, she moved to close her hand around the kitten, but it sprinted to the back tire on the opposite side of the van.

She tracked around to the other side and got down on her knees. "Hey there. Still me. I didn't go anywhere. Here's the deal, I can't go anywhere and risk squashing you, so it would really benefit us both if you'd let me help you."

The kitten darted back to the other tire.

"Not buying it, huh?" She sighed, got up, and returned to the other side. This time, she lay on her belly against the warm asphalt and walked two fingers toward the woebegone creature. Maybe talking would soothe the poor thing. "Look, I get that you're all stealth ninja kitty and everything, kudos on the mad sprinting skills by the way, but I gotta go."

"Rrrowww." Fur bristling, the kitten arched its back, sent her a get-the-hell-away-from-me-*bee*otch-or-you'll-be-sorry-you-didn't-make-out-your-will hiss and swatted a warning paw.

"Seriously, I can't be late again for the luncheon meeting of volunteers who answer the lonely hearts letters written to Cupid. I'm already skating the razor's edge with that bunch over my habitual tardiness and yes, while it is sorta hypocritical of me to give advice to the brokenhearted when I myself have never actually been in love, somebody's got to answer those letters and you don't look as if you've got a mind to do it for me. And even if you were willing, there's the whole no opposable thumbs issue. Sorry if that hurts your feelings, just stating the facts."

The kitten's fur settled back into place and he or she canted its head as if trying to figure what she was yammering about. It was so darned cute and the talking did seem to help.

"If I'm not really qualified to answer the letters and I can't seem to show up on time, why don't I just quit? Good question, Egbert. You don't mind if I call you

Egbert, do you? Unless is Egbertlina. Is it Egbertlina? I can't really tell from here if you're a boy or a girl, but to answer your question, it's this whole family obligation thing. We—just to clarify, that's me and my sister, Natalie—are descended from Millie Greenwood, the woman who started this whole letter writing mess when she wrote a letter to Cupid asking him to help her snare her true love, John Fant and it worked stupendously. He dumped Elizabeth Nielson at the altar for Millie, who was just a poor housemaid. It's terribly romantic."

Her sister, Natalie was enamored of that legend, but to Zoey, it was all a bunch of blah, blah about long dead people, then again, if she were being honest, jealousy could have something to do her lack of interest in it. *She* wasn't the oldest daughter of the oldest daughter of the oldest daughter of Millie Greenwood like her sister. She had no real stake in keeping the parable alive.

As she spoke, Zoey was slowly inching her hand closer to the Siamese.

The kitten's hair flared again.

Zoey backed off.

She fumbled in the pocket of her blue jean shorts for her cell phone, and flicked it on to check the time. Twenty minutes to twelve. No way was she going to make it to the meeting on time, especially since she still had to drive the thirty miles from Alpine to Cupid.

Every Monday, Wednesday and Friday from noon to one-thirty, the volunteers met to answer letters from the lovelorn written to Cupid. The letter-writing tradition had started in the 1930s after the Depression hit and the town had a desperate need of extra income and they did anything they could to encourage tourism. Grandmother Rose had spearheaded the campaign, gathering some of the local women to answer the overwhelming number of letters that people left at the base of the Cupid stalagmite inside the Cupid Caverns. At first, the replies to the letters were left on a bulletin board posted outside the caverns, but that became unwieldy and in the 1940s someone had the idea of doing away with the bulletin board and instead printing the letters and "Cupid's" reply in a free weekly newspaper that was paid for, and distributed by, local businesses. Great marketing ploy, but somebody had to answer all those freaking letters.

Should she call her sister and say she was going to be late? Or roll the dice and see if she could get there in the nick of time if she drove hell bent of leather.

If you get another speeding ticket, they'll cancel your insurance.

Dammit. She ducked her head under the van again. "I don't mean to scare you, kiddo, but this standoff isn't working for me. Something's gotta give, so if you want to spit and hiss, have at it."

The kitten arched its spine, flattened its ears, took her suggestion, hissed long and loud and then darted back across to the other tire once more.

Blowing out her breath, she played ring-a-round the van a third time, went down on her knees, rump in the air and got serious with the kitty. "No more pussyfooting around. You cannot stay under the van. This is non-negotiable."

The Siamese slapped her hand with amazingly sharp little claws, managed to make contact with her index finger and draw blood.

"Ouch." She popped her finger into her mouth. "Anyone ever tell you that you're a vicious little cuss?"

"Hey there Zoe-Eyes," oozed a deep masculine voice.

Only one person called her that. She jumped to her feet, spun around, and came face to face with six-foot-two inches of lean, raven-hair cowboy.

Zoey grinned from ear-to-ear at the sight of her very best friend in the whole wide world. "It's flipping Jericho Hezekiah Chance!"

He held out his arms and she flew across the asphalt to throw herself into them, his familiar scent of crisp cotton, leather, sunshine and desert sand enveloped her in his hearty hug. He smiled down at her.

"How did you know it was me?" she asked.

"I'd recognize that cute fanny anywhere."

Her skin tingled electrically. Whenever he said things like that, her naughty thoughts went to . . . well . . . places where they had no business going. Their relationship was strictly platonic, always had been, always would be, but sometimes she couldn't help wondering if he wanted more from her and that made her want more from him and wanting more was perilous territory.

Zoey pulled back. "It was the Cupid's Rest van. That's how you knew it was me, not my fanny." Ugh, why had she repeated the word *fanny*? She put a hand to her backside. *Stop calling attention to it!* She dropped her arm, forced a laugh.

His smile turned wicked. "Uh-huh. That's it. The van."

What did that smile mean? Was he flirting with her? Once upon a time, she thought so, but then she'd pulled a bonehead move and kissed him and he'd been horrified and things had been weird between them for months afterward. She was not going to make that mistake again.

Put away the second-guessing. He's your friend. That's it.

Too bad, since Jericho was endlessly hot. If he wasn't her best friend . . .

But he was. *Forget it.* With her palm, she shaded her eyes from the sun.

He possessed skin the color of a walnut hull and no matter how often he shaved, he sported a five o'clock shadow. His cheekbones were razor-sharp and his nose had a slight bump at the bridge that along with his dark eyebrows gave him a hawkish appearance. At first glance, no one pegged him for a science nerd, but he spent as much time indoors analyzing, cataloguing and teaching as he did outdoors digging up artifacts. He was a real life Indiana Jones.

"You should wear sunglasses," he said. "Protect your eyes."

"You're not wearing them."

He patted the front pocket of his red plaid western shirt. "Took them off when I spied you. Had to get an unobstructed view. You're a sight for sore eyes."

"Is something wrong?"

"What makes you ask that?"

"You can't hide anything from me. I know you too well. Something's up."

He paused. "Mallory and I broke up."

Oh goodie. Okay, that was tacky. "I'm so sorry to hear that. You guys were two peas in a pod."

"That was part of the problem. We were too much alike."

"What happened?" She held up a stop-sign palm. "No wait, save that story. We'll go out drinking tonight. Wednesday is half-price draft night at Chantilly's. You can tell me all about it then."

"That's okay. I don't need a shoulder to cry on. It was a long time coming. Besides, I also have some very good news." His big smile was back.

"Great. Then we'll go out to celebrate. What's this very good news?"

He spread his hands open wide. "You're looking at

the new project archeologist at the Center for Big Bend Studies."

Zoey let out a squeal and threw her arms around his neck. "Yippee! Jericho this is awesome. I'm so excited for you."

A sudden stillness settled over him that was both patient and predatory, the same darkly fascinating threat as a Big Bend mountain lion methodically stalking prey. What was this? Something was different. There was a hard-edged steeliness to him that hadn't been there before. He'd left Cupid not much more than a boy, but he's returned a fully developed man. Unnerved, she dropped her arms and stepped back.

"Thank you for giving me the heads up about Dr. Keel's retirement," he said evenly, his tone belying the tension she'd felt in him. "It gave me a jumpstart on the compctition."

"Pfftt. With your credentials the competition didn't stand a chance." She clapped her hands, more to get herself back on keel than anything else. When in doubt, rah, rah, rah always worked. "I'm so excited. Is that why you and Mallory split the sheets? You're moving back home."

"Partially," he hedged.

"Will you be living in Alpine?'

"Alpine is closer to work."

"But Cupid's home," she coaxed. "Besides, it's got the added bonus that I'm there."

"Can't argue with that. I'll just have to see what kind of housing is available in both towns."

"There's a room open at the Cupid's Rest for a long term border," she coaxed.

"We'll see."

"Oh." She laced her fingers together, did a little jig. "This is so wonderful. Will you be heading up this summer's field school?"

He nodded. "I will."

"Woot!" She pumped her fist. "You'll be my instructor. Dibs on teacher's pet."

"Fair warning. I'm not cutting you any slack just because we're friends. I'm a tough instructor."

She waved away his threat. "We're going to have so much fun."

"And work very hard."

"Hard can be fun," she teased.

Jericho's face reddened and he tugged at his collar. Ha! She'd embarrassed him. That's what he got for making the fanny comment, but now she was feeling off kilter too. "Um, have they decided yet where they're going to hold the field school? This is my first dig and I'm sooo excited."

"It's a toss-up between a Gilliland Canyon in Big Bend, Nature Conservancy's Independence Creek Preserve in Terrell County, or Triangle Mount in Jeff Davis."

"Triangle Mount? We're talking home sweet home."

Triangle Mount was on private land owned by the August McCleary foundation. "Are we looking to put to rest the rumors that Triangle Mount is really a North American pyramid?"

Lately, on the heels of some unscientific claims that some flatiron mountains in Bosnia were ancient pyramids, there had been much speculation that Triangle Mount could possibly have been a pyramid as well.

"It's mostly bollocks of course," Jericho said. "The theory is something most serious archaeologist dismiss out of hand and because of limited funding wouldn't waste time on, but all scholars must guard against both complacency and a sense of superiority. There's always that rare exception to explore. Besides, it would make a great field school project."

"You gotta admit that it *is* a perfect triangle. Easy to see where the rumors come from and why people are fascinated by the notion of pyramids in West Texas."

"Don't get too worked up about it. Triangle Mount is the dark horse. Director Sinton is leaning toward Gilliland Canyon."

"What determines which dig site we'll chose?"

"Funding for one thing. For another, we need permission. It's easier to gain access to government land. In the past, the McCleary Foundation has been resistant to granting admittance."

Zoey cocked her head. True enough. The August McCleary Foundation was very protective of their land holdings. "Are you setting me up to do the dirty work with cousin Walker for you?"

Jericho scratched his chin, his blunt cut nails rasped appealingly against his stubble. "Well, you are a McCleary and you do have a talent for twisting arms, but honestly, I don't know if Triangle Mount is the best project for us."

"Hey, I've got nothing to lose. In fact, I'll even ask if the foundation will considering chipping in to help fund the dig."

"Let's not push our luck."

"Why not? All he can say is 'no' and we won't be any worse off than we were before."

"It's up to you." He shrugged.

"Consider it done." She snapped her fingers. "Triangle Mount, here we come."

Jericho chuckled. "I love your self-confidence, Zoe-Eyes."

Love.

Why did that word seem to stand out from the others? And why was she feeling warm and squishy inside because of it? Nothing wrong with loving your best friend, right? There were all kinds of love. For instance, she loved Urban Decay waterproof mascara, Cheetos—the puffy kind, Aunt Sandra's to-die-for banana pudding, skinny-dipping in Lake Cupid on a hot summer evening, and laying on a pallet in the back-yard staring up at the darkest night sky in the entire US of A, and wishing when a star streaked flaming bright. Never mind that more often than not, she cast that wish as a single question. *When is my soul mate going to show up?*

"And I'm so happy that you got the job," she chattered, pushing past her feelings. She learned a long time ago that the best way to deal with melancholy feelings was to keep her mind, and her body, busy, busy, busy. "It's great to have you back home. Do you realize how long it's been since we've seen each other in person?"

Jericho put a palm to the back of his neck. "Three years since I moved to Utah for my PhD in anthropology."

"That's right." She playfully swatted his shoulder. "You're a doctor now. We must definitely celebrate. Chantilly's tonight. Be there seven-thirtyish and put on your best dancing boots. We're gonna do some serious scootin'. I haven't had a decent dance partner since you abandoned me."

Jericho smiled, shook his head. "Damn, I've missed you."

"Me too. Missed you that is, not me. How could I miss me?"

"That mind of yours runs a hundred and fifty miles an hour."

"Ya think?" She winked.

"I know so. Chantilly's tonight. It's a date."

Date.

She knew he didn't mean it that way. Why was she

thinking like this? She and Jericho were just friends, but c'mon who could deny the man filled out a pair of Levis in the most drool-worthy way?

His hand rested on her shoulder. "It is good to see you again, pal."

Zoey's lips went cold. Pal. Buddy. Amigo. Friend. A guy who wanted to sleep with a girl did not call her, "pal."

Jericho leaned over and lightly kissed her cheek, a platonic peck. Brotherly. Clearly, nothing had changed for him in three years. Fine. Good. She'd use that as a damper to douse the tiny flame that flickered in her heart. The feeling would pass. It always did. What she needed was a new boyfriend.

"Bye!" She wriggled her fingers and turned back to the van, her heart thudding strangely. She was about to get in when she remembered about the kitten. Maybe she'd gotten lucky and it had taken off when she'd been talking to Jericho.

This time, so that her rump wouldn't be in the air, she crouched and ducked her head underneath the van. The Siamese was curled up asleep. Ah ha. Gotcha now. She reached around to pick it up and the kitten leaped as if she'd touched it with a live wire and darted to the opposite side of the van.

"Not again." She groaned.

"What's wrong?"

Zoey jumped, whacking her head against the undercarriage. "Ow!"

"I'm sorry, I didn't mean to startle you," Jericho apologized. "When I saw you on the ground, part of me said to just let it go. It is Zoey after all, but the curious part of me that knows whatever you do is never boring, had to come over and see what was up."

She rubbed the top of her head, glanced up at him. "You're too sly. You should wear a bell or something."

"Probably my Native American blood. Hunter DNA."

"Yeah, all one sixteenth of it." She got to her feet.

"One sixteenth Comanche," he said. "Strong genes. Stamps the bloodline forever."

"I've heard this brag before."

"So you have. Are you going to tell me what you're doing?"

"Catfishing," she replied.

Jericho rolled his eyes upward and addressed the sky. "I had to ask."

"As it turns out I'm really lousy at it."

"*It* being . . . ?"

"Stubborn kitten doesn't want to be rescued."

"Ah," he said. "I'm finally on board the Zoey thought-train. It's been so long since we've talked in person that I've gotten out of the rhythm. Let's see if I can help."

How many times had he helped her out of a jam? Two dozen at least, probably three if she thought about it long enough. *Ya think by now you should be able to handle your own problems.* You'd think, but she scooted over to make room for him.

Jericho crouched beside her, his scent getting all tangled up with the smell of asphalt and kitten. His shoulder brushed against hers and she caught her breath.

The kitten stared at them, eyes wide, muscles bunched.

"The poor thing must think we're ganging up on him. I'll go to the other side of the van," she said, hopping up quick. Whew. Gotta put some distance between her and those broad shoulders.

Jericho made a low, soothing sound in the back of his throat, but he did not touch the Siamese. The kitten cocked its head. "That's right little guy, come out, come out. We won't hurt you."

He spoke soft and slow and as if by magic, the kitten crept forward. After a few minutes, he put his hand down and the little Siamese came over to nibble on his pinky finger and then finally, curled up in his palm and started purring.

"I'll be damned," Zoey muttered. "You missed your calling. You should have been a cat whisperer."

With the kitten cradled against his chest, Jericho got to his feet. She hustled around the van to join him once one. "It is a boy or a girl?"

Jericho checked. "Boy. You wanna hold him?"

"Yes."

He transferred the cat over to her.

"Hey, there Egbert," she crooned. The kitten looked

up at her with sleepy eyes. It was still purring. Happy now. Apparently they'd just gotten off on the wrong foot.

"Egbert?"

"I named him already. Eggy for short."

"That's dangerous."

"How so?"

"When you start naming animals they have a tendency to become your pet."

"If I can't find his owner maybe I will keep him."

Jericho put a palm over his mouth, amusement deepening his chocolate eyes to coffee.

"Are you laughing at me?"

"Nope." He nodded.

"Liar. You are laughing at me."

He dropped his hand to show that he wasn't smiling, but he had his lips pressed together so tightly she knew it was all he could do to keep from bursting out in a belly laugh.

"What is so funny?" She frowned. Normally, she loved making him laugh, but it was the principle of the thing.

"Nothing."

"You don't think I can own a cat?"

"No one owns a cat. They own you."

"Fine, you don't think I can take care of a cat."

"I never said that."

"You looked both entertained and skeptical. Like it's the most outrageous idea you ever heard of."

"Have you ever owned a pet?"

"Sure. Lots."

"Name one."

"Um . . . I had a hamster once, or maybe it was a gerbil."

"What was its name?"

She crinkled her nose. "I can't recall."

"Apparently he was quite beloved."

"Sarcasm, cheap shot for the uninspired."

Jericho chuckled. "God, I've missed this. Repartee is not the same in email."

"Why do you think I keep trying to get you on Twitter? It's *the* medium for one liners."

"You're the one who excels at one liners."

"True." She tapped her chin. "Your emails do tend to run along the lines of *War and Peace*, the unabridged."

"So whatever happened to the hamster?"

"Got out of its cage and ran away."

He dipped his head, arched one eyebrow, and slowly shook his head.

"What? It happens."

"I seemed to remember you also had goldfish. What happened to them?"

"They died."

He held out his palms. "You're proving my case."

"They're goldfish. How long do they last? A couple of weeks tops."

"Mine lived for twelve years."

"Show-off."

"Simply stating my case."

"Which is that I couldn't possibly be a responsible pet owner?"

"Trying to establish a precedent."

"Natalie and I had a dog once."

"And who took care of it?"

"Natalie, but that's beside the point."

"Is it?"

"Geeze, Jericho, whose side are you on?"

"Egbert's."

"You seriously, don't think I can take care of a cat?"

"Zoey, you can do anything you can set your mind to. I believe that one hundred percent."

"But . . . ?"

"Some people just aren't meant to be pet owners. There's nothing wrong with that."

"Wow, way to stomp on a girl's feelings."

"It's just that you have so many interests. You're always on the go, never at home. A pet requires a lot of time and attention."

He was right. She did have trouble sitting still, but that didn't mean she couldn't own a cat. The deal was, she'd just never really had much of a reason to stay home.

"He might belong to someone," Jericho said. "So the point could be moot."

"I'll take him to a vet," she said. "See if he's been

chipped and I'll put up notices, post on a few social media sites."

"Are you sure you don't want me to take charge of him?"

Earlier, he'd sort of bruised her ego, but now she was just plain irritated. She sniffed. "I can do this."

"Okay. Just offering to let you off the hook."

She looked at the kitten who was staring at her with such a trusting expression that her stomach flopped over. She could be a cat owner. Why not? "Thanks for the offer, Jericho, but I'm in this hook, line and sinker."

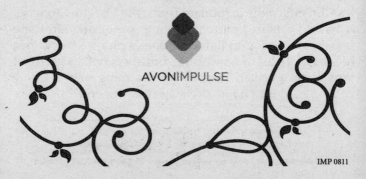